MISTRESS

OF THE

NIGHT

Charlotte Featherstone

D1178471

Erotic Historical Romance

New Concepts   Georgia

Be sure to check out our website for the very best in fiction at fantastic prices!

When you visit our webpage, you can:
* Read excerpts of currently available books
* View cover art of upcoming books and current releases
* Find out more about the talented artists who capture the magic of the writer's imagination on the covers
* Order books from our backlist
* Find out the latest NCP and author news--including any upcoming book signings by your favorite NCP author
* Read author bios and reviews of our books
* Get NCP submission guidelines
* And so much more!

We offer a 20% discount on all new Trade Paperback releases ordered from our website!

Be sure to visit our webpage to find the best deals in e-books and paperbacks! To find out about our new releases as soon as they are available, please be sure to sign up for our newsletter (http://www.newconceptspublishing.com/newsletter.htm) or join our reader group (http://groups.yahoo.com/group/new_concepts_pub/join)!

The newsletter is available by double opt in only and our customer information is *never* shared!

Visit our webpage at:
www.newconceptspublishing.com

New Concepts Publishing, Inc.
5202 Humphreys Rd.
Lake Park, GA 31636

ISBN 1-58608-748-7
March 2006 © Charlotte Featherstone
Cover art (c) copyright 2006 Eliza Black

NCP books are available at special quantity discounts for bulk purchases for sales promotions, premiums, fund raising, or educational use. For details, write, email, or phone New Concepts Publishing, Inc., 5202 Humphreys Rd., Lake Park, GA 31636; Ph. 229-257-0367, Fax 229-219-1097; orders@newconceptspublishing.com.

First NCP Trade Paperback Printing: March 2006

Prologue

Ashbourne, Derbyshire,
1781

"Damn you, Catherine, *push*!"

"I can't," the exhausted woman wailed as another contraction seized her body.

"My lady, you *must* push. The babe is almost out, ye've only the head to deliver."

Cracking open the door to her stepmother's chamber, eight-year-old Celeste gasped at the sight before her. Two midwives were standing at the end of the bed, one holding Catherine's thighs apart, the other lifting and twisting the legs of the babe. Her father was standing to the side of the bed, his meaty fists planted on his hips.

"Catherine, that's my heir. Push, damn you!"

Catherine squealed with pain as the midwife inserted her beefy hand and attempted to deliver the babe's head.

"Out of my way," her father roared, shouldering the midwife away from Catherine's legs. "I'm not just going to stand by and watch my heir die because of incompetent females."

"My lord," Mrs. Noland, pleaded. "You canna just tear the babe from her. Babe's that come breech need a special way of deliverin'. You have to have a care. *The child!*" Mrs. Noland cried as he gruffly took the babe's legs in his hands and twisted.

"Push, damn you," he snarled, lifting the babe's legs high in the air so that she could see the purple, mottled toes curled tight. "And don't you dare defy me, Catherine."

Her stepmother let out a blood-curdling scream and with a savage grunt, her father pulled a silent and bloodied, limp babe from Catherine's womb.

The room was quiet except for the dripping of blood as it rolled off the foot of the bed and splashed with an eerie, rhythmic patter onto the floorboards below. Celeste looked up from the widening maroon puddle to the still and silent form of her brother. Her father, his face ruddy and blotched, swore and started shaking the babe, commanding him to cry, to breathe, to do *something*.

And then he did, a weak gasp, soon replaced by a wet gurgling sound that resonated deep in his tiny lungs. He struggled to breathe, the moist, raking breaths echoed throughout the room, and Celeste stood frozen--stricken, hoping the babe would prevail. And then he suddenly drew up his legs and flailed his arms out wide and let out a loud, impassioned roar that made her stepmother begin to weep.

"Ladies," her father bellowed, holding her newborn brother high in the air for all to see. "I give you my heir. The future Earl of Hardcastle."

Chapter One

London
May, 1814

He'd been the object of her desires for months. Madeline Brydges, the daughter of the Earl of Penrick, stole another glimpse at the man who had occupied her every waking thought and, she admitted, filled her nights with passionate dreams.

"He's going to catch you staring, you know," her friend, Harriett Longbottom murmured beside her.

"No, he won't," Madeline whispered, careful to keep her glances casual and short and seemingly uninterested.

It wouldn't do to attract the attention of the Tabbies. They were always a threat, always milling around, searching for juicy tidbits to gossip about. And her staring at the Earl of Hardcastle would be fodder for the gossip mill. The tale would no doubt spread through Lady Carmichael's fashionable ballroom like fire through a barn.

"He's too dark and brooding," Penelope Mills moaned.

"He's mysterious," Madeline replied, glancing once more at the tall man with black curls. Not curls, really, more like waves. Thick, silky waves that she'd dreamed of touching.

"He's aloof," Harriett warned.

"Merely misunderstood, Harry."

"He's rude," Penelope snorted, "and if you think the way he cut Mary Anne Hastings the other night at the Faversham rout is *misunderstood*, you've gone daft."

"Mary Anne was chasing after him as if she were a queen bee and he was a pot of honey."

"He's insufferable."

"He won't do," Penelope added, flicking open her fan. "Find someone more malleable, someone you can make dance to your tune."

Madeline watched as he stood solemnly, his shoulders resting against the wall of the ballroom. He was tall, almost as tall as his friend, Bathurst, who stood alongside him, but not nearly as big. While Bathurst was broad and heavily muscled, the earl was lithe and sleek, like a full blooded stallion. Proud, regal, and immensely masculine. "

"Madeline," Harriett sighed, "what can you be thinking? Hardcastle isn't husband material. Penelope is right, the earl's a brutish oaf who only looks at women so he may cut them to the quick with his razor edged tongue and icy glares. He'll rip you to shreds within three minutes, and enjoy doing so."

"He won't."

"He will," came the unified voices of her friends.

"He's worth the risk, I think."

"He'll be a challenge," Harriett whispered, peering through the crowd in order to glimpse him. "There's no doubt about that."

Madeline studied the earl from her vantage point across the room. He was surrounded, as always, by his friends, Lords Bathurst and Reanleigh, and their wives. "When have I ever backed down from a challenge?" Madeline asked, watching as the earl's face pulled into a look of pained boredom.

"That's what scares us, you never back down, not even when it's dangerous to keep going. As your friends we really cannot allow you to do something as rash as this. You simply cannot set your cap for the Earl of Hardcastle," Harry lectured.

"I don't see why not," Madeline said peevishly. Really, she was very disappointed in Harry and Penelope. When she had confided in them that she'd chosen her potential husband she had expected enthusiasm, not criticism.

"I don't see the earl making you an agreeable husband," Harry grumbled.

"Let me be the judge," Madeline said, plopping her empty champagne flute on a passing tray. The earl would do, he had to do. Her father had all but blackmailed her into finding herself a husband. If she didn't find a suitable mate by the end of the season, her father was cutting off all support to her beloved Montgomery House. And there was no way in the world she was going to give up her life's work. Those women needed her as much as she needed them and she wouldn't, absolutely couldn't, let something like finding a husband get in the way of the house. If her father wanted her to wed, so be it. But there was only one man for her, and she would settle for no other. She wanted a marriage filled with love and children and she was certain the Earl of Hardcastle would provide her with both. She had an uncanny ability to read people, and she had read Hardcastle perfectly--he was in need of love and affection.

* * * *

"She's lovely."

Blaine nodded his agreement, careful not to move his eyes an inch. "She's turned out well. She was rather nervous, but I do believe she's settled in."

"I'm not speaking of your niece, Hardcastle," Bathurst mumbled. "I'm referring to the young lady you've been staring at all evening."

"I don't know what you mean." Blaine appeared as though he were bored with the conversation when all he really felt was shock at being discovered watching the woman who was quickly becoming a fixation with him.

"You've been all but devouring her since the moment you spotted her, which was at least," Bathurst removed his pocket watch from his waistcoat pocket, and checked the time, "an hour ago."

"You're mad," Blaine scoffed, feeling the faint flush of heat in his cheeks. "I'm keeping an eye on Miranda, nothing more."

"If you were watching Miranda," his friend, Reanleigh drawled, "you would see that she's dancing with Ashton, the most notorious young blood of the season."

"I am watching Miranda." He forced his eyes from the fetching woman by the buffet table, only to have them land on his young niece and a most unsuitable suitor. "The pair of you act as though I were a moonstruck twit pining after the chambermaid."

"Not pining," Bathurst laughed, "devouring."

"I most certainly was not devouring Madeline Brydges. The very thought is preposterous."

"Ah," Bathurst chuckled. "That's the lovely's name, is it?"

"So you were," Reanleigh teased. "'Bout time you took a fancy to someone. It's past time you started thinking about a wife and a family. 'Tis time you saw to the Hardcastle dynasty. You've been holed up in that cave for too long."

"It's not a bloody cave," Blaine said through set teeth, "and I prefer it to mundane society, of which I'm very quickly associating with your company. And furthermore, I'll have you know marriage and brats are the last thing on my mind." He inclined his head, abruptly putting an end to the unwanted conversation. "If you will both excuse me, I need to have a word with my niece."

"By all means," Reanleigh smirked.

"Make sure you pass by the buffet table." Bathurst motioned to the horde of people clamoring for a plate. "With such a crush, there's a good chance you'll get to rub up against her."

"I do not *rub*," Blaine grimaced, disgusted with his friends and their ribbing. "I consider myself a *gentleman*. As such, I do not graze, brush, side along or do anything else to a lady, much less rub up against her in a ballroom."

"Being a *gentleman* is over-rated."

"Yeah," Reanleigh drawled, finishing his champagne in one swallow, "and it doesn't get you the girl, either."

Shaking his head, he left his friends and wondered, not for the first time, how he had let Celeste talk him into sponsoring his niece for her first season. He must truly be mad to think he could pull off such a stunt. It was absolutely ludicrous to believe that he of all people, the social misfit of the ton, could parade around, acting as though he fit in, when in fact he knew he stood out like a sore, reddened thumb.

Sighing, Blaine made his way to where Lord Ashton was preparing to depart from his niece. If only Celeste hadn't cried, if only she hadn't flung herself into his arms, sobbing, grieving for the husband she had loved and lost, hurting over the pain of raising her family on her own.

If there was one person on this earth he truly loved, it was his sister--his half-sister, he corrected. He had never been able to stand idly by and watch her cry. He'd always been affected and last week had been no exception. In fact, he'd been so damned moved that he'd agreed to the plan before he could even think of the pitfalls. And there were, he thought nervously, many pitfalls.

Seeing Ashton leave Miranda at Lady Brookehaven's side, Blaine charged straight ahead, glad at least that his niece was amongst friends. The Dowager Dragon, as he and his cronies had so uproariously named her when they were boys, was his friend Bronley's grandmother and a great asset to him in launching Miranda in the social whirl. While his sister was clearly out of mourning for her husband, Celeste was still prone to fits of crying and melancholy, leaving him and the dowager to see his niece through her first season.

"Hardcastle." The dowager glared at him, her wrinkled hand curling about the head of her walking stick. "I expect you'll have a discussion with Miranda, here, about agreeing to dance with young men of questionable character."

"Indeed, your ladyship." He nodded politely as he reached for Miranda's arm. "Come along, my dear."

"And Hardcastle," the dowager said, leaning close to him, so close in fact, he had to bend to hear her. "I would have a care the next time I took a notion to study a member of the opposite sex. It was most apparent, even from this distance and with my poor eyesight."

"As always, Lady Brookehaven, you are a font of indispensable advice."

"I do try, Hardcastle," she laughed, her hazel eyes dancing mischievously in the candlelight. "One must always stick to one's duties."

Yes, Blaine thought as he steered his niece away from the dance floor, the dowager was forever discharging her duties. Her damnable nose was always in someone's business. She knew everything about everyone in Society, and he might have thought it vastly amusing, or perhaps reassuring where Miranda was concerned, but instead it raised his hackles, made him nervous that perhaps the dowager knew everything about him, too.

"I can't believe you're dragging me off like a prehistoric cave dweller."

Blaine gritted his teeth and increased his pressure around Miranda's elbow. "I'm not dragging, merely steering."

"Oh?" she said mockingly, her full lips turned down into a pout, "so now I'm being treated as if I were a horse."

"If you do not cease this silly behavior at once, I'll do more than guide you. I will have no qualms about pulling you by the wrists, kicking and screaming and causing every possible ruckus so that every damn person present will stop what they are doing and gape at the spectacle you're making."

"You wouldn't dare."

"Try me."

"Where are we going?" she whined. "Why can't we just go outside where no one will hear you yelling?"

"I do not yell, Miranda. You know that."

But, that did bring him to an interesting dilemma. Just where the devil was he going to take her? Blaine knew without a doubt that if he snuck her away some place private he'd only arouse curiosity. The Beau Monde would no doubt put two and two together and decide he was lecturing her about dancing with Ashton. And the last he thing he wanted was for the ton to always be watching his niece, waiting to see if she would defy him, which she would no doubt do as soon as he turned his back.

Looking about the crowded ballroom he settled his gaze upon the buffet table. He knew for certain Bathurst and Reanleigh would be watching him, waiting to see if he would *rub against*

Lady Madeline.

He supposed he could return to the dance floor. It might not hurt to lead her out, act as though naught was amiss, assure the ton his niece was the model of decorum and a paragon of female virtue. He snuck a glance at the still simpering and pouting Miranda.

Ever since her father had died, Miranda had become a stranger to him. She'd turned into a tempestuous, smart-mouthed creature who delighted in giving her mother crying jags, and himself fits of apoplexy. It wasn't like Miranda to be so petulant. He knew it had to do with missing her father, and yet, he couldn't stand to sit back and watch her ruin her life. He didn't want that--he knew all too well what it was like to feel like an outcast. To feel different. To be lonely.

"Well?" Miranda said waspishly.

"You will walk to the buffet with me and you will be polite and smile. I will tolerate nothing less, do you hear me?"

"Fine," she bit out, stomping beside him. "But I'm not eating anything. I've all but lost my appetite."

"Do you know, my dear, I think I should let Ashton court you. Why, I wager one week spent in your company will be enough to cure him of his evil propensities."

"I cannot believe you said that."

"Believe it, Miranda. My tongue can be just as forked and poisonous as yours. Whomever did you think you inherited the talent from?"

Her look of pure astonishment amused him, it almost made his dangerous exposure to the seeing eyes of the Beau Monde worth it. Almost, but not quite.

* * * *

"Look," Harriett hissed, "*he's* coming."

"For Heaven's sake, Harry, lower your voice. We don't need to have everyone know I've got Lord Hardcastle in my sights."

"I'm certain everyone does know," Penelope smirked. "You haven't taken your eyes off him all night. In fact," she teased, leaning over the table as she reached for a lobster patty, "you've been pre-occupied with the earl for months."

Nearly a year now, Madeline mentally corrected her friend. It was a year ago that she had first spotted the mysterious earl, standing alone in Lady Lancaster's drawing room. She had been immediately drawn to him, to the aloofness he cloaked himself in, to the aura of mystery he tried so hard to create. He had looked haunted, lonely, vulnerable. She hadn't been able to shake the memory of his clear gray eyes as they had flickered to hers, briefly looking at her, before he had once again assumed his polite, indifferent mask.

She watched as he neared the table, his young niece in tow. There was something challenging, something mysterious about the man that attracted her beyond what she had ever felt before. She'd had plenty of offers from gentlemen in the last few years-- one did not reach the ripe age of four and twenty without such offers, but she'd rebuffed them all. They hadn't caught her attention, hadn't evoked her fantasies in quite the way the earl had.

Her father always had plenty to say about her refusals, but she had placated him with a smile and reassurances that she would indeed one day marry and provide him with a grandchild. A grandchild who would inherit the Brydges ancestral home, Sanbourne Hall in Sussex.

"Pretend you're reaching for a pastry." Penelope murmured in her ear. "Lady Reanleigh is looking your way, with what, I would say, is barely concealed interest."

Madeline swallowed deeply and reached for a cream and strawberry filled tart. The last thing she wanted was to attract the attention of Hardcastle's friends--especially his friend's wives. The earl would surely rebuke any and all of his friend's wives' match-making attempts.

It was the truth that all his bosom bows seemed to dote on him. No, doting wasn't quite the right word. More like protective. They seemed to guard him whenever he ventured out into society, which was, she thought with a frown, much too infrequent.

"That's enough," Penelope hissed, "you've got at least half a dozen sweets on your plate."

"Oh," she said, surprised as she looked down at her plate. "I guess I lost count."

"I suffer from the same malady," a feminine chuckle reached her from across the table. "I'm afraid I have a sweet tooth, too."

"Lady Bathurst," Madeline smiled, seeing her sidle up to the table with Lady Reanleigh beside her. "How nice to see you again. You're looking very well."

"Thank you. You do remember my very good friend, Lady Reanleigh, don't you?"

"Of course," Madeline smiled. "A pleasure, madam."

"Good evening," the marchioness said, her infamous crooked grin in place. "And to you too, Miss Mills, Miss Longbottom."

Madeline watched as her friends smiled and inclined their heads politely.

"Ah, there you are," Lady Bathurst smiled, grabbing hold of Hardcastle's arm as he reached the table. "Lady Madeline, have you been introduced to the Earl of Hardcastle?"

Madeline's eyes darted to the right to see the man of her dreams standing directly before her, a narrow table filled with sweets and fruit separating them. Her heart jolted, then started to race as she dared to look at him. Not glance, or make a sweeping gesture with her eyes, but really look at him.

He was beautiful--masculine beauty personified. His hair was a mass of silky black waves, the color so dark it reminded her of coal. His brows were bold, perfectly arched, and his lashes, the same coal color as his hair, were thick and full, fringing the most perfect gray eyes she had every seen. Eyes the color of a snow laden sky in November.

"Lady Madeline," her name swept past his thin, hard lips in a whisper, the sound strangely evocative to her. "A pleasure."

"My lord," she said far too tremulously. Good Heavens, what was the matter with her? She felt strangely breathless, as if she were weightless. She felt her cheeks flame, her lashes begin to flutter. She *never* fluttered her lashes, had never acted like the giggly girls out for their first season, not even when it *had been* her first season. What had gotten into her?

She watched him take her proffered gloved hand in his, watched breathlessly as he lowered his lips to her knuckles. She sucked in an astonished breath when she felt him slide a finger down her glove, along her skin and begin to stroke the inside of her wrist. His lips hovered above her hand for what could only have been seconds, but which felt like minutes before he looked up at her, meeting her gaze. His eyes now looked almost a pale blue and his lips twitched in the barest hint of a smile.

"Enchanted."

"Th ... thank you," she stammered, clearly at a loss for words and indeed, any thoughts or actions.

"Miss Greenwood," Lady Reanleigh said, addressing Hardcastle's niece. "I do believe Anna Richmond is attempting to gain your attention and in a most shocking display of wildly moving arms. Here," the marchioness whispered, taking the plate from her and resting it atop the table. "Lady Bathurst and I shall navigate you through this crush and help you to save the poor girl's reputation."

Madeline forced her eyes away from the earl, watching as the threesome made their excuses and headed to the dance floor. Her breathing was still harsh and rapid and she used the time to regain her composure. Never had an introduction left her breathless, panting for more. But then, never had a gentleman made so much of a simple kiss. It was as if they were the only two people in the room, their eyes studying each other, learning, trying to discover the other's secrets and hidden desires.

"You will excuse me, Lady Madeline, ladies," Hardcastle bowed before them.

He couldn't just leave, not like this. "Do you dance, my lord?"

"Maddy," she heard Harry's hushed admonishment, felt Penelope jabbing her at the same time, reminding her she was being far too forward.

"No, I do not," he replied, his eyes once again cool and hard.

"How about something to eat, there's every possible delicacy here. Can I tempt you?" she smiled, then winced when she realized it sounded like she was offering him an invitation.

He smiled then, not just a mere twitching of lips, but a full grin, one that made his lips soften and blinded her with a dazzling array of white, straight teeth. "I'm afraid not. Excuse me, ladies."

With a curt bow he was gone, disappearing into the crowd and into the night.

"Fortnight, my toes," Penelope scolded, "you'll be lucky to capture his attention before you turn into an ape leader yourself."

"Are you wagering I cannot capture the earl's interest?"

"No," Penelope challenged, her hands on her hips. "You can get his attention, there's no doubt about that, but can you make him love you? For that is the real challenge."

Madeline sucked in her breath and searched the room for him. He was going to be difficult. He was arrogant, prideful, aloof and the biggest hindrance of all was the fact he didn't want anyone to get close to him.

She watched him take his usual spot by the wall, only footsteps away from the door, his polite mask once again firmly in place. She continued to stare at him, wondering if it was possible to make the mysterious Lord Hardcastle love her.

And then she felt his gaze on her, saw him return her look, but it was not one of his casual, almost scathing glances that he showed to everyone else, it was a look of longing, of need, of…. Madeline swallowed hard as she watched him look her over from the top of her head to the tip of her toes. The look conveyed hope. Hope that maybe she would be the one person to penetrate his iron façade.

And it was then that Madeline realized that the Earl of Hardcastle was going to be a worthy cause.

She had been helping those in need for too many years to miss the signs, the silent cry for help. She had experience with those whose pride refused to beg for such relief. She just needed to reach out to him, and he needed to let her.

"I mean to have Lord Hardcastle for the rest of my days," she said firmly. "I'll have his love. You mark my words, I *never* back down from a challenge."

* * * *

'Can I tempt you?' Bloody hell, she could tempt the Almighty himself. Just one toss of those flame colored curls and a flick of turquoise eyes was enough for him to willingly succumb. Damn it, why did she have to be the most fetching female he'd ever seen?

Blaine sighed and sank into his favorite chair, his companion, Shadow, coming up on his haunches, laying his head on his knee in faithful canine affection.

Why the hell couldn't he get the picture of her full red lips and beguiling smattering of freckles out of his damn mind? Because, he thought, raking his hand through Shadow's pelt, he wanted her. Not just a body to enjoy for an hour, or an image to think about while he satisfied his needs, he wanted her. *To possess her*, to make her his. Each time he saw her, the feeling was more stark-- urgent. His need increased with every glimpse of her and her flame red hair. A year ago, at the Lancaster party, she had caught his attention as no other had ever done. Numerous months later she still intrigued him. He had been fascinated by the joy that shone in her eyes, the love of life she seemed to show in all she did and everyone she looked at. She was everything that was light and dazzling. She was popular and fun, delighting in the entertainments of the ton, while he lived in the dark and shadows.

He'd been aware of the dangerous waters he was treading, but he hadn't realized how far above his head he was until tonight.

When he had taken her hand in his, he'd wanted to do much more than simply glide his finger along her skin. He'd wanted to tear the glove from her hand, to press her palm to his mouth, to smell the scent of her as he kissed her skin, before pulling her to him, enveloping her in his arms, tasting her throat, her jaw, even, he thought, her lips.

He should have been shocked to admit the words; he'd never felt the desire to connect with someone as he did with Madeline. It was a sacred rule of his--when satisfying his carnal appetites, he never partook of their mouths. He never exposed himself to the intimacy of lips touching and nipping--tongues, hot and wet, searching, mingling and then finally joining. He'd wanted no part of that sort of intimacy with a woman. He'd forbid himself that pleasure long ago. Intimacy led to feelings and feelings led to trust, and it was only a matter of time before trust and feelings were replaced by deeper, darker, emotions.

No, his affairs were discreet one-night dalliances with the demimonde. There were no emotions, save physical desire, involved. The willing participants wished nothing more of him than his money, and he wished for nothing more than a willing body to slake his natural male inclinations.

Shadow closed his eyes and whimpered, that deep heart-wrenching sound from his belly, echoing exactly what he, himself was feeling. He knew he was getting himself all tied up in knots. Knew without a single doubt that he should put the girl out of his mind, but he couldn't. Every time he closed his eyes, he saw her before him, her full red mouth tempting him, beckoning him to explore her, to take what he had never wanted from another woman. She was his fantasy, a temptress, a Houri. She was, he sighed, resting his head back against the chair, his weakness.

"My lord," Ringwald called, striding into the study, a silver tray in one hand and the evening paper tucked beneath the other. "I've brought your tonic."

"Thank you, Ringwald."

Blaine watched his valet place the tray on the table beside him with a flourish. Who would credit it looking Ringwald that he had once been a boxer. A fisticuffs fighter turned into a gentleman's gentleman. When he had found him, nearly fifteen years before, Ringwald had been a bloodied broken mess left for death in a marshy ditch on the edge of his estate.

Never one to see another human being suffer, he'd brought him home, to the extreme disapproval of his father, and had nursed him back to health. Ringwald had been faithful to him ever since and as his valet he was nothing if not discreet. Ringwald was, in fact, silent as the tomb.

"Your spectacles, my lord." Ringwald handed him the silver wire frames.

"Thank you." Blaine stiffened as he looked down at the offending object. He hated being weak, hated how he had to pamper himself in order to ward off another one his 'bouts'. But damn it to hell, he didn't know of any other way. The dozens of physicians he'd seen in his lifetime had yet to provide him with any treatment, let alone a cure.

"The dog," Ringwald nodded to Shadow, "has been doing a very great amount of whimpering these past days."

"It has not escaped my notice," Blaine drawled, stroking his faithful companion. "He can always sense it, the change in the atmosphere, the shifting of currents."

"I believe, my lord, if you might permit me, it is a change in you that the beast takes exception to."

"How so?" he asked, meeting the clear blue gaze of Shadow. "What is so very different about me now, my friend?"

"Permit me to say, milord, that you're, well…." Ringwald coughed, his big callused hand covering his mouth. "Well, you can be somewhat of a prig, a touch miserable if you don't mind my saying."

"I suppose you're correct, Ringwald. I seem to recall feeling rather miserable and acting like a snarling bear before sliding back into a relapse. Perhaps that's what alerts Shadow."

"I've taken the liberty, my lord, of increasing the strength of the valerian in the tea, on account that the dog has started again."

"Thank you, Ringwald. As always, you're indispensable."

"My lord," he bowed, and left the room.

Reaching for the cup, Blaine took a large swallow and grimaced. When the devil was he going to acquire a taste for aniseed and licorice?

"Ah, Shadow," he sighed, putting the cup back into its saucer and stroking the animal behind his ears. "What is a man to do? It is somewhat unnerving, you know, waiting for it to come, seeing the signs all around and not being able to do a damn thing to stop it."

The dog whimpered in reply, then began to shake, a series of deep growls slipping past his lips, before barking and prancing about the room.

"Ah yes, something is burning. I smell it too. And the heat, it's so very hot in here."

And Madeline, was she truly here, was the vision real? Was the temptress actually walking into his study, her unbound hair floating around her like flames, her arms outstretched to him, begging him to come to her?

"Milord." Ringwald ran into the room, chasing Maddy away, ruining the image of her disrobing for him. "Sterling," Ringwald bellowed for the butler. "For the love of God man, get help."

Chapter Two

"Thank you, Mr. Sedgewick."

Madeline rose from behind her desk and watched as her portly man of affairs crammed a stack of papers into his already overflowing folio.

"Do consider it, my lady. The Morning Lane project will not get underway until the investors have all the monies needed. If they don't have an additional ten thousand pounds, the project will not come to fruition and your large investment will sink like an overloaded ship on the Thames."

"An apt analogy, Mr. Sedgewick," Madeline said through gritted teeth.

"I do detest bringing you unfortunate news. But really, my concerns were most overwhelming."

"I thank you for your concern, Mr. Sedgewick. You may return in a fortnight, I'll have my answer then. Surely the developers can wait that length of time?"

"I'm off to their offices as we speak. I shall send word around if it looks like they will need a decision sooner."

"Very good, Sir. Good day."

"Good day. And do not worry over much. Montgomery House shall make it through this rough spot."

Madeline watched the short little man waddle across the rug and let himself out of her study. With a hopeless sigh, she sunk down into her chair and rested her head against the desk.

What was she going to do? She'd already invested twenty thousand pounds in the Morning Lane project in the hopes she would see a huge profit. A profit that was very much needed to do repairs to the house. And if she wished her dreams of expanding the home and its services to become a reality, she needed the housing project to start immediately.

"'Ere now." Mrs. Noland, the house's midwife and housekeeper came into the room carrying a tray laden with biscuits and a huge pot of tea. "Don't despair, luvy. We've plenty of time to come up with an idea to save this place."

"Thank you, Maggie," Madeline whispered without looking up. "But, I do believe Montgomery House might be beyond saving.

Father has only given me half of our agreed upon monthly stipend and now it looks as though the townhouse project in Cheapside is not going to come about."

"Eh?" Mrs. Noland asked, nearly dropping the tray on the carpet. "Sedgewick assured you it was a sure thing. He all but guaranteed you a packet on your investment."

"I know," Madeline groaned as her head lay atop the desk. "I might have put the cart before the horse, Maggie, and with Montgomery House's savings. Had I known Papa would stop funding the house I would never have invested my savings into the Morning Lane project."

"What's this about losing money?"

Madeline looked up from her crossed arms to see Phoebe, the ton's most infamous courtesan, turned instructor of grace and lady-like deportment, glide into the room.

"Madeline, here, is having some doubts about that investment she ventured into."

"Morning Lane?" Phoebe asked, passing her a cup of steaming tea. "What's happened?"

"The developers need another ten thousands pounds before they start the project. Unfortunately, Mr. Sedgewick tells me that they are unable to come up with the funds."

"I see," Phoebe said, her brown eyes widening with concern. "And I suppose he came to Montgomery House to solicit the extra ten thousand."

"Yes," Madeline nodded, feeling her black mood deepen further. "And we can't afford it. Not with eight babies due this month and the extra linens and help it will take. Already I've seen an increase in expenses after taking Mary and Helen in. I hadn't accounted for those extra mouths to feed, I'm afraid," Madeline groaned, rubbing her temples, vainly trying to come up with a plan. If only her father hadn't halved her monthly income. If he would just believe that she was searching for a husband. If only she hadn't promised him a grandchild to inherit his un-entailed fortune and estate.

"I'll not take any wages this month, luvy. My pension from my last employer is more than enough to see me through."

"I couldn't ask that of you, Maggie."

"And it's not as though I need to dress myself in the finest silks and muslins. After all, I have no one to impress," Phoebe demurred, artfully arranging her skirts.

"If only that infuriating man would see fit to fall in with my plans," Madeline exploded before she could stop herself.

"Who?" Maggie asked, "Sedgewick?"

"No," Phoebe corrected, "She means her Papa."

"Neither," Madeline mumbled, as she stood up from her chair and paced before the desk. "The earl. The man I intend to marry." The man who was going to father her children, she silently added.

"Oh," Phoebe murmured, sipping her tea as elegantly and decorously as if she were a duchess. "*That* man."

"Well," Maggie, hedged, clearly uncomfortable with the topic. "Perhaps he has his reasons, luvy. Not every man wishes to marry."

Madeline huffed, not liking the fact the earl had evaded her at every ball for the past fortnight. "What is wrong with me, I ask? What is it that offends him so? Is it my red hair, do you think?"

"The earl," Phoebe began, her voice croaking slightly, "is known to be elusive and mysterious. You cannot expect him to fall at your knees, declaring his undying love simply because he slipped his finger down your glove."

"He looked at me," Madeline blushed, "in … in *that* way."

"Men frequently do that, Dearest. It doesn't exactly mean they wish for the union to be consecrated by God in a church."

Madeline did flush then, furiously in fact. Was that what the earl had been thinking? Had it just been something carnal she'd seen in his eyes? Was it lust that had changed his eyes from gray to almost blue?

"'ere now, sit down. You'll wear out that lovely carpet. Now then," Maggie began after Madeline had once again taken the chair behind her desk. "Let's discuss this all calm like."

"What am I going to do? I can't lose the house. I can't let these poor unfortunates onto the streets with no one to help them get by."

"You just never mind about that, luvy," Maggie said soothingly, patting her hand in a grandmotherly fashion. "Phoebe and me have a plan. We'll come up with the blunt, you leave it to us."

"But how-"

"Now, don't you worry about the particulars, you've enough on your plate. You've promised your father you'll get yerself a fine husband and give him a packet of grandchildren. You worry about that, and we'll get the money, won't we, Phoebe?"

"Indeed," Phoebe smiled, her courtesan charm evident. "I have many influential contacts. Some, I daresay, would love to hear about a chance to invest in what is most likely to become a very lucrative housing project."

"But I do not want you to have to go to back to-"

"Oh, do not worry about that, Madeline. Phoebe Knightly no longer sells her body for men's pleasures. But, I could," she smirked, "consider renting out my company at the theatre or private parties."

"But you shouldn't have to."

"You saved me from a life of destitution, Madeline. When you came across me that day in the park you took the time to sit with me--a whore. I was thirty-three years old and had just been given my *conge* from my lover. I had nowhere to go, no prospects to see me through. But you saved me, and I shall never forget it."

"Now then," Maggie said, squeezing her hand. "You let us take care of the money and you take care of capturing that man's heart. If that's who you want, then by God, go get him."

* * * *

"Well, I'm here. What's this all about, Cissy?"

His sister, Celeste, raced into his arms, her sobs echoing in the quiet drawing room. "Miranda," she choked, drenching the lapels of his morning coat. "She insists on accepting invitations for excursions with Ashton. I've tried to tell her, but she won't listen. She just does what she pleases."

"Miranda," he called, his voice booming loudly up the stairs. "Down here this instant, young lady, or I shall come up there and fetch you."

"Yes?" Miranda asked, instantly appearing in the doorway, her hands fisted on her hips in a defiant and decidedly saucy manner.

"Do not think to act such a way with me, Miranda. I know your games and I can assure you, two can play at them."

"You're not my father!" she yelled back, her toe stamping into the rug. "I don't have to take orders from you."

"You will do as I say as I am now your nearest male relative."

"You are not. Henry is."

"Henry is seven years old."

"Henry is now the Marquis of Greenwood."

"Henry wears shortpants and wets the bed," he shot back, becoming more irritated by the moment. "And since your father left you and Henry and your mother in my care until the Marquis of Greenwood reaches his age of majority, you are indeed mine to command."

"What is the matter with you, Miranda?" Celeste asked, fresh tears streaming down her face. "I don't understand you."

"What is the matter?" Miranda shouted. "You deny me the opportunity to do anything fun. I want to go riding, you say no. I want to walk in the park and you say no. I want to-"

"But all those things were with Ashton, Miranda," Celeste argued. "You know how I feel about that young man. Find another suitor."

"Ashton?" Blaine asked, studying his nails. "Hasn't he tired of you and your churlish behavior yet?"

"What do you know about him?" Miranda said with a haughty toss of her blond curls.

"I know he won't marry you."

"And who are you to say?"

"I do believe," Blaine said, his exasperation finally showing, "that we have been down that road."

"May I go to the park?" Miranda suddenly asked.

"With whom?" He already knew the answer.

"Lord Ashton."

"Fine," Blaine said, stroking Shadow's head. "Be ready in ten minutes. I'll accompany you."

"*You,*" she cried, the words sounding choked from her.

"You go with me or you may stay here. Celeste, I was planning on taking Shadow for a run. Would you care for a stroll?"

"I'd be delighted," she said, mopping up the traces of her tears. "Let me get my parasol."

"Eight minutes, Miranda, and we're leaving, with or without you and your saucy mouth."

"I can't believe I have to been seen with that ghastly beast in the park," she pouted, glaring at Shadow.

"Believe it."

"You're just hoping for the chance to embarrass me, aren't you? You won't be happy till you've succeeded."

"Trust me, Miranda, if I wished to embarrass you, I could. In the most horrific way imaginable and it would have nothing to do with the beast. You have," he said, glancing at the mantle clock, "six minutes in which to cease your grumbling and make yourself presentable. You look in a state, and I, my dear, have no wish to be embarrassed by *you.*"

* * * *

"I thought," Harriett puffed breathlessly, "we were going for a stroll."

"We are," Madeline said, charging through the gates of Hyde Park. "A brisk stroll."

"Where's the fire?" Penelope asked, tugging on Madeline's reticule and bringing her to a halt.

"I thought a vigorous walk would clear my head."

"Well," Harry huffed, fanning her reddened face, "I'm about to swoon from lack of air."

"Sorry," Madeline mumbled, studying the elegant couples that strolled past them. "I was lost in thought."

"What's on your mind?" Penelope asked, starting to wander down the path, their stride slow and unhurried, allowing Harriett to catch her breath.

"Montgomery House."

"Your father has decreased his allowance again, has he?"

"Yes," Madeline sighed, kicking a pebble with her boot and sending it spinning down the path. "He wants to push me into making a decision. He thinks I'm spending far too much time at the house and not enough time husband hunting."

"Have you told him about Hardcastle?" Harry asked, her breathing at last restored.

"Yes. He had the audacity to laugh."

"Well," Penelope said, shading her eyes against the blazing sun, "he does have a point. I mean, the earl is not noted to be in the market for anything, much less a wife."

True, but she was certain the earl only pretended to not want a wife or family.

"Here he comes," Harry hissed.

"Here who--*oh*," Madeline said, her voice dropping an octave, as she saw Hardcastle strolling with his sister, Lady Greenwood, a magnificent dog at his side and a pouting, scowling Miranda behind them.

"Good day." Lady Greenwood smiled as they met on the path. "A lovely day for a stroll, is it not?"

"Good afternoon, ladies," Hardcastle mumbled, before bowing to them.

Madeline met his eyes, but he looked away, intent on studying the toe of his polished Hessians.

"May we join you?" Lady Greenwood asked, releasing her hold on her brother's arm, only to reach for Miranda's hand, and bring her forward.

"Of course," Penelope replied, falling into step with the Marchioness. "Madeline had us walking so fast that poor Harry was forced to stop to take a breath."

"My brother is the same," Lady Greenwood smiled. "I'm afraid his strolls are rather like gallops."

Madeline looked to the earl again but he failed to meet her eyes. Instead he walked slowly, allowing the women to go ahead of him, while he and the dog trailed behind.

"That's a lovely animal," Madeline said, stopping to pet it. "May I-"

"No," he said, gripping her hand about the wrist as she bent to pet the dog. "He's…" he said awkwardly, finally meeting her gaze, "he's not always receptive of strangers."

"Oh," she whispered, looking away from the cool gray eyes of the master and into the ice blue eyes of the dog. "What a beautiful creature. Such intelligent eyes. Such a beautiful coat."

"He's part timber wolf," he replied, his fingers still encased around her gloved wrist. "My friend, Stanfield brought him back from Upper Canada when he was but a pup."

Madeline looked into the clear blue eyes that stared back into hers. She could see the animal's nostrils flaring, catching her scent on the breeze, his watchful eyes scouring her, committing every bit of her to memory.

"He was only a pup, not yet weaned when Stanfield found him whimpering beside his mother. She was dead. Caught in a trap set by the fur traders."

"And he's been your faithful companion since?"

"Yes." Hardcastle stroked the beast's head affectionately. "He follows me wherever I go."

"May I?" she asked, removing her glove and extending her hand to the animal.

Before he could answer, the animal left Hardcastle's side and was sniffing her, his head cocked to one side as he sniffed and studied her. And then, with a whimper he licked her hand.

"Amazing. He's never willingly gone to anyone other than myself since he's matured."

"I have a way with those that are misunderstood," Madeline smiled, kneeling before the wolf, her ungloved hands raking through his luxurious pelt. "What is his name?" she smiled when she felt his head nudge her hand for another pet.

"Shadow."

"A fitting name for so proud and mysterious a beast. Oh," Madeline said as her hand brushed against something picky and hard. "You've a burr in your fur."

"Has he?" Hardcastle asked, removing his gloves and searching through Shadow's pelt. "Where?"

"Over more," Madeline said, watching as his hands missed the spot yet again. "No, there, a bit higher."

"I don't feel anything."

"Here, let me." With a deep breath, she took his fingers in her hand, the warmth and softness of them surprising her, making her feel off balanced. He looked at her then, his gray eyes softening. "It's right here," she said shyly, guiding his hand to the burr. "Do you feel it?"

"Yes," he said, his voice gravelly and harsh. His eyes, she noticed, continued to hold hers instead of inspecting Shadow's pelt. "Yes, I do feel it."

He made no attempt to move his fingers from beneath hers and neither did she. She felt a tremor of excitement course through her as he moved his hand atop hers, only to thread his fingers between her shaking ones.

She watched breathlessly as he looked up from their entwined hands, his eyes once again meeting hers, his thumb stroking her knuckles.

"You have enchanted the beast, my lady."

Madeline looked down to where their hands were joined in Shadow's pelt, the thickness of it disguising their entwined fingers from casual passersby. No one was looking, or indeed paying them any attention. Even Penelope and Harry and Lady Greenwood had continued up the path, heedless of the fact they straggled behind.

It was only her and the earl, their fingers locked tightly together, the heat from each radiating and absorbing into the other.

He continued to stare and again, Madeline was stunned by the emotion in his gaze. Shocked to see his breathing increased and the feel of a tremor of his fingers against hers.

"I have come to learn, my lord, that some beasts are needlessly misunderstood."

"One must be careful with beasts," he said, the curtain once again drawing across his eyes, shielding his need from her. "Some beasts," he began, removing his hand from hers, "are not what they seem. In fact, Lady Madeline, you don't always get what you see."

Striving to regain his sensibilities, Blaine reassembled his mask and motioned to the path. "We are falling behind."

Her questioning eyes roved over his face once more before she stood, straightened her bonnet and took her place beside him.

He'd made a grave error in believing he could continue to meet with Madeline and not become emotionally involved. What the devil had prompted him to say such a thing to her? Surely she realized that he had been referring to himself and not Shadow when he had talked of beasts.

"Your niece is taking the death of her father very hard," Madeline murmured alongside him as they strolled along the path. "I felt much the same way when my mother died. I was Miranda's age. I miss her very much. I'm certain Miranda misses him just as much."

Blaine said nothing. What could he say? He hadn't experienced the same feelings of regret when his father had died three years before. He had been rather relieved when the bastard had decided to cock up his toes in his mistress' bed.

"I suppose she has a reason for acting out," Madeline continued, shielding her eyes from the sun in order to study Miranda better. "Forgive my impertinence, my lord, but I cannot help but ask if she was close to her father?"

"Yes," he said, bristling at her forwardness and not understanding why the hell he felt compelled to answer her. He was divulging personal information about his family--he never discussed them and never talked about himself. And yet here he was with Madeline, speaking of things he never would have--in fact, things he never had. The topic of his parents, most especially his father had been off limits for years. He'd long ago banished their painful memory from his brain, all but forgetting them and how they had treated him.

His mother was still alive. Estranged, but well, living in self-imposed exile in France, returning yearly to play doting grandmamma to Celeste's two children. He chafed at the thought of her, surrounding herself with his half-sister's children. Catherine was *his* mother, but she couldn't bring herself to love him. Catherine had cared more for her husband's child with another woman than she had for her own flesh and blood. Of course, Celeste had been easy for Catherine to love--she was normal. She didn't embarrass her, or mortify her with behavior, 'akin to that of an idiot'.

The remembered barbs still stung, still hurt as much as they had when he was twelve. Mentally he shook himself. He didn't want to recall the taunts and sneers and the feeling of inadequacy. Especially when he was strolling beside Madeline.

"You and Miranda are very close, are you not?"

The question took him off guard. He already felt off centered.

Memories of his mother and her cruel treatment of him always did that. He might have been successful in banishing the memory of his parents, but he'd never figured out how to make the pain of their treachery disappear. And now he had Madeline strolling beside him, digging into his past, attempting to uncover his secrets.

How had she known? How had Madeline guessed that he and Miranda shared a special bond? He'd been fifteen years old when Celeste had borne Miranda. He'd been thrilled with his niece, doted on her, played with her and delighted in her cherubic smiles. She'd loved him despite the dark secrets inside him. Little Miranda had been the first person beside Celeste to truly look at him without sympathy or horror. She had loved him. And then her father had died and she had started to hate him. Had begun, he thought, with a pang of hurt, to be ashamed of him.

"Forgive me," she said shyly, a faint hint of pink dusting her cheeks. "I only wish to be of assistance. I understand, you see, what your niece is going through, and I can only assume she loves you a great deal. Why ever would she try to drive you away if not to protect you and herself?"

"What are you saying?" he asked, halting her in the middle of the path. "How do you come to understand Miranda so well?"

She shrugged, her turquoise gaze meeting his. God, her eyes were lovely. It was like looking into a tropical lagoon. Hypnotizing. Soothing. Beckoning him to their deep depths.

"I have a knack for understanding others. Call it a gift, or intuition, but I can tell you that Miranda is choosing to be willfully stubborn. Somehow she's decided that everyone she loves will be taken from her and she cannot bear the pain of that. So, she's chosen to drive her loved ones away, thus preventing her heart from breaking once again."

His gaze reluctantly left Madeline to search the park for his niece. He watched her walk beside Celeste, her head lowered, her shoulders hunched. For the first time in months he saw her in a different light. She was indeed in a dark place full of fears and insecurities. He knew it to be true. It was like he was looking into the mirror seeing his own reflection shining back at him.

"How did…." He looked back at Madeline, her eyes seeing far too much. He shouldn't have exposed himself in such a way. She was dangerous, far too observant and intelligent. If he wasn't careful she would discover what he was.

"My lord," she asked, touching his sleeve, stepping nearer to him. So close in fact he could smell her, the scent of soap with a hint of lemon reached him. "I fear I have overstepped my bounds. Forgive me."

"Good day, old boy."

Blaine looked away from Madeline's hypnotizing eyes to see his friend Bronley and his wife strolling in the park, pushing a pram.

"Dev," Blaine nodded curtly. "Rebecca."

"Good day," Rebecca smiled, her eyes lighting when she saw Madeline standing beside him. He wanted to groan. He'd seen that amused sparkle in her eye before.

"Lady Madeline," Bronley demurred, taking her hand in his. "It has been far too long."

"It has indeed, Lord Bronley."

"We've just come from visiting Grandmama."

"And how is the dowager marchioness?" she asked.

"As saucy as ever, right Hardcastle, old boy?"

"I fear I must refrain from comment."

"Congratulations, Lord Bronley, Lady Bronley, on your newest arrival." Madeline peered into the pram, her eyes widening in wonder. "Such a beautiful baby."

"Thank you", Rebecca gushed. "Would you care to hold her?" Rebecca asked, picking the babe up.

"Oh, I'd love to," Madeline cried as if she were a child being handed a sweetmeat. "I adore children."

Blaine watched with growing horror as Madeline held the child, cooing and remarking as if it were natural to her. As if the infant actually belonged to her. He saw Bronley send him a sidelong look and he felt the prickles of heat rise under his collar. He knew what that look meant, had seen it countless times and he wished no part of it.

"Isn't she lovely, my lord?" Madeline asked, her face flushed with joy.

"I suppose," he said gruffly, stepping away from her, fearing she might plop the babe into his arms. "At least this time she hasn't spit up all over herself."

"Really," Rebecca frowned. "I assure you, all infants spit up. I'm afraid even your offspring will do the same."

His offspring? There would be no children sprung from his loins. He'd never wanted them, had never wanted to think about having his own. There would be no babe to carry on his curse, of that he had promised himself. There was no inducement in the world for him to bring an innocent babe into the world only to suffer through the same hell as he.

"I say, you look remarkably at ease, there, Lady Madeline. Motherhood will suit you."

"Do you think so, Lord Bronley?" Madeline asked, clearly in awe of the compliment. "I do love children. I hope to be blessed with many."

"Many, eh?" Bronley slid him another look. "Well, Lady Madeline, best of luck to you."

"Would you care to hold her, my lord?" Madeline whirled around, shoving the baby at him. He felt himself shrink back, as if she held a hissing snake in her hands and not a gurgling infant.

Again he felt off centered, disjointed. He didn't like the feeling, the loss of control. He wanted out of the park, wanted to be rid of the sight of Madeline with a baby in her arms.

"You will forgive me, Lady Madeline, but I find infants tiresome at the best times. I must go," he said curtly, bowing before her, his sensibilities at last returning. "I have an appointment."

He did, indeed. Another trip to Bethlehem Hospital was where he should go. A visit to Bedlam always cured him. Always reminded him that he could never allow another human being into his life--into his heart--and, most importantly, into his soul.

"Never mind him," he heard Rebecca say jauntily, as he strolled away from them. "He's never liked children. I'm sure he'd prefer to see his title die into obscurity than provide it with an heir."

"Rubbish," Madeline scoffed, "what rational man would willingly let his title die out?"

His decision to never marry or procreate was infinitely rational, he thought as he strolled away. What sane man would willingly bequeath his curse to his offspring? No, there would be no children from him and that, he vowed, was an irrevocable promise.

Chapter Three

"With your last generous donation, my lord, we were able to add another twenty cots and numerous blankets and pillows. We also brought in the services of a Joseph Gibbert, a very influential physician who specializes in brain disorders."

Blaine followed John Jenkinson, the superintendent of Bedlam down into the dark and damp bowels of the mad house. Nervous energy flickered along every taught nerve, culminating in a shiver down his spine. His brow began to sweat and he felt his throat constrict as they walked through an invisible shroud of stench and human decay.

"We're trying to make repairs to this wing. My predecessor misguidedly believed these patients were beyond help, that they needed virtually no creature comforts, thus the deplorable conditions."

Blaine felt his breath whoosh right out of him as he took in the putrid state of the cells before him. Overcrowding and harsh conditions had made the patients more demented and confused. The never-ending darkness played to their agitation; the dim candlelight only fueled their dementia, making them see monsters in each and every flickering shadow--visions that terrified them.

He forced himself to look from cell to cell and see the faces behind the madness. To see what they had once been before the darkness of insanity had claimed them.

It was a pitiful sight. More than pitiful, it clearly defied words. The hopelessness, the despair he saw shining behind the glazed look of madness disturbed him, made him confront what it was it was like to be consumed by demons.

He hated Bedlam, despised the fact that such a monstrous place was needed. He hated his father for bringing him here as a child every Sunday afternoon and taunting him with accusations, with parallels between himself and the inmates. Finally, he abhorred the fact he needed to come and remind himself of just what might happen to him if he were to be exposed to the prejudiced and ignorant eyes of the *ton*.

"Gertrude was recently brought to us," Jenkinson mumbled, whipping out his handkerchief in order to hide himself from the rank odor of urine, feces and rotting food. "She suffers from the falling sickness. Quite violent, in fact." He motioned to a cell where a woman, no more than thirty, sat huddled in the corner. Her thin shift was stained and tattered, revealing pale skin marked with festering lesions and rodent bites.

"Her family committed her. They say she suffers from voices before she succumbs to her fits. Her husband says he fears the devil is at work."

Typical, Blaine thought, looking away from the woman as she rocked back and forth, her breasts spilling out from the tattered neckline. Ignorance abounded. In these modern days, where they could light the streets with gas, produce silks and wools with alarming speed using machinery and wage war across vast areas of lands, they were still forced to think of some maladies as the devil's work. As possession.

He shuddered, wondering how many people had been wrongfully committed to the asylum under the guise of demonic possession. How many people had died alone in their cells, perfectly sane, pleading with the Almighty to save them from Hell? How many God-damned aristocrats had stood before these very cells on a Sunday afternoon and paid to watch the idiots, the insane, the possessed, perform their freakish acts and laugh at them as they did?

And then he heard it, the familiar cry, the thumping of flesh against stone. He darted his eyes back to Gertrude, back to the writhing, shaking form of the pathetic wretch, her eyes rolling, her tongue lolling out, blood trickling down her chin as she bit it in the height of her fit.

It was haunting, horrific and it scared the hell out of him.

"I've seen enough," he said gruffly. "You'll receive a draft for five thousand pounds. See to it that conditions in these cells are vastly improved by my next visit."

And then he left, fled through the dark tunnel as though the devil himself was hard upon him, ran as though the contagions would leap from the patients and infect him.

Flinging open the doors of Bedlam, he stepped out of the darkness and into the sunlight, gasping, inhaling the scent of air, air that was free of foul decay and human suffering. He took another breath, mentally replaying what he'd seen and promptly lost the contents of his lunch.

* * * *

"Nanny," Blaine called as he crossed the small drawing room

and placed a kiss on her papery, wrinkled cheek. "At last I find you at home."

She blushed as he squeezed her hand before taking up the settee across from her. "Have a seat. Can I pour you a cup?" she asked, holding up the teapot.

He nodded and looked around the small room, which was cozy and neat and filled with warmth. He reached for the cup and stared into the face of the woman who had raised him. The woman who had loved him as if he were her own flesh and blood.

Maggie Noland, or Nanny Noland as he had called her since he could talk, had been his mother's midwife. She had been at his birth and acted as his nurse and nanny, also playing the role of his mother, grandmother and now, treasured friend.

He studied her gleaming eyes and realized he never felt more at peace than when he was at her side, drinking tea and feeling completely at ease and unguarded. She knew all there was to know about him, all his dark secrets and sorrows. There was nothing to hide from Nanny--she knew it all.

"I thought you were to accompany Miranda to the Somerset ball this evening?"

He shrugged and sipped his tea.

"Surely you're not going out without a cravat and waistcoat?" she teased, passing him a tray filled with biscuits and mincemeat tarts. "The *ton* will have hysterics witnessing you in your state of dishabille."

"I'm tired of balls and soirees and uncomfortable clothing. It's fatiguing always having to be on my toes, searching for escape routes and pretending enjoyment."

"Only pretending?" Nanny chuckled, her wrinkled lips curving into a lopsided grin. "I'm certain it isn't always such a trial."

No indeed, he thought, biting into the tart. It wasn't always torture to stand along the walls and pretend he wanted to be there. Not when *she* was there. When Madeline was present in a ballroom, he did want to be there. In fact, he wanted to be nowhere else but in the room, watching her, wishing she could be his.

No, that was wrong. There was somewhere he'd rather be. He'd rather be on the dance floor, sweeping Madeline up into his arms during a waltz. Holding her close so that he could feel her against his chest, smell the scent of her as it clung to the air between them. But that would never happen. He couldn't let it happen. So, instead, he contented himself with covert stares and nights filled with longing.

"So what brings you to an old woman's house at this time of night?"

"It's barely eight o'clock, and you're not an old woman. Besides," he mumbled, biting off another chunk of his tart, "you're never home. You're always working at that home. You'd think your pension wasn't enough to keep you."

"Dear boy," she laughed, pouring him more tea, "I want for nothing. The pension you give me is nigh on scandalous, and the servants you've hired do all my work. What, may I ask you, did you think I would do with my time?"

"Shop, read, travel abroad."

"Bah," she waved his comment aside. "I would waste away from idleness. I enjoy the home. It's good for me and I like that I'm able to do good for the poor souls who enter its hallowed halls."

"Tell me about this home," he asked, settling himself against the cushions. "You spend an extraordinary amount of time there."

"It's a home for women who've found themselves in dire straits. The proprietor has a heart of gold, she can't refuse anyone. I do some of the housekeeping and of course, I deliver the babies."

"Babies," he said, choking on his tea. "Good grief, it's a foundling hospital?"

"No. It's more than that. It's a home, a school, it's...." she paused, then looked at him, emotion welling in her eyes. "It's almost like a family. It's a Godsend and the lady behind the idea is the most wonderful, caring woman I've ever come across."

"I assume the clients are ladies of the night and their offspring?"

"Oh no," she countered. "You wouldn't believe the girls who cross the threshold of Montgomery House. They're from all walks of life. Governesses, lady's maids, why, we even have a vicar's daughter who found herself with child."

He arched a brow and smiled. "A motley assortment at best."

"Yes," she laughed, "but we do rub along rather well. We all work together to run the house and get the chores done. The women work hard to learn a new way of life and I'm pleased to say that the success rate of Montgomery House is very high."

"I must visit you there," he said, setting his cup on the table and reaching for another tart. "If for nothing else than to see what sort of place can house these poor unfortunates."

"Of course. If you ever find yourself in Leicester Square, stop in at number thirty. The girls would be more than happy to entertain you."

"You're teasing me."

"And you're baiting me," she laughed. "Tell me," she asked, sobering. "Are you well? I saw Jenkinson the other day, he said you paid him a visit."

"I donated some money for repairs."

"You went to torture yourself."

"Merely to remind myself of my precarious state."

"Isn't it time your parents' prejudices left you? How much longer will you go on believing their hateful words? You're not a monster. You're a man. Nothing more, nothing less."

"If the ton knew what I was, they would not think twice about having me committed."

"The ton is full of foolish imbeciles. They've no right to accuse you of anything."

The familiar feelings of helplessness and hopelessness once again welled up inside him but he ruthlessly forced them aside. "I would not wish for Celeste and her children to suffer the humiliation. Especially when Miranda is seeking to marry. I cannot afford for their names to be associated with the stigma."

"Excuse me, ma'am," a maid said, peering around the door. "But there's a lad here that wishes to see ye."

"Bring him in, Mary."

Blaine watched as a lanky youth, no more than twelve, loped into the drawing room, his tattered woolen hat scrunched between his hands. "The missus has asked me to fetch ye, Mrs. Noland," he said, a hint of cockney accent infusing his words. "Abby's time's come."

"Let me get my bag, Daniel," Nanny said, rising slowly to her feet. "If you'll excuse me?"

"Of course," Blaine said, already standing. "But let me take you in the carriage."

"I'll take a hack," she mumbled, hurrying about the room, gathering her black leather satchel.

"You will allow me to take you, or I shall see to it that you stay here."

"Well, *milord*," she huffed, affection twinkling in her eye. "You're a right devil to be ordering me about."

"Indeed, it was rather high handed of me," he grinned, taking the satchel from her. "But I did promise to look after you, did I not?"

"And you do a good job of it. One wonders when you'll start looking out for your own happiness. Now," she commanded, wrapping her shawl about her shoulders and giving him a good glare. "On to Montgomery House, babies don't always wait."

* * * *

"That's enough, Jacob," Madeline scolded as she took a sticky bun out of the five-year-old's cherubic hand. "You've already had one."

"I'm still hungry," he complained, rubbing his belly.

"You, sir, must have a hollow leg. One more," she said, mussing the boy's golden curls, "and don't tell the others I let you have it."

"I won't, missus," he said, sliding from the chair and running off in the direction of the stairs.

"I wonder when Maggie will get here?" Phoebe asked as she stared out the window. "Daniel's been gone quite some time."

"She'll be here," Madeline assured, checking on the stirring babe in the bassinet that lay beside her.

It had been two hours since Abby's pains had started, and already she was close to delivery. They could hear her, her screams and cries getting louder with each pain. Madeline knew it wouldn't be long before the child was delivered. She just hoped Maggie would make it for the grand entrance.

"I never get used to the sounds of childbirth," Phoebe whispered, visibly shuddering as another pain-filled scream rent the air. "I don't understand why women keep doing this over and over again."

"Well," Madeline said, lifting the fussing infant from her bassinet, "some women wish to be mothers more than anything."

"Yes, but, the pain."

"The pain is a small price to pay," Madeline whispered, as the infant quieted and settled her head against the curve of her neck. "I would think the joy of bringing life into the world far outweighs a few hours of pain."

"Hmm," Phoebe said, unconvinced. "But then you have a squalling infant to take care of. I can't abide that endless crying."

"Little Emily has quieted," Madeline smiled as she stroked the baby's downy head. Thinking how satisfying it would be to have a child of her own. A child with black waves and mesmerizing gray eyes. But Hardcastle, it seemed, was against having a family. He'd paled and nearly tripped in his haste to get away from her when she had tried to pass him Anna. Had she misinterpreted his actions? Perhaps he simply didn't feel comfortable around other people's children. Many men were like that. Surely he wouldn't be opposed to holding his own children? It was utterly impossible to think he would never have them, as Lady Bronley had suggested. The man was an earl after all, he had a title to pass on. No man wanted his title to die out. Not even her father had easily resigned himself to that fate.

"And then there are the soiled linens and the feedings," Phoebe continued to complain. "They are forever in want of something."

"They only wish to be loved, Phoebe," she said against the babe's brow. "That's all any person really wants."

"Well-"

"Where is she?" Maggie huffed as she waddled into the room. "I'm not too late, am I?"

"No, she's…." Madeline stopped mid-sentence and forgot to breathe. "Lord Hardcastle!"

"Lady Madeline," he said, shocked to see her as much as she was to see him.

"Oh good," Maggie said breathlessly, reaching for her satchel. "You've saved me the introductions. Do carry on."

Both of them watched her trod up the stairs, satchel in hand. Maggie Noland had long disappeared before Madeline could even thinking of talking.

"Allow me to introduce you to-" she stopped when she saw Phoebe was no longer in the room. "She must have left. I was going to introduce you to Montgomery House's governess."

"Oh," he said awkwardly, as he looked about the room. She saw him wince, then shudder as another one of Abby's screams splintered the strained silence.

"Perhaps, my lord, you'd like to take a turn about the gardens?"

"Yes," he nodded, bolting out of the room.

"My lord," she called after him. "This way."

"Oh right, he mumbled as he sailed past her. She smiled to herself as she watched him practically run for the door. Men, they were such a weak a lot.

* * * *

"So," he began as he strolled about the small garden, "you didn't tell me you were the proprietor of Montgomery House."

She shrugged and rubbed her arms. She should have brought a shawl. The capped sleeves of her ball gown were not enough to keep the chill of the wind away.

"You're cold," he said, removing his jacket and striding over to her. "Take this. No, I insist," he said when she shook her head. "You'll freeze to death in that ball gown."

"Thank you," she murmured as she sat on the stone bench,

luxuriating in the heat of the jacket and the scent of him--soap and a hint of sandalwood. "I'm afraid I got called away from the Somerset ball and I forgot my shawl."

"Do you often get called away?" he asked, reaching for a leaf above him, yanking it from the branch. "Do you attend all the births?"

"Sometimes. Not always. Abby," Madeline motioned to the house, "is special to us. She was taken advantage of by a man who should have known better. I wanted to be here to help her."

"Ah," he nodded, the glossy leaf twirling about his fingers, "the vicar's daughter."

"Yes, how did you know?"

"Mrs. Noland," he said, gazing up to look at the moon that lay hidden between the trees. "I was there when the lad came to fetch her."

"You must be Maggie's previous employer," Madeline said, astonished that Maggie would leave out such an important fact. Especially when Madeline had all but been planning to ensnare his lordship into marriage. Why, the woman had never once hinted that she knew the man, much less worked for him. It was very strange that Maggie would be so elusive about her connection with the Earl of Hardcastle.

"She was my nurse and nanny, a favored member of our household and I see to it that she lives a comfortable life. Tell me, how did you come to find yourself proprietor of a house for poor unfortunates?"

Madeline shrugged and looked at the toe of her slippers. He looked so devilishly handsome standing in the moonlit garden, his linen shirt contrasting sharply against the inky night. More than once she'd caught herself staring at his naked throat, wondering what the patch of skin would feel like beneath her fingers. He had made no excuses for his dishabille, had not even mentioned it. His casual dress enticed her. He looked dangerous in only his shirtsleeves and black trousers.

"This is a very large house," he said, staring at the brick façade and large windows. "I imagine the lease is exorbitant."

"No," she said, swallowing hard, trying to look away from the way the moonlight illuminated his strong arms through his shirt. "I own it. My mother's father bequeathed it to me upon his death. He made his fortune in trade and he wanted it put to good use."

"And you enjoy helping people?"

His tone was quiet and somewhat mocking, as if he would laugh at her.

"Yes, I do," she said rather sourly. "I find extreme gratification in helping those less fortunate than myself."

"I have offended you." He reached for her hand, gently pulling her up from the stone bench. "Forgive me. I had no intention of hurting you."

"I … that is.…" she stammered as he brought her before him, his fingers entwining with hers.

"Forgive me?" His lips brushed her knuckles in a whispered kiss.

"Of course," she said, trying to stop her hand from trembling in his.

"Will you dance with me?"

Madeline stared at him, clearly stunned by his sudden request. How many times and how many balls had she pined away, waiting for him to ask her to dance? That he should ask her now, out in the moonlit garden thrilled her beyond what she thought possible.

They stood together, him looking down at her, her gazing up at him, their fingers locked tightly together. The wind went still around them and the moon slipped behind a cloud, shrouding them in darkness.

Damn it, what had he done? He'd been thinking of her in that damn ball gown, her pale skin illuminated by the moon, her flame red hair enticing him, making him wish to run his hands through its thickness. He couldn't get the image of her wrapped in his arms, twirling beneath the moonlight out his mind. He could never risk the chance of dancing with her at a tonnish event, shouldn't even be tempting fate now, but she looked so damn beautiful in her green watered silk gown that he thought he had to feel her against him or go mad with longing.

Her turquoise eyes searched his face, her full lips trembling with nervousness, or perhaps excitement. Jesus, he wanted to kiss those lips, to feel them against his, to slide his tongue into her mouth and feel her respond to him.

He shouldn't be doing this, he should never have come. He wasn't dressed as a gentleman, wasn't acting as one should, but he didn't give a damn. This was Madeline and he wanted to feel her against him, to discover if she would feel as good in life as she did in his dreams.

"My lord?"

"My name is Blaine. Call me by my given name."

"Blaine," she said, tasting his name upon her tongue. The resulting sound was a hushed whisper, sweeter than anything he had ever heard.

"May I?" he asked, reaching through his gaping jacket and fitting his hand around her waist. "Just one dance, Madeline, that is all I ask."

"Yes, Blaine," she said breathlessly as he twirled her around, the pace slow and unhurried as he brought her closer to him, so close he could feel her heart beating through his shirt. He closed his eyes and savored his name on her mouth, her fingers on his arm, her warmth against his chest. He felt at peace, at one with her. Felt as though he could risk all and let himself fall in love with her-risk laying open his secrets and letting her in. He'd give anything to feel her beneath him, to feel himself inside her.

"I have wanted you to ask me to dance, my lord," she said, her voice low and quiet, almost impossible to hear above the sound of his raging blood. "But you never do. You never even speak with me when we're out in Society. You act as though we've never even met."

"I…." he trailed off, catching a scent of her as it wafted up between their bodies. "I'm out of my element amongst the ton, I'm afraid."

"And yet you are a wonderful dancer, as accomplished as any other gentleman I've danced with."

"I'm," he swallowed thickly, unsure of why he wanted--no needed to explain his behavior to her. "I am not comfortable amongst the ton. I'm a solitary person, I keep my own counsel, and prefer to do so."

"You're lonely."

He stopped then, shocked by her words, by her perception of him. He'd made himself vulnerable, let himself weaken as her soft body melded with his. She saw too much, knew too much.

"This," he said, his voice cracking with desire, with the pain of what he knew he must do. "I can't…."

"Just let me in," she whispered.

"I'm afraid you would not like what you see."

"Trust me," she said, her tempting mouth only inches away from his.

Unable to stop the feelings of desire, of desperation, he grasped her hand and pressed her palm to his mouth. Closing his eyes, he savored her warmth and the scent of her. He could be happy with Madeline-content to spend the rest of his days with her, if he wasn't so scared about her discovering his secrets. If he wasn't so terrified of her turning from him.

"You don't know me," he whispered, sliding her hand down his chest to rest over his bounding heart. "I'm not the man you think I am."

He saw the image of her in the drawing room, the sleeping babe curled against her. Saw the happiness, the completeness in her eyes and knew what she longed for. She intended to marry, intended to bring life into the world. Madeline was a nurturer, put on this earth to be a wife and mother. And she would be, but not *his* wife, nor the mother of his children. He could never marry her, could never fulfill her dreams of motherhood. She was not the sort of woman one dallied with, she was the sort one married and therefore, not destined for him.

"I can't," he breathed, releasing her hand as though he'd been burned. "I cannot give you what you want. I will only make you miserable."

"No," she said, reaching for him as he stalked away. "You're wrong."

"I cannot give you what you need, don't ask it of me."

"You may give up on me, my lord," she whispered, reaching out and grasping his wrist. "But, I too have made up my mind, and nothing will deter me, not even your secrets and your fears."

"Be careful what you wish for. Dreams have a way of turning into nightmares."

Chapter Four

Rubbing her eyes, Madeline peered up from her account ledgers. Sedgewick had appeared that afternoon at Montgomery House, informing her that the investors of Morning Lane were prepared to give her a fortnight to come up with the additional ten thousand pounds and not a day more.

With a sigh, she looked down at the figures and wondered where in Heavens the money would be found. Checking her arithmetic, Madeline was frustrated to see that it was indeed, correct.

Blast! Why was her father making it so difficult for her? If only he hadn't halved her monthly stipend. If she'd had the full amount she was certain she could scrap up the ten thousand, but it had been three months since her father had cut back the house's funding. Three months since he'd issued his ultimatum--marry or lose his backing for Montgomery House. *You're consumed with that damn house, Madeline. It's time you moved on with you life.*

How her father's words irritated her, and his method of forcing her hand was not in keeping with how he usually dealt with her. She had promised, and she kept her vows. He needn't worry. She was four and twenty, hardly on the shelf. And she had promised him. But apparently, her father was not happy with the course she had set for herself. He wanted results, and the results were her married off by the end of the summer.

"Well, you've got yourself into a fine kettle of fish," Madeline grumbled aloud. Not only was her beloved house about to go under, along with her very large investment for the Morning Lane project, but it seemed her hopes for the husband she'd so desired was about to go up in smoke also.

Glancing at the package sitting atop her dressing table, Madeline shoved back her chair and strolled to it. Untying the neat bow, she parted the paper and unfolded Blaine's jacket, bringing it to her face to smell what was left of his scent.

It had been a week since they'd danced in the garden of Montgomery House. A full week since she'd even seen him. The rogue had been conspicuously absent from society. It was, she thought, as though he had fallen off the face of the earth.

Rubbing her cheek against the soft wool, she remembered how it had been between them. She had seen a need in him, a desire to reach out to her and then he had shut her out just as quickly as he had reached out. *Blast the man!* He was being far too difficult, far too secretive. He acted as though he was a pariah, a monster among men. And that was perfectly ridiculous. There was nothing wrong with the Earl of Hardcastle. Perhaps he was a bit aloof and more than a touch arrogant, but really, she could decipher no medical malady. Well, perhaps a touch of ennui, but what male of the ton didn't suffer that from time to time?

The man was an enigma. One minute he was looking at her as though he would kiss her senseless, the next he refused to even talk to her, much less look at her.

Folding the jacket and hiding it back inside the wrapping; Madeline sat down and contemplated her situation. She had to marry, there was no question about that. She could not lose Montgomery House. She'd invested too much time, too much love to let it slip through her fingers so easily. She had worked side by side with her mother for years, making a success of Montgomery House.

She could not fail now. Failure of any of kind was insupportable. Her future consisted of Montgomery House and a husband. She wanted that husband to be Blaine. And yet, he had told her in no uncertain terms he did not share her visions of the future. And she must marry. Yet the very thought of a marriage of convenience sickened her. She didn't want to live the rest of her days in a cool and distant relationship. She wanted a husband she could love, one that would love her. She wanted a home, a family. She wanted Blaine. From the very first time she had seen him, Madeline had felt a strange and inexplicable attraction to him. She was drawn to him, not just to his athletic body and handsome face, but him, the man behind the mask.

Her father had given her till the end of the Season to choose herself a husband. It was June, nearly eight weeks left before the close of the Season. Surely she could get Blaine to wed her? How difficult could it be? He was already softening, already reaching out to her. Asking her to dance had proved it, despite what he thought. Surely a man possessed of such passion could not resist forever?

Eight weeks, she thought, blowing out the candles and padding silently back to her bed. Eight weeks to discover Blaine's secrets and make him fall in love with her. It would work, she mused, nuzzling beneath the blankets. It had to work, because she had no intention of losing either Montgomery House or the Earl of Hardcastle.

* * * *

"Your father seems to be in high dudgeon," Penelope whispered over the tip of her fan. "He keeps glaring this way."

"Pay him no heed, Penny. He's merely trying to intimidate me into doing his bidding."

"What bidding?" Harry asked, stealing a look at the Earl of Penrick. "I say, Maddy, he has the same ferocious set to his brows as you do when you're bent on a mission."

Madeline looked to the group of men gathered in the middle of the ballroom. In the center was her father, conducting his Whig business with his cronies and sending her scathing glances when he thought no one was looking.

He was displeased with her, she knew that. But really, what did he expect? She wanted to marry Hardcastle, not one of her father's underlings.

"He's trying to push Lord Tynemouth on you, isn't he?" Penny asked.

Madeline shuddered, noticing how Tynemouth kept glancing her way. "He wishes to make a political alliance, and I'm to be the bait. Of course, he misguidedly thinks Tynemouth and I will suit."

"He is handsome. Lovely eyes."

Madeline arched a brow in annoyance. "If you find Tynemouth attractive, Henny, why don't you dance with him?"

"We haven't been introduced. And, I'm afraid, he only has eyes for you."

"Well, he can keep his eyes to himself. I'm not interested."

"Viscount Stanfield looks at you quite a bit."

Madeline searched the room for Hardcastle's friend. He was standing beside Blaine, his intriguing green eyes raking boldly and inquisitively over her before slowly moving away. "It means nothing," Madeline said, praying she was correct. Nothing could make her pursuit of Hardcastle more complicated than his friend thinking she was making eyes at *him*.

"Here he comes."

"Oh, no," Madeline groaned.

"Oh, yes," Penny laughed.

"Good evening, Lady Madeline," Lord Stanfield said before bowing. "Miss Mills, Miss Longbottom."

"Good evening," they curtseyed in unison.

"May I have this dance, Lady Madeline?" Lord Stanfield asked, gallantly reaching for her hand.

She smiled uneasily and closed her fan. Accepting his hand, Madeline allowed him to lead her onto the dance floor for an invigorating Scottish reel.

"It's been ages since we've met, my lady," the viscount said, spinning her around and stepping behind another couple.

"I believe," she said, when they were partnered together again, "it was last year, at Lady Lancaster's card party. Pray tell me, how is Miss Lancaster?"

He smiled a roguish grin, his white teeth flashing behind his full lips. "The last time I saw her she was quite well. Although I confess it's been some time since we've met. I understand you've taken my friend's niece under your wing," he said, twirling her once again.

"I suppose," she murmured, wondering what thoughts were behind his questions. "I've merely taken the opportunity to show Miranda the way amongst the ton. We seem to have been attending the same balls this past week."

"Imagine that, attending the same soirees and routs as Hardcastle's niece. What a coincidence."

Madeline sucked in her breath at the thinly veiled innuendo. "What do you propose by the comment, my lord?"

"It was merely an observation."

"If you have something to say, Lord Stanfield, say it. Pray, do not beat about the bush."

"I have only the highest of compliments to pay you," he said, glancing to where Hardcastle and his other friends stood against the wall. "Are you by any chance going to the new exhibit at the museum tomorrow?" he asked, pinning her with his intense green gaze. "I understand it's to be quite an event."

Was he asking her to attend the opening with him? Good heavens, what if he did think it was him she had in her sights?

"You should go." He cast another glance in his friend's direction. "Bound to be a crush. You never know who you'll meet there."

The music ended, and Lord Stanfield walked her over to the edge of the room, only footsteps from his friends and Blaine.

"Perhaps we shall meet up at the museum tomorrow? The crowds should have dissipated by two o'clock, don't you think?"

She nodded, her mind feverously trying to decipher just what he was telling her.

"Perhaps tomorrow, then."

And without another word, he left her, standing alone with Hardcastle only feet away.

"Madeline," she heard her father's voice rumble behind her. "I have someone who wishes to dance with you."

"Papa," she said, smiling as her father's eyes, filled with challenge, met hers. "I would be delighted."

She was relieved when she saw his anger suddenly evaporate. She didn't dare defy him again, not after their row that afternoon. Not after she had flatly refused to listen to his prattling about the unsuitability of Hardcastle in the role of his son-in-law.

"Lady Madeline," Tynemouth smiled, his friendly brown eyes widening. "Shall we?"

"Indeed," she nodded, smiling at her father as she strolled past him with the young viscount.

Drat! This was the last thing she wanted to do. She didn't want to give Tynemouth a reason to be encouraged. She didn't want him always sniffing about her skirts and bothering her at every function. If he was always hanging about, how in the world would she ever get close to Hardcastle?

"You look very fetching this evening, Lady Madeline."

"Thank you," she mumbled, automatically searching the room for Hardcastle.

"Are you going to the museum tomorrow? I thought I understood from your father that you were."

"I suppose," she said absently, watching as Blaine pretended boredom before a gaggle of women who stood conversing with Lord Stanfield.

"Would it be too forward of me to ask you to accompany me?"

"Just look at what you've done. You've torn your frock!"

Ignoring Tynemouth, Madeline peered over his shoulder to see where the ruckus was coming from.

"You stupid, stupid girl.

Seated on the chair, directly beside the women hovering around Lord Stanfield and Hardcastle, sat Alexandra Billingsworth and her mother, who was viciously berating her. She saw Alexandra start to cry, and then saw Hardcastle raise his chin, his firm lips hardening, his polite mask at last giving way to distaste.

"You little idiot," Lady Billingsworth continued on, her voice louder with each insult. *"You're a disgrace. I'm ashamed of you."*

Madeline watched, completely taken aback as Blaine closed his eyes, his face paling as if he were bearing the brunt of Lady Billingsworth's cruel tongue. And then to her astonishment, he excused himself from his friends and female admirers and headed straight for Alexandra. Madeline thought sure her mouth dropped open when Blaine bowed gracefully before the girl, extending his hand to her in an invitation to dance.

"Lady Madeline?" Tynemouth asked nervously, his voice a touch tremulous. "Would you permit me to escort you to the museum?"

"What--oh yes, yes," she mumbled, watching in amazement as Blaine strolled onto the dance floor with the awkward, lumbering Alexandra Billingsworth in tow.

A wry smile curled her lips. It was the most gallant thing she'd ever seen anyone do. He was a solicitous partner, his thin lips giving way to an amused smile, his face never once betraying the fact that the nervous Alexandra was trampling his toes. He whispered something in Alexandra's ear and Madeline felt her heart swell when the girl smiled brightly, her whole face lighting up, giving her the look of newfound confidence.

He was an amazing man. He despised dancing, feared being out amongst the ton, all eyes focused on him. And yet, he'd done it. He'd put his fears and secrets behind him and saved an awkward and shy debutante from the merciless ton and a scornful mother.

Aware of a curious tingling down her spine, Madeline chanced a glance over her shoulder and met Blaine's cool, gray eyes. He took his time looking at her, his eyes sliding down the length of her body, only to settle on her face with his brow arched in perfected hauteur. What the devil was that look about? She had done nothing to incur his silent reproof. She tried to catch his attention again, but the insolent man flatly refused to acknowledge her, absolutely refused to even look her way.

That was it, she thought, wishing she could stamp her feet in frustration. She was going to get to the bottom of his scathing glances. She promised herself by the end of the ball she was going to learn just what thoughts were going on behind that brooding mask.

* * * *

The exasperating man had left! He was utterly frustrating, completely rude and arrogant and if Madeline had him standing before her this very minute she'd give him a tongue lashing he'd never forget.

"Dratted man," she muttered beneath her breath as she leaned over the balustrade, searching the gardens below. "Always disappearing at the most inconvenient of times."

"I see your lovelorn pup has at last given you a minute of peace."

The mocking sound of Blaine's voice washed over her shoulder. She felt him behind her, a dark, dangerous aura radiating from him. She didn't know why, or what had caused this abrupt change in him, but she knew for certain she had never seen him in this mood before.

"Lord Tynemouth has departed for the evening," she said, not bothering to look at him. Instead she watched the couples below walk along Lady Carstairs' lavender trimmed paths.

"How unfortunate," he drawled, "you must be crestfallen to be deprived of his company."

She could almost see him huffing and puffing in his arrogance. She knew he had crossed his arms over his chest and knew her cavalier attitude towards him was making his anger bubble further. But she was heedless of the warning, however. She was angry herself and she was more than a little put out with his treatment of her this evening.

"I'm sure we'll meet up another time. He's good ton. I can always find him in the right places."

"I see you're common to your breed."

Madeline whirled around, her eyes blazing. She saw him, bathed in shadows as he leaned against the wall, one leg bent, his boot resting against the bricks. His arms were folded across his chest and his gray eyes flashed at her, their color reminding her of metal.

"And just what do you mean by that?"

"Merely that you follow the same path as others of your sex. For a while I thought I had made a mistake. I'm infinitely relieved to discover that my perfect record of never being wrong still stands."

"You're too arrogant for words, my lord," she said archly. "What are you attempting to imply?"

"Merely that your actions were predictable. Like others of your sex, you use feminine wiles to get what you want when the object you desire is denied you."

"How dare you," she hissed, unable to believe that the man standing before her was ever in need of saving. *Blast him!* He was quite beyond redemption. Never had she been talked to in such a fashion. *Never.* And she had dealt with many far below his station who lacked the education and social graces that he did.

"You disappoint me, Madeline." He pulled away from the wall and stalked out of the shadows. "I thought you were different from all the brainless fluff that frequent the ballrooms."

"Ugh," the sound was a strangled cry of shock and outrage. She couldn't believe his arrogance as he stood before her, his mocking face peering into hers. This was the man she loved? The man she had wanted to spend the rest of her life with? His tongue was sharp as a knife, and he was, effectively shredding her to bits.

"Very disappointing." His emotionless eyes raked contemptuously over her again. "I rather thought that out of any of them, you would be the one to prove yourself up to the challenge."

And then he left her, his elegant stride carrying him from the balcony and into the ballroom only to disappear amongst the fluff of the ton.

* * * *

The carriage lurched and stopped as it made its way across Town to the museum. The process was slow going and more than tedious owing to the great amount of carriages, all on their way to the grand unveiling. He must be utterly mad to entertain the thought of going out amongst the fashionable set. Everyone was going to be there, watching and seeing, and waiting.

Blaine leaned his head back against the velvet squabs and groaned. *Please*, he pleaded with his maker, don't let *her* be there.

"Are you ill?" Miranda asked.

"I'm fine," he said, peeking at her from beneath his lashes.

"Well, you don't sound fine."

"I'm fine," he bit out, closing his eyes in an attempt to stamp out his lingering anger.

"Humph!" Miranda pouted. "And he says I'm in distemper."

"Miranda," Celeste warned. "Watch your tongue."

Yes, he thought, *do watch it, or I'll gladly slice it out of your mouth.*

Damn it, he was in far too foul a mood to be traipsing about a bloody museum gawking at musty artifacts. He didn't give a damn if the Historical Society had unearthed a treasure trove of antiquities they thought belonged to King Arthur. Arthur and his knights were a fable, a meaningless tale, a bloody lie--just like everything else in life.

He stirred, rubbing his shoulder against the velvet. It was all *her* fault he felt this way. Until the Maddening Madeline Brydges strolled into his life he'd never let his emotions get the better of him, in one way or another. He prided himself on his control, the ease he had in being able to make himself feel nothing but empty amusement. He'd only ever allowed himself to feel mild sexual attraction, moderate enjoyment, and most definitely never anger. But Madeline had taken all that away from him. She made him crazed with lust, mad for the hope of a future free of loneliness, and she'd damned well made his temper soar out of control.

And that had been the reason he'd acted like a bastard. Jesus, he still couldn't think of what he'd said to her without wanting to shrink in shame. He'd been vile, utterly pompous and conceited-- and he'd delighted in it. He relished her shock, the look of hurt as it crossed her face. He'd gloried in the fact that he'd turned her and her unwanted attentions away from him. He was free of her, free of her haunting green eyes and tempting mouth. His secrets were safe, his heart would be safe. He could live his life in the quiet solitude of his own private hell without her unsolicited intrusion.

And yet, that was what had kept him up all night, tossing and turning, pummeling his pillow, fighting the vision of Madeline married to another a man. Of Madeline carrying another man's child.

"Uncle Blaine," Miranda said, concern evident in her voice when he groaned aloud again. "You aren't going to-"

"I'm fine," he snapped. "Would you both stop clucking like a pair of mother hens. I'm attempting to sleep, if you must know."

"Sorry," Miranda said, looking out the window. "I only meant to help."

"Pardon me," he mumbled back, forcing his temper to subside. He really needed to get a hold of himself. It was always dangerous to get worked up into a state. Any emotions were dangerous, but a temper, well, that was the most perilous emotion of all. What he really needed to do was to get the Maddening Madeline out of his mind for good. That would solve everything.

"Lady Madeline has invited me to take tea with her and Lady Hester tomorrow afternoon. Would that be acceptable to you, mother?" Miranda asked.

"Of course, Dearest," Celeste murmured. "How sweet of Lady Madeline to include you."

"Oh, she is the nicest person. It was so thoughtful of her to introduce me to Georgiana Longbottom. We've become fast friends."

"She is a very caring young woman."

Blaine felt Celeste's eyes burning a hole in his face. He could just imagine the expression she wore. Sympathy mixed with anxiety. It was always the way she looked at him when she was concerned for him.

"Lady Madeline runs a home for poor unfortunates, did you know that?" Miranda asked, heartily warming up to her topic of Lady Madeline.

"I had heard," Celeste mumbled, trying to curb Miranda's exuberance.

"Well," Miranda announced, "Lady Madeline says that we can accompany her to Covent Gardens when they set up their table on Faire Day. We have to be properly chaperoned, of course."

"Of course."

He wished to God Miranda would stop touting the chit's merits and just stuff it. He was sick of hearing her name, tired of feeling ashamed of his deplorable behavior and what it had done to the saintly Madeline. But to yell in frustration would be too telling. He'd be giving far too much away if he gave into the urge. So instead, he allowed himself to suffer through half an hour of listening to the saintly acts of Madeline Brydges and praying to his maker that he would not meet up with the temptress of his dreams.

Chapter Five

"My ancestors hail from the north," Lord Tynemouth droned on. "Durart Hall overlooks the peaks. Lovely part of Derbyshire."

Madeline smiled, nodding to a group of Tabbies who were busy looking her way. "Have you been to Derbyshire? I wondered if you've ever happened to come across Durart Hall?"

"I've been many times to Derbyshire, my lord. I'm afraid I've not had the pleasure of seeing your ancestral Hall."

"Well," Lord Tynemouth smiled, squeezing her arm as he maneuvered her through the crowd. "We will have to see what can be done about that."

Madeline forced a smile on her lips and feigned interest in the numerous rows of artifacts lining the gallery. She wasn't one to be in raptures over antiquities, but she did love the romance of King Arthur. His Knights of the Round Table were everything that was good about humanity. Their vision for equality and justice was simply visionary.

"Lady Madeline, Lord Tynemouth."

Madeline looked up from a display case of swords to see Lady Bathurst waving. "Isn't it a crush?" she asked excitedly, squeezing her husband's hand in her exuberance.

"Indeed." Madeline watched as the earl affectionately squeezed his wife's hand in return. "As a member of the Society, Lady Bathurst, you must be thrilled to be part of this discovery."

"Oh, indeed. I was quite shocked when the Duke of Roth stumbled across them."

"Well, it's vastly interesting," Tynemouth said, looking about the room. "And a crushing success."

"Yes, well, we were counting on success. Please, Lady Madeline, let me introduce you to my husband."

"A pleasure, Lord Bathurst," Madeline curtseyed.

"Intrigued," the earl murmured, his deep blue eyes sparkling behind black lashes.

"Say, old boy," Lord Bronley came up and slapped Lord Bathurst across the shoulder, "you haven't by any chance seen-- *ugh*," Bronley grunted, shaking his foot as though someone had trod over it. "I say, hello, Lady Madeline, didn't see your there."

"Good day, Lord Bronley," Madeline grinned, unable to help herself. "I'm afraid toes are bound to get stepped on. This crush is quite something."

"Indeed," he mumbled, looking about the room.

"Lady Madeline," a voice demurred behind her. "So nice to see you here this afternoon."

Madeline whirled around to see a familiar pair of green eyes looking back at her. "Lord Stanfield," she said, flushing as he looked her over with his perceptive gaze. "I did manage to make it."

"And found someone to escort you, how resourceful of you. Tynemouth," Lord Stanfield nodded, letting his gaze drift from her to her escort. "I say, isn't that Lord Hastings over there?"

"Why, yes," Tynemouth said, craning his neck to see through the crowd. "I believe you're correct."

"I heard he's the best bet to be our Prime Minister. I understand he's very influential in the Whig party."

"Indeed?" Tynemouth mumbled thoughtfully, studying the elderly lord through the throng of people. "Lady Madeline, you won't mind if I leave you for a moment? I'd like to say a few words to Hastings."

"Oh, I wouldn't mind."

"Thank you," he mumbled, raising her hand to his mouth. "I shan't be long."

"A political hound," Stanfield whispered in her ear. "I've no doubt it would become rather tiresome after a time, wouldn't you agree, my lady?"

"Yes," she said, bristling at the closeness of him. "I suppose you're correct."

"Lady Madeline," Lord Bathurst drawled, "since you're without an escort, would you care to take a turn about the room with us?"

"Allow me to step in for Tynemouth," Lord Stanfield announced, whisking her away with a firm grip on her elbow.

* * * *

"Aren't these amazing?" Miranda exclaimed as she studied the glass cases.

"Quite," Blaine said, resisting the urge to loosen his cravat. *He was bloody hot.*

"Wonderful workmanship," Celeste said, admiring a jeweled brooch. "And to think it was just lying buried in the dirt."

"A harrowing thought, indeed."

"Are you unwell?" Celeste asked, watching as he hooked his

thumb beneath his collar and loosened his cravat.

"Fine," he mumbled, straightening the knot in an attempt to look presentable.

"I'm going to go stand with Georgiana Longbottom," Miranda announced.

"Fine."

"Would you mind if I went over to the next booth? They have an assortment of textiles I'd like to see."

"Fine," he barked again, struggling with his blasted cravat.

"Blaine are you certain-"

"Fine!" he bit out, completely frustrated. *"I'm fine."*

Celeste stared at him long and hard before sighing and moving away. Damn it to hell, he wanted out of there. He was tired of the people, sick of always having to keep an eye open for a door to escape out of. *Damn it,* he just wanted to get home and enjoy a snifter of brandy in peace and quiet.

"I say, old boy, I wondered where you'd got to."

"Dev," he said, forgetting about his cravat. "Where have you been?"

"Must have missed you in the crowds. Say, you haven't seen Bathurst have you? We got separated."

"No," he grumbled, studying a jeweled dagger in the case before him. "I haven't."

The dagger was really quite something. Exquisitely carved, with what he thought resembled Arabic script on the hilt. Lowering himself so that he was eye level with the case, he studied the dagger, trying to interpret the script, when a pair of arresting and most disturbing green eyes met his through the opposite side of the glass case.

"Madeline," he said softly, rising to full height.

"Lord Hardcastle," she said, her tone cool and aloof. "Pray, do not let me disturb you." Her eyes, slightly shadowed with circles, raked over him before she turned and walked away from him.

He swallowed hard, hating to see the hurt that shone in her eyes. Damn it, why had he needed to treat her so harshly? Why couldn't he have left well enough alone? He should have left the ball after his dance with the Billingsworth chit. But, no, he'd wanted to stay and torture himself with visions of Madeline and Tynemouth together, smiling and dancing and doing everything he wished he could do with her.

He'd been so damn jealous, so damn angry that he'd deliberately set out to hurt her--to push her away from him so he didn't have to think of her, to confront his feelings and accept what she did to him.

"I need to get out of here," he growled to his friend. "Is there an empty room around? A library? A storage room? A bloody broom closet?"

"A closet, did you say?" Bronley asked, his eyes dancing mischievously. "Well, I think I saw something that might be suitable over there."

Blaine watched as Bronley pointed to a door at the opposite end of the room. With a nod of thanks he left his friend for the safety of solitude.

* * * *

"In here did you say?" Madeline asked, pointing to the door.

"Yes," Lord Bronley smiled. "I do believe that's where Bathurst said the ladies rest area was set up."

"You don't mind, do you?"

"Of course not. Please, take all the time you need. There's nothing like a little privacy to raise ones spirits."

With a grateful smile, Madeline let herself into the room. Closing the door, she leaned against it letting out a long suffering sigh.

"Madeline."

She opened her eyes to see Hardcastle leaning against the wall, his hat in one hand, the other one rifling through his already disheveled hair.

"My lord," she said, feeling awkward and excited at the same time. "I … I did not know you were here. If I had, I would never have dared-"

"You're presence is not unwelcome."

"Well, I … that is.…" she trailed off, suddenly off balance. She didn't know what to say. He wasn't the arrogant beast of the night before, if he had been, she was prepared for him. He wouldn't get away with speaking to her in such a fashion again. But he hadn't. His voice had been quiet, slightly shaky, almost as if he were uneasy, unsure of what to say.

"My lord," she said, wetting her lips, hoping she was doing the right thing. "I wanted to tell you how gallant you were in asking Miss Billingsworth to dance last evening. I do believe you had quite an impact on her. It's the nicest thing a gentleman can do for a lady."

He sighed and looked up at the ceiling. Madeline followed his gaze, wondering what of interest was up there. When she saw it was nothing but smooth plaster, she looked away and decided to peruse the books on a nearby shelf. Obviously his lordship did not do well with compliments, or perhaps it was his less than subtle hint that he did not wish to discuss the subject further.

"I cannot abide the berating of children by their parents," he finally said. "It was most painful for Miss Billingsworth, and I could not stand by and watch her be destroyed by her shrew of a mother, or the taunting fools of the ton."

She didn't know if he realized how much he'd revealed about himself with that statement. She wondered if he knew how his voice cracked, hinting at a past hurt by his own parents.

He'd sympathized with Alexandra Billingsworth because he'd also suffered at the hands of his parents. Somewhere in his past he had lived through the same taunts and jibes. She was coming to understand him, to see why he held himself apart from society. At some point his parents had told him he was inferior, maybe, perhaps, even an embarrassment.

"I can't remember a time where I displeased my parents so much they would berate me in front of their peers."

"I could never please my parents." She heard him toss his hat onto the table and sigh as he leaned against the wall. "I wasn't what they wanted."

Intrigued, yet aware she was treading very deep water, she plunged forward. "Surely you didn't have to suffer as poor Miss Billingsworth did last night?"

She heard him suck in his breath, imagined him stiffening, struggling to draw the shade of secrecy once again. He had unwittingly exposed his past, and he had at last checked himself.

Madeline replayed all she knew about him, all she'd seen of him. His outburst and cruel jibes last evening were uncharacteristic of him. He'd been lashing out, trying to distance himself from her, trying to make her turn from him. Blaine was hurting, he was in need of understanding and love, and yet he refused to take it where it was offered. He gave in only so far before snatching his hand away and drawing himself back into his dark depths.

"I do not talk of my parents. The past is history, and history can never be re-written."

He had been hurt. She could hear it in his voice, feel it as the tension in the room tightened and closed in on them. She felt his anger and pain coil within him only to radiate out to her. He was so in need of love, and yet, she didn't know how to reach out to him, how to give him what he needed. He wouldn't let her get close enough to help him.

"I should leave you," she said, not knowing if she was doing the right thing, leaving him alone with only his tortured past to keep him company. But then, what could she say if she stayed? She didn't know what words to use to breach his tough shell.

She heard his steps, soft and sure behind her, then suddenly felt his breath against her neck. "Don't leave," he whispered, pressing his face against her exposed skin. "Don't run from me."

His breath and lips caressed her neck, while his fingers lightly traced the neckline of her pelisse before trailing down her spine.

"Forgive me, Madeline. Forgive me for what I said last night."

She nodded and with a tremulous swallow, allowed him to nudge her head to the side, resting it against his shoulder as his lips softly, reverently, nuzzled her neck, followed by light flicks of his tongue.

"I wanted that dance to be with you, Maddy. The whole time I was dancing with her I thought only of you, wishing we were the only two people in the room so that I might do this to you."

Her pulse leapt and surged as he continued to caress her neck, his fingers, light and teasing trailed down her throat, stopping at the peak of her breast, only to travel back up the column of her throat.

"Tell me," he said, bringing her back tight against his chest, his tongue, hot and teasing flicked along her bounding pulse. "What is it you desire?"

Her brain screamed that it was him she wanted. That she wanted his kiss. But this was neither the time, nor the place. It was too dangerous, anyone could walk in and catch them. She didn't want to trap him, she wanted him to come to her willingly, to reach out and consciously take her in his arms, to invite her into his life, his heart.

"Tell me." His hand traced her breast, then cupped her and she whimpered, trying to think despite the heavy fog of desire clouding her brain. Never had she felt anything quite as mind numbing as Blaine's hands roving her body. Never had she been more aware of the fact that she was a woman--a woman with desires.

"God, how I want this," he said thickly, stroking his thumb along her nipple, making it pebble hard. "And this." he slid his hand down her bodice to the flat plane of her belly where he kneaded the small mound. "And this," his voice was a low rumble in her ear as his fingers traced the curls of her sex through her thin gown. "I want this so much. So much so that I cannot sleep. So much that I am constantly thinking of you, of your lips, your flame red hair, the way your skin feels. So much that I lie awake, hard and aroused, torturing myself with thoughts of how you will feel beneath my hands, my lips, my body. I dream of how you will taste, Madeline. I dream of the taste of your sex, the feel of you on my tongue. Tell me, would you let me taste the desire I create within you?" A whimper caught in her throat and he tightened his hold on her while he kissed her shoulder. "Tell me what you want, Maddy."

"I want a future. A future with you. What," she said, feeling her legs tremble when he cupped her once more. "What do you see for us in your future?"

He stopped then, his hand splayed across her belly as his hot breath came in short pants against her.

"You shouldn't have asked me that." He abruptly moved away from her, his hands grasping the bookcase, steadying himself and caging her. She wished she could see his face, to know what expression he wore, but he didn't turn her to face him, instead, he pressed himself against her, his breathing much too rapid and much too harsh. "You should have asked me what I wanted from you, Madeline. I was prepared to bare my desire before you and tell you what I wanted was you. I would have told you that I wanted you naked beneath me, that I want to feel myself slip inside your body. I would have owned up to the fact that I dream of your seduction while I lie alone at night in bed."

She felt herself tremble at his words, felt her desire flare further, wondering what she could do to get him to take her in his arms and kiss her. But then his voice, which had been husky with emotion, with physical desire, changed, replaced with aloofness. "You asked what I saw for my future, Madeline, and I can tell you I see nothing. The picture before me is black and empty, and infinite. I have no future."

* * * *

"Look hard, boy, this is your future. This is what you've got to look forward to."

Blaine shook off the memories of the day at Bedlam, the feel of his father's strong fingers gripping his neck, forcing him to stare at the patients. As he looked up at the portrait of his dead father, he was still able to feel the viscous tightening of his sire's hand on his neck. Even now, at thirty three he still trembled at the sight of him.

George Henry Hartley, the eight Earl of Hardcastle had been a big man, a towering giant with wiry gray hair and burly sideburns. He'd been possessed of big shoulders and fists the size of prized hams.

As far back as he could remember, Blaine had been aware of his father's hatred for him, cognizant even at seven that his father was ashamed of him. *His idiot son. His halfwit heir.*

Taking a long swallow of brandy, Blaine stared into the gray eyes of his father and felt the old pain swell within his breast. His father had told him he was nothing, that he would never be anything but a sniveling simpleton writhing on the floor of Bedlam. How his father had taken delight in telling him how worthless he was, that he'd never grow to be a man of any consequence. But he had shown the old bastard. He'd gone off to Eton and he'd learned, excelled in fact, in every area of study. He'd been terrified of the other boys learning his secret, but he'd braved it, wishing nothing more than to show his father he could succeed.

He'd found confidence in his early years at Eton, and after Bronley, Stanfield, Reanleigh and Bathurst had entered his life, he'd begun to change. Begun to believe that the world might not be as cold and terrifying has his father had let him believe. But then the old bastard had ruined it all by bringing him home during the holiday break. He'd dragged him to Bedlam and forced him to confront his secret.

His body had changed that winter, and so to, did the nature of his illness. It had been Christmas Eve and the dinner was about to be served. His father had been in a vile mood all day, and Celeste and his mother had been sitting at the table, nervously fidgeting with their utensils. And then Blaine had smelled it, that oddly familiar scent of burning bread. His muscles had tightened and jerked, begun to shake beyond his control and he'd look to his mother to help him. But she had sat there staring at him, a look of horror on her face, her lips twisted in repulsion. He'd seen the same look on the visitors to Bedlam as they watched the inmates, their madness spiraling out of control. He'd watched, frightened, sickened as they sat transfixed in horrified fascination watching the inmates. He recalled looking around the table, seeing that his family was staring at him the same way the ton did the insane idiots in Bedlam.

He'd spent the next two days in bed, weak and exhausted, almost unable to gather the strength in order to make it to the chamber pot. For two days he lay in bed, listening to his father rail at him about him being an idiot, a *God-damn embarrassment to me, and the Hardcastle title.*

Unfortunately, his sire had not been able to see past his own prejudices and embarrassment in order to admit that he'd fathered a child with epilepsy.

The falling sickness had been the bane of his existence since birth. For the first twelve years of his life it had been a subtle shaking of the head and hand, or a mere drifting off as if he were day dreaming, but having no recollection of doing so. The quacks and medical men his father brought before him thought it was something he'd outgrow, something he did to seek attention and stave off boredom. None of them knew or understood the nature of his illness.

The year he'd turned twelve was when his *fits* had taken a violent turn. No longer was it a localized twitching or staring off into some unseen land. The episodes were short and violent, with complete loss of physical control and consciousness, culminating in days of indescribable fatigue and weakness.

His father had thought him truly possessed then, had threatened to commit him. The very thought had terrified him. Blaine had imagined his cell in Bedlam, saw the members of the aristocracy out on their Sunday stroll taunting him, laughing at him. He'd thought of slowly growing mad, losing his humanity and letting the madness consume him until he was nothing more than a caged animal, crawling on all fours, cowering in the corner of his cell. But in the end his father had been too ashamed to admit that his heir, was a *possessed idiot.* He hadn't committed him to the lunatic asylum. But he had imprisoned him. His father had relegated him to his own private hell to wage war alone and frightened with his demons.

He'd gone back to Eton then, to continue in his studies and attempt to forget about his father and the fact that his mother had betrayed him by washing her hands of her only child. He continued to excel, but was unable to carry on to university with his friends, his disorder having increased around the time he sprouted in height and his voice changed. Instead, he'd tutored himself at his ancestral home in Derbyshire, devouring books and learning what he could on his own. As a result, he was fluent in six languages, and instrumental in deciphering secret codes for the Foreign Office during their campaign to oust Napoleon. He'd been credited with saving thousands of lives, both of soldiers and the intricate network of spies who risked their lives to send him information.

And still, it hadn't been enough to satisfy his father.

"Your tea, milord," Ringwald said, setting the silver tray on his desk.

"Thank you, Ringwald."

"A package has just arrived, milord. Shall I bring it in?"

"At this time of night?" he asked, looking at the clock atop the mantle.

"A lad was here. I hope you don't mind, but I sent him off with a few shillings, his jacket was threadbare."

"Of course. Bring this mysterious package in, if you please." He glanced once more at his father's portrait, shuddering as he felt the bastard's cold eyes following him back to his chair. He should have bloody well burnt the thing when he wanted to, but he'd acted out of deference for Celeste. The bastard was her father too.

Ringwald handed him a package wrapped in brown paper and coarse string. Blaine waited until his valet left the room before opening it. He studied the bundle in his lap, noticing his direction was written with a neat hand, the writing small and infinitely feminine. Shadow whimpered before resting his muzzle on his knee. "Yes, I believe you're correct, my friend. I think it might be from *her*."

Blaine continued to stroke Shadow's ears, while staring down at the package, memorizing every little detail of her writing, every curl, every flourish. It was silly, he thought, to take such delight in his name scrawled across the paper, and in her hand. He was being absurd, much too foolish. She was everything that was light and good, and he was everything that was dark and haunted. It wouldn't work--couldn't work. He would only turn her away with his moodiness and monstrous fits. He didn't want her to see him that way. He'd rather forsake her than expose her to his weakness. It was far better she have only their stolen moment in the museum to remember, than him, convulsing unconscious before her.

Shadow whimpered again, this time the dog sniffed the package, nudging it with his wet nose, urging him to open it. With a sigh, Blaine pulled the string and parted the paper, only to see his jacket and a folded missive atop it. A hint of sandalwood and lemon met him as he lifted his coat out of the paper and brought it to his face, remembering the way she had looked in it. The wool smelled of her and him, an intriguing blend of bodies, making him wonder if his bed would smell the same way after he'd made love to her. He thought then of their bodies entwined together, their scents mingling as if they were one.

But that was just a dream, a fantasy he'd created while satisfying his needs with his hand. He'd dreamt of her, thought of her naked and willing in his bed. There was no fear, no frightening reminders of his illness. Only desire existed in his dream. Passion like none he'd ever thought to find.

Reaching for the letter, he slipped his finger along the fold. He wished he could rid himself of the memories of Madeline's supple body pressed against his, the delicious taste of her skin on his tongue as he licked and laved, took and wanted.

'Love will find a way through paths where wolves fear to prey ... M'

Sighing, he closed his eyes and rested his head against the chair. "She's a romantic. She doesn't realize what she's getting herself into."

Shadow looked up at him and whimpered, before resting his head once more on his knee. "She thinks I'm mysterious and alluring, she doesn't yet know that my mystique quite transcends any darkness she's ever known. But still," he said, rising from his chair and strolling to the bookcase. "I find that I'm drawn to her, that I can quite easily forget that I am a beast when I'm looking into her beautiful eyes and drowning in their depths. What is a man to do when confronted with such temptation?" he asked, pulling a slim leather volume out of the shelf, and walking back to his chair. "I suppose," he said, opening the book and taking a sip of his tea, "that one could please the lady and read the poem."

Shadow swallowed and slid to the floor, only to lay his muzzle on his boots. "Do you suppose, my friend, that this is merely co-incidence, or do you think that Fate has brought her to me?"

Shadow merely sighed and closed his eyes, drifting off into canine slumber. How was it, Blaine thought, as he read the familiar lines of Byron's, *Giaour*, that the lovely Madeline had known just what to say to him? She must be truly destined to be his, because it was virtually impossible for her to have discovered his penchant for Byron. No one knew, not even his friends. The only living being that had ever heard him recite the works of Byron was Shadow, and he was fairly confident that his faithful companion had not breathed a word to her.

With a smile, he settled back and enjoyed the poem, the Turkish tale of love, passion and deception and he reveled in the fact that this time, Fate might just be working with him.

Chapter Six

Madeline set her teacup down on her saucer and beamed at Phoebe. "I'm happy I decided to come to the house this afternoon. Who would have thought I'd be welcoming two more babies into Montgomery House?"

"Indeed," Phoebe shuddered. "All that wailing and screaming. I confess I had to escape to the garden."

"I'm pleased all is well. It's always such a perilous journey."

"Speaking of dangerous journeys, how goes yours with the earl?"

Madeline couldn't help but sigh. Her whole plan was fizzling before it had even started.

"I take it he's proving difficult?" Phoebe asked while she poured more tea. "It's not surprising. He always was untouchable."

"Did you know him?" Madeline asked, almost fearing the answer. She didn't know why, but she had the worst sensation in the pit of her stomach. It was as if she were hanging by her nails, waiting for a dreaded answer. She didn't want to think of Phoebe with him, in fact, she didn't want to think of him with any female that wasn't her.

"I was acquainted with him," Phoebe said, visibly stiffening in her chair. "You understand that my position as part of the *demi monde* prevented me from being wholly accepted. I only had contact with those who wished it. But I did have an opportunity to study him from time to time, and was amazed by the control of him, the way he could hold himself up in front of them despite their hushed whispers."

"Why do you think he needs to hold himself apart? What troubles him so?"

"Who can say?" Phoebe shrugged and reached for a lemon biscuit. "He is a solitary person, keeping to himself and holding his own counsel. I doubt there is a single person he's confided in. I don't think he's ever needed anyone."

Madeline tapped her fingers against the desk. That was a load of rubbish, not needing anyone. Every human being needed someone. Hardcastle was no different in that respect. He just refused to believe he needed anything, much less anyone.

"Does he," Phoebe started, then cleared her throat. "Does the earl know what it is you desire, Madeline?"

"Well, I believe so," she mumbled, wondering if the earl was too obtuse to see she desired him for her husband.

"Madeline," Phoebe whispered behind her napkin. "Sometimes men don't understand subtlety. Sometimes women need to be very brave and straightforward, telling them what they wish for."

"I did tell him I wished for a future together."

"And what did he say, Dearest?"

Madeline shivered as she remembered his words, haunting and painful. 'I have no future'. It had been the most disturbing thing she'd ever heard, and the despair she'd felt coming from him had made her heart twist in her chest.

"Perhaps he thinks you wish for a...." Phoebe coughed in her hand. "Mayhap he thinks you wish for a … a dalliance."

"A *dalliance*," Madeline cried, springing from her chair. "I wish to marry him, not trifle with him till he grows tired of me."

Phoebe reached for her hand, stilling her from pacing. "That is the problem, isn't it, Dearest? He isn't interested in that, is he?"

Madeline felt the stinging sensation prick her pride. She hated to have to admit that Blaine had no more interest in marrying her than fly over the moon, and yet, it wasn't as though he was immune to her. They had shared that incredible embrace the day at the museum.

"Sit," Phoebe commanded, "we're going to have a discussion, and it's going to be very frank, and you're going to learn all about the nature of men and women."

"Now?" Madeline asked, her face flushing fiercely. "I have to go. I've promised father that I would attend Lady Fraleigh's soiree with him this evening."

"It won't take long," Phoebe smiled, squeezing her hand affectionately. "But I do believe it will be worth it. After our discussion, you'll be able to look at the earl in a very different light and use that to your advantage."

"You're going to help me to seduce him?" Madeline asked, her face now flushing furiously. "I don't want to trap him Phoebe, I want him willingly."

"Not trap, Dearest," Phoebe grinned, "Entice. I'm merely going to teach you how to capitalize on some of those very male tendencies."

* * * *

"You look lovely tonight, my dear. You remind me very much

of your mother."

Madeline smiled and reached for her father's hand. "Thank you, Papa."

"I'm glad to see you've been allowing Tynemouth to pay you attention. He's a decent man, Madeline, he'll make you a good, solid husband."

Madeline nodded and looked out the window. She hated what she was doing, but there simply was no other way. She had to make her father think she was pursuing others instead of Hardcastle. Her father flatly refused to hear her pleas or her arguments about Hardcastle's merits and suitability as a husband. Her father had left her with no choice. If she was to marry and produce a child to inherit Sanbourne Hall, then it had to be with a man she cared for. A man she loved. And the Earl of Hardcastle was the man she was losing her heart to. She had long since pinned her hopes on marrying Hardcastle, and no other man, no matter how *solid* would do.

"Tynemouth has invited us to Derbyshire. I've accepted the invitation on your behalf."

She whirled her head to look at her father. "When?" she asked, trying to stem her flow of anger.

"Three weekends from now."

"But that's Lady Brookehaven's charity weekend. Montgomery House is this year's recipient. I've promised to be there to help organize it."

"By all means help organize it," her father said as he tugged on his gloves. "But you will not attend it. That Brookehaven party is nothing but a glorified curtain for gratuitous indulgence and lascivious pleasures. You will not be seen at such an event."

"You cannot mean-"

"I mean that you will accompany me to Derbyshire, or you'll have no further assistance from me with that damned house, do you understand?"

"Yes," she mumbled, feeling the frustration rising in her breast.

"That house has done nothing but consume you since the day we found Nanette. You're wasting away, Madeline, and I won't stand by and watch it happen. You're *saving* yourself into spinsterhood, and that isn't what your mother intended when she decided to let you help her with her causes. You cannot rescue everyone, my dear."

"That isn't true," she lashed back, remembering the words he'd said as they stood staring down at the lifeless body of Nanette.

"Everyone can be saved. Everyone is worth saving."

"Not at the cost of your future. Your mother, God bless her soul was the most caring woman I've ever met, and God knows that I loved her--still love her, but this is not what she wanted for you. Your mother didn't want you to forfeit your own happiness to save those less fortunate. She wanted you to fall in love, to get married and make her a grandmother. She didn't want you sacrificing your own happiness in order to make others happy."

But in marrying Tynemouth and giving up Montgomery house, she was sacrificing, she was relinquishing her dreams of marrying Hardcastle, of marrying the man she loved, the man she wanted to be with for the rest of her life. If what her father said was true, her mother hadn't wanted her to wed for duty. And in marrying Tynemouth she would have none of what her parents had shared-- only a political alliance and a congenial relationship. Their children would be nothing but heirs, pawns in the political games of parliament. They wouldn't be a family, which was what she wanted, which was what she had with her own parents.

"Do not look so forlorn," her father said, patting her knee. "All will work out. You'll see, my dear, Fate has a way of setting things to rights."

* * * *

"You look lovely, tonight, my lady. You quite take my breath away."

Madeline smiled politely, forcing herself to suppress a grimace. She didn't want to be dancing with Tynemouth, or be the recipient of his ever increasing compliments.

"Has your father spoken to you about your visit?"

She stiffened in his arms. The last thing she wanted to discuss was that. She had absolutely no intention of journeying out to Tynemouth's ancestral home, and certainly not the weekend of the Brookehaven party.

"My parents are looking forward to spending some time with you. And I must say, I too look forward to getting to know you better without the eyes of the ton always watching."

This was getting worse by the minute. She shouldn't be doing this, letting him think she might entertain the idea of marriage to him. It was wrong, it was dreadfully deceitful. She hated duplicity of any kind, and yet here she was, tricking Tynemouth into believing that she might be open to his offer of marriage.

"I understand you met my sister at Lady Hester's tea today. I must say, Francesca was rather taken with you."

She did grimace then, thinking of how his sister had all but welcomed her to their family. Francesca had talked endlessly about how well she would love Druart Hall and the surrounding countryside. It was no wonder the ton was watching, waiting with bated breath for the banns to be read.

"You've been rather quiet this evening, Lady Madeline. Might I enquire after your health? You aren't ill, are you?"

Yes, she should say that. Say that she was feeling dreadfully tired, that her head pounded and she felt feverish. But then he would likely take her to her father and he would in turn whisk her home and that would leave her without so much as a flash of Hardcastle.

The damnable man, she thought angrily, had yet to make an appearance, and Miranda and Lady Greenwood had been there for two hours at least. She'd been scouring the room all evening for just a glimpse of him.

"Lady Madeline," Tynemouth asked, his lips very near her ear. "Shall we take a turn about the gardens? Perhaps a breath of fresh air is in order."

Not yet ready to leave without seeing Hardcastle, she nodded and allowed Tynemouth to escort her to the French doors, and out onto the balcony.

"Lovely night," he said, breathing deeply beside her. "I love the smell of spring. Don't you?"

She chanced a glance at him and her guilt once again assailed her. Tynemouth was a good man. A decent man like her father had said. And yet she could not bring herself to feel anything more than friendship for him. He was handsome she supposed, in a typical way. His brown hair was cut short and immaculately styled. His face was angular and clean shaven. His eyes, which were clearly his most pleasing feature where large and brown, reminding her of a faithful puppy. She sighed again and looked away. He'd make someone a perfectly decent husband--just not her.

"I hope you'll love Druart Hall as much I," he said, his gloved hand sliding along the balustrade to rest atop hers. "I'm certain you'll find much to occupy your time."

"My lord," she said, taking a deep breath. "I do believe that we should come to some sort of understanding."

"If you'd like," he said, sliding her a sidelong glance.

How could she tell him that she had no intention of meeting him in Derbyshire, much less marry him?

"Let me ease the burden for you, Lady Madeline." Tynemouth squeezed her hand reassuringly. "I understand that Montgomery House is a very important aspect in your life, and you may be assured that I won't interfere in those activities."

"Well, that is very generous of you," she said, gulping in surprise.

"I'm well aware that many men might take exception to such a thing, but I'm not of that stock. Contributing to charities is a vital task and an admirable trait in any politician's wife."

"Yes, well...." she said, freezing as she heard the word, *wife* cross his lips.

"I get the impression that the idea of visiting Derbyshire is not as palatable to you as I had originally thought."

"Oh, it isn't that," she said, unable to bear the look of regret that crossed his trusting eyes. Oh, this was getting much too deep. Much too deceitful.

"Perhaps you might be so good as to tell me what is really troubling you."

"Well, the Brookehaven charity ball is that weekend. And Montgomery House is the recipient. You understand, don't you?"

"Say no more," he said, smiling with what she thought might be relief. "The first thing about alliances, my dear, is that they must be agreeable to both parties. Since you have a previous engagement, allow me to plan your excursion for another time, perhaps the week after?"

His look was so hopeful that Madeline couldn't crush it with a refusal. So, instead she nodded and murmured her thanks.

"Would it be too much to hope for an invitation to this charity weekend? I'd like the opportunity to assist in the continuation of such a worthy cause."

"Of course," she said, following him back into the ballroom. How could she refuse?

"I'm sure we can find just as much to amuse ourselves with at the Brookehaven ball, as we could in Derbyshire, isn't that right?"

* * * *

"He's trying very hard, isn't he?" Penny said, motioning to Tynemouth who stood across the room boldly staring at her.

"Oh, Penny, it's just terrible. He won't be dissuaded."

"An admirable quality in a politician. Much less so in a suitor."

"It's horrible," Madeline groaned. "I don't want to hurt him, yet I cannot marry him. I can't, Penny."

"You should think about it. It's not as though Hardcastle is falling at your feet."

"Irritating man," she mumbled under her breath. "He's proving most difficult."

"And Lord Stanfield is proving just as attentive as Tynemouth. Here he comes."

Madeline looked over the top of her fan only to see Lord Stanfield marching towards her. He was being rather attentive, but not as other gentleman had. In fact, he acted more the part of a friend than a smitten suitor.

"May I steal your friend away, Miss Mills, I'd like a private word."

"Of course. I wouldn't mind in the least."

"We'll just be a moment," Lord Stanfield said, taking Madeline's elbow and leading her to the balcony that she'd only moments ago returned from with Lord Tynemouth.

"My friend sends his regrets he can not be here this evening."

"Your friend?" she asked, feigning ignorance. He raised a brow, his green eyes quickly seeing through her façade.

"My friend is, unfortunately, indisposed this evening. He requested I give you this."

Madeline felt him slip something into her hand, then bow before taking his leave. With a deep breath she opened her palm, only to see a small folded paper lying in her gloved hand. With shaking fingers she opened the missive and stared at the most beautiful words she'd ever read.

'He lived--he breathed--he moved--he felt;
He raised the maid from where she knelt;
His trance was gone--his keen eye shone
With thoughts that long in darkness dwelt'. With thoughts that
burn--in rays that melt.

It was, Madeline thought, a tear escaping her eyes, the most precious gift she'd ever been given.

* * * *

Blaine parted the branches of Lady Fraleigh's apple tree and watched as Madeline, bathed in glowing lights from the ballroom, read his missive. It had been a foolhardy thing to write, but as he sat in his study the evening before, immersed in Byron's epic *Giaour*, he couldn't help but be moved. To feel as though they were kindred spirits, using their shared love of the written word to convey what they felt.

He'd known what she meant by her missive. He feared the words as much as he savored them. He had been moved by them, had felt the need, the desire to let her love him, to bring her into his life and into his bed. But all too soon his fanciful thoughts were replaced by reality.

He'd been nearing the end of the poem, the candles had burned low, the last log on the fire had been reduced to glowing embers and his tea had long turn cold. He had felt the familiar shudder as he closed the book, smelt the faint odor of something burning before he the rhythmic shaking of his body consumed him. He'd been awakened as Ringwald, and two burly footmen hefted him up from the floor.

The entire house had been in uproar with Sterling, his butler, ordering his bed turned down, and the maids, clucking and shrieking to do his bidding. It was then, as he struggled to walk up the stairs with some measure of dignity, that he'd finally admitted to himself that bringing Madeline into his household was a fatal decision. He could not subject her to the chaos, the disruption of life when one of his fits decided to strike. He couldn't allow her to see him in such a state, and he knew, without a doubt, he could never completely hide his condition from her.

There was only one thing to do. He had decided upon it that very morning. He had to give her up. To forsake his dreams of having her in his life, in his bed, in his heart.

He'd written the words from Byron, hoping to give her a glimpse of what was inside his heart. She *had* awakened him from his darkness. She had made him see, made him want as no other woman had ever done. But in the end it wasn't enough. Nothing was enough to banish his demons.

Stepping closer, he watched as she clutched his letter to her breast. He would never forget, never stop thinking--stop dreaming of her.

With a sigh, he looked at her one last time, committing every inch of her face to memory. Memorizing for eternity the way she looked, her brilliant eyes sparkling in the moonlight, his words and thoughts clutched tightly to her breast. She was beautiful, remarkable. She was everything he would have desired in a wife, but he was not what she needed. He could never make her happy and she deserved that above anything. Madeline Brydges was the beauty and he was nothing more than the hideous beast.

With one last glance, he left the garden, wondering when the pain of regret would abate. When, he asked, as he stalked to his carriage, would he realize that forgetting her was the right the thing to do?

Chapter Seven

"Three days and still he shuns me," Madeline huffed, blowing an errant curl from her face.

"Dearest," Phoebe demurred as she placed a pile of embroidered handkerchiefs in a box. "A lady must always act aloof. You must distance yourself. That's surely what Hardcastle is doing."

"Distance myself," Madeline scoffed as she lifted a box full of linens from her desk and placed it onto the floor. "Why in the world would I wish to distance myself? I don't understand. He sends me the most beautiful, passionate poem I've ever read and then he wishes to distance himself from me? Whatever for?"

"Because, Dearest, that is how the game is played."

"What game?"

"The games of lovers. You don't expect him to fall at your feet begging for your hand, do you? You have to make him want to give in. You have to give him a reason to defy his past behavior and come out into Society to claim you."

"Games, secrets, poems," Madeline grumbled, reaching for another box to fill for the Faire Day at Covent Garden. "I don't understand any of this. Why can he not be more like Tynemouth? With him, everything is straightforward."

"They are two very different men. Tynemouth is a man with a mission. He needs a wife, a political mate. He's confident and amusing and he'll be a good husband to you. He has nothing to hide. Hardcastle on the other hand is deep and mysterious. He never looks at a woman, never tries to be outgoing or sympathetic. Simply put, he's not looking for love."

Madeline stared down into the empty box. "I just wish I could understand what was going on inside his head."

"What is Hardcastle's greatest weakness?"

"I don't know. I have yet to get to know him well enough to learn that."

"Nonsense," Phoebe scolded. "You've been studying that man for a year."

"Arrogance, I suppose."

"Why is he arrogant? You must ask yourself these questions in order to understand him."

"I don't know," Madeline moaned. "I don't understand men the way you do."

"All right," Phoebe said, calming her with a gentle squeeze of her hand. "I'll tell you only because I can see you're working yourself up into a state. Now," Phoebe continued, running a hand along her skirts. "Hardcastle's arrogance stems from vulnerability. You've discovered he doesn't want anyone to get close to him, he doesn't want anyone to know the *real* him. Now, if arrogance and vulnerability are his weakness, then his pride is his strength."

"What does pride have to do with anything?"

"Pride, my dear, is what makes the male species *very* male. It's what separates the men who we feel affection for, from the men we fall head over heels for."

"Pride and arrogance are faults. They cannot be considered strengths of character."

"On the contrary, Dearest, pride in a man is a very great asset to a woman. Along with pride goes possession."

"How in the world is a possessive nature supposed to help a woman?"

"Because a man who is possessive cannot rest until the woman he desires is his. All men have a propensity for possession, and your Lord Hardcastle is one of them. He's possessive about his privacy and his secrets. In fact, his possessive nature has even been directed at you. He wouldn't have lashed out at you after seeing you dancing with Tynemouth if he didn't already think of you as his."

"I've been raised believing that a possessive, greedy nature is a sin."

"Not greedy, merely a sense of ownership, of mastery. A man like Hardcastle won't rest until he has what he wants. It may take some time before he can bring himself to admit that what he wants is you. But when he does, nothing will stop him. For now, I'm afraid, you'll have to play by his rules."

"*His rules,*" Madeline mumbled, attempting to process all of Phoebe's insight into the male brain.

"Unfortunately, that's where the arrogance falls in. He won't allow anyone to talk him into something before he's ready. Not even you, Dearest. By the way," Phoebe said, reaching into the desk drawer. "This is for you, compliments of Lord Faversham."

Madeline took the envelope and gasped at that sight of pound notes lying inside. "However did you manage this?"

"That's the thing about men and their possessive nature, they cannot stand to be bested. Lord Faversham hasn't quite got over the fact that I was never his to possess. He'd like the opportunity to try once again."

"This is unbelievable," Madeline whispered. "He gave you a thousand pounds because he couldn't stand to be bested?"

"No, silly, because he's trying to win me. See, every man will go about it in his own way. This is why I'm telling you that you need to read between the lines where Hardcastle is concerned. He wants you, Madeline, you just have to look deep where he's concerned. He'll show it, no matter how hard he tries not to. Unfortunately, a man as masterful as Hardcastle is going to be very subtle. That's where you'll have to learn to spot the clues for yourself."

"Miss," Ten-year-old Holly cried, running into her study. "You must come quickly, an enormous bouquet has arrived."

Madeline caught Phoebe's mischievous smile just as Maggie was carrying in the most exotic collection of flowers she'd ever seen.

"Heavens," she said breathlessly as Maggie set the arrangement down on her desk. "I've never seen the likes before."

"Lovely," Phoebe mused, turning the vase around. "All shades of whites and creams. An interesting collection of flowers. Quite different from your run of the mill posies."

"Anemones and white bleeding hearts, oh, and is that a white lilac? I adore lilacs."

"There's a card as well, luvy," Maggie announced, passing her a square envelope.

'And though his note is somewhat sad,
He'll try for once a strain more glad,
With some faint hope his alter'd lay
May sing these gloomy thoughts away.'

"Lovely," Maggie sighed wistfully as she strolled from the room. "I always was a fool for a man who adores poetry."

"And clearly from one who is well versed in Floriography as well."

"Beg pardon," Madeline mumbled as she read the lines once again.

"Floriography," Phoebe enunciated for her as if she were one of her pupils. "The language of flowers. His lordship says quite a bit with this bouquet, if indeed, it is from his lordship."

"Yes," Madeline flushed, clutching the note to her chest. "It is. Tell me what the flowers mean."

"Well," Phoebe said, stroking the anemone. "Anemone usually

means forsaken." Phoebe looked up, her brow arched knowingly. "And yet he's included some Nutmeg Geranium, that generally denotes an expected meeting."

"Which flower is that?" Madeline asked excitedly.

"The greenery, Dearest," Phoebe laughed teasingly, grasping handfuls of the trailing plant. "And there is the bleeding heart that usually means fidelity. The most telling of all though, is the tuberose."

Madeline watched as Phoebe reverently ran her finger along a magnificent stalk of flowers, their white buds tinted the barest hint of pink.

"Have you ever smelt a tuberose, Madeline? They're quite the most decadent, delicious scent you'll ever come across."

Madeline reached over and sniffed delicately from the blossoms. "Oh, my," she whispered, surprised at the heavy, exotic scent clinging to the buds. "It's wonderful--it's very ... sensual."

"And very expensive. Almost impossible to find. The rarity combined with the sensuality of the scent makes the meaning that much more intriguing."

"Tell me," Madeline whispered, sniffing the flowers once again.

"It means--*dangerous love*."

Madeline sucked in her breath and stared over the top of the flowers to where Phoebe stood grinning. "Now, it's up to you to put the clues together. The earl has most definitely sent you a message."

"Miss Knightly," Holly called as she ran once more into the room, this time carrying a posy of red roses. "These just arrived for you."

"Thank you." Phoebe smiled, taking the flowers from the girl. "Run along now, dear. Cook is set to serve lunch."

"You're blushing," Madeline teased when Holly left the room. "I can't believe it."

"It's been some time since I received a bouquet."

"Well," Madeline asked. "What do red roses mean?"

"Passion," Phoebe mumbled, showing her the card.

"*I have to see you. I must.-F.* Lord Faversham sent you those?"

"Hmm," Phoebe nodded, smelling the flowers. "It's not quite Byron is it? But," Phoebe said with a smile, her cheeks painted a pale pink, "it'll do."

* * * *

"Lovely day for a stroll, is it not?" Tynemouth asked as they walked arm in arm along the path. "I much prefer walking than maneuvering a carriage about the park. Such a crush at the fashionable hour."

"Mmm," Madeline murmured absently. Her mind pleasantly engaged elsewhere-on the meaning behind a very large and very expensive arrangement of flowers.

"I received my invitation to the Brookehaven affair. I thank you again."

"You're welcome."

"I say, does that dog strolling beside Lord Hardcastle resemble a wolf?"

"Where?" Madeline nearly shouted, before checking herself. "I mean … how strange."

"Indeed," Tynemouth glanced at her, his mouth set in a firm line. "Very strange."

"I do believe that is his niece walking beside him. And who is that on her arm?" Madeline asked, trying to curb her racing pulse and redirect Tynemouth's attention away from her.

"Why, I think that's Renfrew. Decent chap. I've fenced with him a time or two at Angelo's."

"Oh," Madeline murmured as they came upon each other.

When they met, Miranda was all enthusiasm, making introductions and grinning from ear to ear. From the corner of her eye, Madeline couldn't help but notice the way Hardcastle looked her over, couldn't help but see the way his cold eyes raked along Tynemouth, his chin raised in a defiant manner. He reminded her of a wolf, preparing to rush in for the kill. All senses were alert, his gloved hands fisted closely at his sides, nostrils flaring in barely suppressed vexation.

'Read the signs. Look deep within.' Madeline remembered Phoebe's instructions, and did just that. She studied him from the periphery of her vision, watching as he towered over everyone, his anger bubbling, barely controlled, his aloof mask slowly sliding away.

Tynemouth grasped Renfrew's hand, shaking it vigorously. "Heard you bested Ashton in a winner take all."

"Well," Renfrew grinned, sliding a glance towards Miranda. "The incentive was worth it."

Madeline saw Blaine arch a brow, clearly exasperated listening to the polite ramblings, of which, he was most definitely not included.

"That's a beautiful book." Madeline motioned to the leather tome clutched in Miranda hands.

"It's Shakespeare's sonnets. Lord Renfrew has loaned it to me."

"How wonderful," Madeline said, carefully studying Blaine from beneath the safety of her bonnet brim. "There's nothing quite like poetry to stir ones emotions and imagination, is there? May I see it?"

Tynemouth stepped in to reach it for her, his hand resting along the small of her back, when he was prevented from moving by a ferocious snarl.

"I do believe he doesn't care for the fact I was nearing Lady Miranda," Tynemouth said, dropping his hand away from the book. "I say," Tynemouth muttered, as he moved closer in an attempt to protect Madeline from Shadow. "The beast appears as though he's going to strike."

"You are correct," came a quiet, yet mocking reply. "The beast is quite desirous to pounce. Shadow," Blaine called, stilling the wolf and bringing him once more to his side. "Come. It is never wise," Blaine suggested, his voice dark and lethal, "to provoke a beast. One can never be assured of what he is capable of. Especially when the right provocation presents itself."

"Well…." Tynemouth stammered. "That's … that's not the type of animal that should be strolling loose. Women and children are about for God's sake. He could rip apart someone's throat."

"He could." Blaine continued to pet Shadow and Madeline could feel the coolness of his eyes as he sent her a scathing glance. "For now, he's quite under control, Tynemouth. I believe your throat is safe at the moment."

"It's not my person, I was fearful for," Tynemouth stormed, his spine straightening. "I'm referring to Lady Madeline."

"Lady Madeline," Blaine muttered, his cold eyes flickering to her. "Why, I quite forgot you were there. You look," his eyes insolently roved her body, "quite different from the last time we met."

She felt Tynemouth stiffen beside her. Saw the way Blaine's eyes challenged her, daring her to say something about the day in the museum.

He was lashing out, hurting her to hide his vulnerability. She had looked between the pages, read between the lines as Phoebe had suggested. He didn't like to see her out with Tynemouth. He might not be ready to admit that he wanted to be with her, but his actions told her loud and clear he certainly didn't want her to be with anyone else.

"My lord," she said, attempting to meet his sharp wit. "I'm

certain I must look very different. Why, I believe the last time we met, I gave you my back."

His lips twitched then, despite the fact Tynemouth had taken hold of her hand and was feverously trying to steer her away. She saw admiration shine in his eyes before he hid it from her. "Ah yes. I remember it rather well as a matter of fact. Tell me, have you read Byron's *The Bride of Abydos*, yet? I was led to believe you were a lover of the printed word."

"No I-"

"You should. It's a Turkish tale of dark passion and deceit. Something you would fancy, I wager."

"'I' believe I've had the opportunity to read some of it, and I confess what I did read quite took my breath away. Perhaps I might read it tonight. I had planned to spend the evening at Montgomery House, tallying the accounts. Perhaps I'll have a few moments of privacy tonight."

He bowed before her, his eyes slowly looking up from the dark fringe of his lashes. They were cool, but not cold and she knew then that he had understood her, and the silent invitation she'd just offered him.

"It is a lovely tale, written to be enjoyed by candlelight and a blazing fire. I hope," he whispered against her knuckles, "that you will enjoy it."

And then he left, Shadow obediently following beside him, his strides long and purposeful and utterly determined.

"I say," Tynemouth said, glaring at Blaine's retreating form. "That was quite the most bizarre conversation I ever heard. I can't decide what exactly he was talking about."

Good. Madeline took Tynemouth's arm one more time and strolled down the path. At least she didn't have Tynemouth to worry about. All that need concern her now, was whether Hardcastle would show up this evening.

* * * *

Bloody hell, he should not be doing this.

Blaine sat in his carriage, his hands wiping his face in frustration. What the devil was he doing out front of Montgomery House? Damnation, anyone could see him, any one of the house's residents could find him alone with Madeline and then what the hell kind of mess would he find himself in?

He'd have to marry her, that's what would happen.

He shuddered at the thought and almost raised his fist to knock on the trap door to signal the coachman to move on. And then he saw the image of her standing beside Tynemouth, the irritating pup's hand touching her as though she belonged to him and he thought better of it.

For the first time he allowed himself to think about the considerable rage he'd felt at seeing them together, at seeing Tynemouth possessively grip her as though he needed to protect her from him. The anger was still there, as well as the desire. Every time he thought about the way she'd smiled at him that afternoon he'd been consumed with desire, with the overwhelming need to sacrifice his own rules and kiss her senseless. Those maddening lips and those endearing freckles had played havoc with his self-control. Damn it, he was still struggling with it, still wondering how he found himself here, hiding in his carriage.

"Milord," the coachman called from beneath the collar of his greatcoat. "We've arrived in Leicester Square. I'll return for ye in a hour, as ye asked."

With a resigned sigh, Blaine reached for the door, alighting into the warm night. Reaching into the cab for the leather satchel, he called to Shadow then shut the door of the carriage, watching as it pulled away, the clacking of the hooves ringing out in the still night.

Casting a furtive glance over his shoulder, he was relieved to see that the windows of Montgomery House's neighbors were all in darkness. It was late, and no doubt the majority of the merchant residents had long ago bedded down for the night. Let's hope, he thought as he walked around the side of the house, because if they weren't, he'd find himself betrothed faster than a street urchin could filch a meat pie.

Chapter Eight

Where was he, Madeline fumed, slamming the cover of her book shut. Surely he was coming? How could he not?

Did he not understand the extraordinary lengths she'd gone through to be at Montgomery House at this hour? Why, she'd actually had to lie to her father. *Lie!* She never lied, and yet she had barely batted a lash when she looked her Papa in the eye and told him she needed to go over the account books and finalize plans for the market at Covent Garden the next day. Her father had reluctantly agreed, insisting on dropping her off and picking her up after his Whig meeting broke up. He had sent James with her, his most dutiful footman. Thank Heavens the chamomile tea had worked on the burley man, else she would not have been sitting here in the garden, waiting in vain for the man of her dreams to appear.

Unable to sit still a moment longer, Madeline tossed her book on the wrought iron table and got up from her chair. Pacing along the path, she snapped off the blooms of lavender and catmint that brushed against her skirt. Inhaling the soothing fragrance, she tried to steady her nerves, but she was afraid. What if she was wrong about the earl and his feelings for her?

She desperately hoped she was correct in her assumption that Blaine desired her. She certainly desired him. She felt different when she was with him, it was if she was aware of the fact that she was a woman when he was with her. He made her think of things that no man ever had. He made her yearn for things only a man could give a woman.

"She walks in beauty, like the night. Of cloudless climes, and starry skies."

Whirling around, she saw him standing beneath the oak tree, his gray eyes glistening in the flickering candlelight. "My lord." Her pulse leapt as she watched him step closer, his eyes roving along her face, then sliding down the front to her gown. "Byron's, *She Walks in Beauty*. I vow he could have written it for you, looking as you do now, your dress illuminated by the moon and the candles. Had he seen your lips, the color of ripe cherries, your eyes, the same shade as tropical lagoons, he would have penned it for you."

She forced herself to stay planted where she was and yet she had the almost irrational urge to move away from him. He looked dangerous--potent, far more skilled at seduction than any other man of her acquaintance. He'd spoken only words, compared her features to things she'd heard before, and yet she felt as though she was hearing it for the first time. She was being seduced--lured into temptation by metaphors and steely gray eyes.

"I...." she stammered and swallowed, striving for an air of decorous grace when all she really felt was giddy excitement. "I thought you might not come this evening."

"I tried to stay away." He captured her hand in his. "But I could not. I had to see you once again beneath the moonlight."

A whimper drew her attention away from his lips against her hand, and searching into the darkness she saw Shadow step forward, his blue eyes boldly looking out at her through the shadowed darkness.

"I hope you don't mind. He wanted to see you, too."

"Of course not," she said, holding her hand out to Shadow. He came immediately, licking her fingers then nudging her hand for a pat.

"What have you in the sack?"

"Ah," he murmured, casting a glance at the house, ensuring all the curtains were drawn. "You will see, my *Rat Ki Rani?*."

"What language is that? I've never heard something so strange, yet so evocative."

He smiled at her, his thin lips curving in a lopsided grin. "Arabic." He pulled a crimson velvet square from the bag and placed it on the grass beneath the tree. "It is Persian to be precise."

"You speak Arabic?" she asked incredulously. "Where ever did you learn it?"

"Self taught," he replied, pulling two pillows, a bottle of claret and one glass from his satchel. "I speak six languages, as a matter of fact, but none of them are as exciting to the senses as Persian." He took the candelabra from the table and motioned towards her with his free hand. "Come. We shall make this our Harem."

"Harem?" she squealed as he pulled her forward, helping her to sit on the pillow.

"Yes," he whispered, his breath grazing her neck. "Harem means 'Forbidden Places'. Surely you and I, completely alone beneath the moon and stars constitutes a forbidden place?" He offered her a glass of wine and reached for the book at his feet.

"Now, ask me what *Rat Ki Rani* means."

"What does it mean?" she said asked with a smile as she licked a drop of claret from her lips.

He stared at her for a long while, his gaze focused on her mouth before he slowly looked into her eyes. When at last he spoke his voice was gruff, almost harsh in its intensity. "Mistress of the Night." He reached for her hand and brought it to his lips. "In India the tuberose blooms are known by the name. You're wearing my blooms in your hair." He nodded to the sprig of tuberose she had impulsively tucked into a curl. "We're together, alone in the blackness of night, therefore, you're my Mistress of the Night, and I have you, at least for an hour, safely tucked away in my Harem."

She felt her hand tremble in his as he rubbed her knuckles across his lips, heard her whimper of surprise as he pressed her hand to his cheek and closed his eyes, his black lashes fanned across his cheek. *"The Bride of Abydos,"* he said in a deep, husky voice, "shall I begin?"

"Yes," she said breathlessly, entranced by the sight of him so close beside her, the scent of him, soap and sandalwood clinging to the air between them. She watched him open the book, his head mere inches from her shoulder as he sprawled out, his leg bent casually, his elbow propped with a pillow.

"Know ye the land where the cypress and myrtle...."

Madeline relaxed against the tree trunk as she listened to Blaine's deep, rich timbre. He had a lovely voice, a voice designed to entrance, to enthrall those with its lush sound. She marveled as his voice inflected every emotion of the poet, the words bringing on new meaning. She studied him as he read, his long, tapered fingers turned the pages with unpracticed ease. His hair, black as coal shone nearly blue in the candlelight that flickered beside him. The top of his head was bent, nearly level with her breasts. He was so close that with every whisper of the breeze she wished she had the boldness to run her fingers through his silken hair. He was handsome and passionate, romantic yet brash. He was everything she had ever wanted and more.

"He lived--he breathed--he moved--he felt-"

"Blaine," she whispered, placing a hand on his shoulder when he'd finished the passage. "Will you read that again?"

He looked up at her, his eyes flickering with warmth--with life. He dropped his gaze and looked at her hand, then brought his lips to her fingertips, kissing them with the barest grazing of his lips.

And then he read it, the sound of his voice the most enthralling thing she'd ever heard.

She sighed when he finished. "Every night I have read your letter, delighting in the words and in awe of the power of them. I have been overcome by their beauty. But nothing," she whispered, raking nervous fingers through his hair, "nothing compares to the sound of hearing them in your own voice."

"Every night I have imagined saying them to you," he said, sitting up and taking her face in his hands. "Never did I dare to hope they would affect you in such a way."

"They have." She spoke the truth before she could stop herself. Phoebe had said to stay aloof, to draw him out and play the game. But she couldn't. She didn't play at games, she wasn't cunning or deceitful and she wasn't ashamed of her feelings. They were natural, honest, and pure.

"Maddy," he kissed her cheeks, then her jaw. "You cannot know what it is like to want what you cannot have."

"I would not deny you." She framed his face in her hands and stared into his tortured eyes. "It is not in my power to deny you."

"You must," he hissed, his lips only inches from hers. "You don't understand. I *know* this must not happen, yet I cannot stop it."

"I can't stop, either," she said, sliding her hands along his face to run her fingers through his hair. "I don't want to stop, Blaine."

"Maddy." He whispered her name in such a way it made her shiver. There was a need in his voice, it was more than sexual desire. It was something far more elusive. She looked up and met his eyes, surprised by the heat in his eyes, shocked to see his lip quivering. His fingers were locked firmly against her face, his eyes focused solely on her lips.

"I have...." he mumbled, then stopped, licked his lip, his eyes never once straying from her mouth. "I want...." he lowered his mouth, his breath hot against her lips, his eyes open, alert, watching--seeing. "Don't push me away," he groaned, lowering his head so that his lip trembled against hers, "not now ... not ever."

And then his lips were upon hers and Madeline felt as if she had never felt anything softer, sweeter or more beautiful against them.

"Mmmmm," he heard himself moan, cursing at the absurdity of it while at the same time slinking down to the ground and taking her with him.

It was like nothing he'd ever thought to experience. Her warm and pliant lips beckoned him to explore deeper and yet he knew to do that, to enter her mouth and kiss her intimately would be his demise. He'd already risked too much by coming to see her. He'd shown too much of his need and now he was displaying too much of his desire, the urgency he felt when their lips touched and held.

Her hands glided down his head and over his shoulders, his muscles tensed, then flexed as her fingers danced, feather-light along his throat and over his chest. Jesus, he was hungry, far hungrier than he had ever been in his life and he had yet to even slip inside her mouth and taste her.

Slanting his lips over hers, he groaned and brought her closer to him, nearly crushing her against his length. She whimpered and kissed him back with untutored exuberance. Unable to stop himself, he let his finger slide down her throat, resting against her bounding pulse. It leapt beneath his thumb, thrilling him into recklessness. He parted her lips then and entered her mouth, feeling the heat of her, tasting the sweetness of the claret on her tongue. Her pulse surged once more, quickening as his tongue mingled and danced with hers.

He'd never thought to have her in such a way. But as he kissed her and she kissed him back, an increasing frenzy of give and take, he realized he had needed this, he needed to taste her, wanted to savor the feel of her, the taste of her on his own lips. He didn't give a damn what he sounded like, or how dangerous this might be to his vows of never risking his heart. He wanted her-- completely.

Feeling bolder, he became more aggressive in his strokes, more demanding as he tasted her, mimicking with his tongue what he so wanted to do with his cock that was now throbbing mercilessly in his trousers. She gasped at the intimacy, at the unmistakable innuendo of this tongue thrusting in and out of her sweet lips. She stilled beneath him, and he cursed himself for being vulgar and impatient. What the hell had he been thinking? She was an innocent and his dreams, his fantasies about them together had been far from pure.

He stopped, forcing himself to open his eyes. Beautiful turquoise spheres stared back at him and then she closed them on the sweetest whimper he'd ever heard. He devoured her then, taking, commanding that she give him more. He couldn't get close enough to her, couldn't kiss her deep enough to satisfy his need for her. Tongues danced, and his fingers began to trace the cleft of her breasts, to feel her smooth skin beneath his fingers. He wanted to trail his tongue along her silky skin, yet he couldn't bring himself to leave the warmth of her mouth. He was addicted, consumed by the taste of her as they shared their lips and tongue. He knew he shouldn't have succumbed, she was already creeping into his heart and he knew, as he plunged once more into her mouth, glorying in her moan and the fisting of her hands in his hair, that she was more than likely already there.

"Maddy," he groaned, leaving her mouth and trailing his lips down the column of her neck.

"Yes," she sighed, answering his silent question. "Yes," she breathed again as he pulled the silk of her bodice down over her breasts, baring her white flesh in the moonlight. Coral nipples crinkled in the air and he lowered his head to her full breasts and ran his lips lightly over the tight buds. She fisted her hands in his hair as he blew softly against them and she arched invitingly as he nuzzled his mouth and chin between the inviting cleft.

His tongue came out in short flicks as he kissed her breasts and he smiled into her flesh as she arched rhythmically beneath him. His hand journey down her side and over her belly and he felt, as well as heard her breathing quicken. Felt her body grow restless as she pulled at his hair, motioning him to take her into his mouth. He cupped her sex through her gown at the same time his tongue swirled around her straining nipple, she moaned and he couldn't help but cup her firmer and bring her nipple deep into his mouth, suckling her. Hot wetness seeped through her gown, warming his palm and he sucked harder, aroused by her body's response to him.

She clutched his hair in her fist and he let her swollen nipple slide out from between his lips. He licked the tip, slow at first, then with longer strokes, like a cat licking a bowl of cream. She was writhing now beneath him, and he slid his finger along her swollen sex, through her thin skirts and rubbed his thumb along her clitoris, knowing that the added stimulation of the fabric would have her panting hard beneath him.

"Oh God, Blaine," she said in a strangled breath.

"Give me what I want, Maddy," he encouraged, circling her nipple with the tip of his tongue. "Come apart in my arms and let me watch you."

Instinctively she widened her legs and he continued his circular stimulation of her clitoris while he tongued her nipple. He watched the play of emotion on her face, watched the way her tongue trailed across her lip before her mouth parted on a silent scream and her back arched and her head tipped back.

A fresh flood of arousal seeped through her gown and he brought her nipple into his mouth, sucking her fiercely, making her body bow tighter and he felt her breast swell in his mouth and her clitoris become erect against his finger. And then she shook, and he watched her through hooded eyes as he pleasured her into her first shaking orgasm.

Shadow stirred restlessly beside them, a low grumbling parted his canine mouth, baring his white fangs.

"Lady Madeline?" a voice called out into the darkness. "You out here?"

Tearing his mouth from her breast, Blaine shielded her body with his and motioned for Shadow to remain beside them. Their breaths were panting, the hot air caressing their throats as he peered around the tree to see a large frame looming in the door of the house. "Who is that?" he asked harshly, unable to believe he was breathless.

"James," she whispered. "My father's footman and my chaperone for the night."

"Some chaperone. He's let me have my way with you for far too long."

"Lady Madeline?" the footman called again, his voice rising in fear.

"I'm here," she called waving from behind the tree as she untangled herself from his arms. "Just reading."

"Readin'? In the dark?"

"I have light." she smiled, taking the candelabra from Blaine's hands. "See?"

"Oh," the footman said, clearly befuddled. "His lordship should be arriving any moment."

"I'll be right in. Just let me get my book."

"Right then, but don't dawdle. You know his lordship doesn't like to be kept waitin'."

Blaine waited until James had closed the door before he reached for her and brought her tight against his chest. "Just one more kiss, my Mistress of the Night, so that I may have the taste of you on my mouth. So that when I wake up, I'll know that this wasn't just a dream."

* * * *

"That'll be three shillings," Madeline proclaimed.

"Three shillings," the elderly duke grumbled, "for a pile of linen and thread?"

"Just pay the lady," a deep voice growled from the crowd. "You can afford it, Roth. It's a small price to pay for a lady's happiness."

"Just mind yer own, Faversham,' Roth snarled before placing the shillings in Madeline's outstretched hand. "Never could understand females and their fripperies."

"Thank you, Your Grace," Madeline called out to Roth as he trudged to the next booth. She smiled when she saw him raise his wrinkled hand in the air and dismiss her with a haughty wave.

"Well," Lord Faversham drawled as he walked up to the table, surveying the wares for sale. "At last I've come face to face with *the* Lady Madeline."

"Lord Faversham," she smiled, slightly un-nerved by the gleam in his brown eyes.

"Where would your lovely associate be this afternoon?" he asked, picking up an embroidered handkerchief and studying the work.

"Associate?"

"Miss Knightly."

"She's … well.…"

"Here," Phoebe called from behind a box.

"Ah," Faversham smiled, his eyes turning a warmer shade of brown, reminding Madeline of melted chocolate.

"Good day, Lord Faversham," Phoebe said while emptying her box of linens on the table. "Have you come to peruse the merchandise?"

"Indeed," he purred. "Although some of the merchandise is somewhat elusive. Some might even say frustratingly so."

Madeline stared in wonder at the conversation. Lord Faversham was clearly bent on having Phoebe and Phoebe, well, she looked as though she couldn't have cared less. She just continued heaping more hankies and kerchiefs on the table, completely ignoring Faversham's smoldering looks.

"How much would it take, Lady Madeline, for you to release your associate for the day?"

Madeline gasped, but Phoebe plunged in, her beautiful courtesan smile in place. "Five thousand pounds," Phoebe declared. "That's the amount we need to invest in a project to assure the future of Montgomery House."

"Done."

Madeline stared in wonder, how had she done it? With a smile and a flick of her blonde head, Phoebe had managed to get the notoriously close-fisted lord to open his pocket book.

"Madeline," Phoebe whispered, removing her apron. "Mrs. Noland is here and Helen is expected any moment, you don't mind, do you?"

"Of course not," Madeline sputtered. "But really, you don't have to … I mean, if you don't want--*how did you do that*?"

"That's the way the game is played," Phoebe grinned, then patted her hand. "And believe me, Dearest, I *want* to go with him."

With a sigh, Madeline watched them traipse away, grinning at the spring in Phoebe's step.

"He's a right devil that one," Maggie came up to stand beside her. "I fear Phoebe may have met her match in him."

"I just hope she knows what she's doing," Madeline whispered. "He won't marry her. Despite the fact his wife gave him his heir before she died, he won't marry beneath himself. She's going to get hurt."

"The road to love is never easy," Maggie murmured, staring at her with keen eyes. "It's fraught with pain and sorrow and sometimes it feels as though it might never work out. But love is something you just can't abandon. True love doesn't give up, doesn't loosen it's on hold ye. Don't you forget that, luvy."

Madeline reached for Maggie's wrinkled hand and clasped it tightly in hers. "Why did you not tell me that you were a member of Hardcastle's staff?"

"I didn't think it pertinent," she mumbled, looking away. "I didn't want you to think I might have any influence over him."

"Do you?" Madeline couldn't help but ask. "Does he listen to what you have to say?"

"He's a man, luvy. Do men ever listen to women?"

"Maggie," Madeline sobered. "Do you know what secrets he keeps?"

"A smile to rival that of the sun."

Madeline jumped in surprise at the sound of the voice behind her. Darting her eyes from Maggie she watched as Tynemouth lounged against the table, a posy of daisies in his hand. "For you," he proclaimed.

"Thank you," she smiled, idly sniffing the flowers, disappointed when they held no scent. "They're lovely."

"They remind me of you, bright and cheery. The yellow centers remind me of the sun and your smile."

He certainly wasn't poetic and his flowers were nothing like Blaine's exotic and lush bouquet. He was trying very hard, but really, how could he be a rival to the enigmatic earl?

"So, you're selling these items for Montgomery House?" Tynemouth asked, looking through the linens. "I'll take three, one for my mother and each sister."

"Well," another familiar voice rang out. "Here's the gel I've been looking for."

"Lady Brookehaven, a pleasure, madam."

"I've sent a missive round to Montgomery House, I'd like to meet tomorrow to discuss the plans for the charity weekend. These things take thought, you know. We just can't expect the weekend to plan itself."

"It would be my pleasure."

"I've asked Rebecca and Isabella to be there also. I presume you know Rebecca? My grandson's wife?"

"Yes," Madeline demurred, remembering having met Lady Bronley.

"And Lady Bathurst is my godchild. Don't know if you know that. I've invited her as well."

"It presents no difficulties for me."

"Hmm," the dowager nodded, her jowls dancing as her hawk like eyes came to rest on Lord Tynemouth. "I say, Tynemouth, I'm surprised to see you here."

"Just assisting Lady Madeline with her endeavors," Lord Tynemouth smiled politely, appearing to be not the least bit disturbed by the dowager's imposing presence.

"Hmmm" she murmured again. "Saw your father the other night at the Gordon soiree. He told me you've a mind for politics."

"Indeed," he smiled. "I'm a protégé of Lord Penrick. He has kindly taken me under his wing. He's been introducing me to all the right people."

"Oh?" Lady Brookehaven declared, her intelligent eyes passing between them both. "How interesting. I hadn't realized."

"Madeline."

Madeline looked up to see Miranda rushing towards her, dragging Lord Renfrew with her.

"Miranda," Madeline laughed, reaching for her hands. "What a pleasant surprise."

"Well, I had to come. I told you I would. Oh," Miranda exclaimed, catching sight of Lady Brookehaven. "Pray forgive me, your ladyship. I didn't see you."

"Apology accepted, gel. Hardcastle," Lady Brookehaven said with a nod. "Nice to see you."

"Good day, Lady Brookehaven."

Madeline looked up to see Blaine standing before her, his gray eyes watchful, yet wary as they slid from the dowager to her. She met his gaze, her heart beating faster when she saw the cool hauteur melt into something far more welcoming.

"Lady Madeline," he said softly, removing his hat, and inclining his head. "A pleasure."

"Lord Hardcastle," she replied, trying to disguise the way her fingertips trembled when he reached for them. "Good afternoon."

"How was your evening at home last night? I seem to recall you were staying in to read Byron's, *Bride of Abydos*. Did you enjoy it?"

"It was … very enlightening. I'm quite at a loss for words to explain it."

"Some things," he said, his lips twitching, "transcend words."

"Quite right," Tynemouth interjected jovially. "Why, just the other day Lord Hastings gave a rousing speech. It wasn't so much his words as the animation of his voice. The passion with which he spoke."

Madeline couldn't help but grin as she watched Blaine close his eyes, a look of barely concealed sufferance played across his features.

"Lord Tynemouth," Lady Brookehaven began, "stroll along with me and tell me about this Lord Hastings. I've heard fascinating things about the man. I've even heard he could be our next Prime Minister."

The dowager ushered him along with a flick of her cane and motioned for Miranda and Renfrew to follow her as well. "Come along, Renfrew. I've a feeling that we just might learn something of importance here. And Miranda, you can help carry my purchases. I'm an old woman, you know, and I can't always be traipsing about saddled under a mountain of shopping."

Madeline watched the dowager shoo them along, Tynemouth clearly attempted to protest, then, finally resolved, began to discuss the merits of Lord Hastings.

"Well, milord," Maggie chuckled, her eyes twinkling with unconcealed affection. "It's high time you've come out to do your duty."

"Nanny," he smiled, his white teeth flashing in the sunlight as he gripped her hand and brought it to his lips in a most gallant gesture. "What is your fancy? I'll purchase anything you like."

"Bah," she waved him away, "You've given me enough

already, but, if you wouldn't mind, luvy," she turned and addressed Madeline. "I'd like to go and see Hester Griffith. She's got some evening primrose that I wouldn't mind a snipping of."

"Ah … no," Madeline said, forcing herself to stop staring at Blaine, at the way his silky waves blew in the gentle breeze in delightful disarray. She had the disconcerting urge to run her fingers through his thick locks like she had the previous night, feeling the strands slide between her fingers.

"I thought of you all night," he whispered softly, pretending to peruse the merchandise once Maggie had taken her leave. "I awoke with the taste of you on my lips and the scent of you clinging to my skin."

"I couldn't sleep, either," she whispered shakily, her fingers discreetly grazing his amongst the linen and lace. "I thought about what we did."

"And does it shame you?" His fingers stopped moving against hers, his eyes flickered up to hers. His gaze was so intense, so knowing, that she felt like shrinking back from it. There was something dark and disturbing in his eyes as he looked at her, almost as if he were trying to see through her, as if he were daring her to regret what they had done.

"Did humiliation greet you with the dawn?"

"No," she refuted, her voice a hushed whisper. "I have no regrets."

"I was filled with remorse when I awoke this morning." He spoke softly, stroking his finger along the top of her hand.

Had she not pleased him? She knew she had been clumsy when he'd first kissed her, but surely he didn't expect her to be adept at the skill? He couldn't be telling her he regretted the time they shared, not when she couldn't stop thinking about it or stop herself from remembering the way he'd held her, the way his tongue, warm and insistent had felt in her mouth and on her breast, the way his fingers had mastered her body.

"From the instant I awoke, I was filled with regret that I could no longer feel you wrapped tightly against me."

"I'm not ashamed of what we did, or how I acted. I.…" she wet her lips and checked to make certain that no one could hear what she was about to say. "My only regret is that I might not have pleased you. That I might … that I was clumsy in my ignorance."

"Madeline, will you meet me tonight? I don't care where. I'll do anything to see you again, I'll go out amongst the ton, I'll meet you in any garden, just say that I can see you again."

"The Thorndale's. I've promised to attend Lady Thorndale's musicale."

"Till tonight then, my Mistress of the Night. I shall be anxiously waiting for you." He brought her fingers to his lips. "This is quite dangerous, my sweet. This attraction might well go beyond what either wants."

"What is desire if not dangerous and illicit?" she sputtered, as he kissed her fingers once more. "That is the very nature of desire, is it not?"

"I hope you do not have cause to be disappointed. Desire and Passion have a way of doing that, once the initial flames turn to smoldering embers."

"I will never have cause to regret anything I do with you, milord. Will you?"

She wasn't certain, but she thought he might have murmured, *'I don't know'* before he released her hand.

He reached into his jacket then and produced the most exquisite sprig of tuberose. "For you," he brought it to his lips before laying it atop Tynemouth's posy. "Till tonight."

"Till tonight," she mumbled, watching him walk away, languidly picking his way through the crowd. When she could no longer see him, she looked down at the creamy flowers he'd place atop the daisies. *Dangerous Love* amongst *Innocence*. She felt herself shiver, wondering at the meaning behind the flowers, wondering how two men could see her in a different light.

She looked up then, aware of a strange tingling down her back. She scanned the crowd, all nameless faces bumping and pushing before her. And then she saw him, alone by an empty table. Their eyes met and held, locked across the distance. He was so devilishly handsome standing in the sunlight, his broad shoulders outlined in the sun's rays. He removed his hat again, his hair blowing in the breeze and she most definitely forgot to breathe. He was, she thought, as he bowed one last time, utterly perfect.

Chapter Nine

What the bloody hell was he thinking? He must have finally descended into madness, for what other reason could there be for him to be standing in Lady Thorndale's music room, bereft of his friends for protection, hoping to catch a glimpse of Madeline?

This was dangerous. More than dangerous, it could mean the end of his reputation, the destruction of Miranda's dreams of marrying Renfrew if it got out he was possessed.

The *Beau Monde* would have no qualms about ostracizing him and his relations. Despite the fact that most members of the ton were well educated, they still held beliefs that his illness stemmed from the devil, that evil possession was the cause. He couldn't afford to ruin his family's reputation, or his niece's happiness because, simply put, he was a panting lust-crazed fool for Madeline Brydges.

But he was. Crazed. Lustful. Damn, he'd had the most erotic dreams of her last night, all of them more than he'd ever admit to, and all of them taking place in a Turkish Harem. Damn it to hell, why did he have to give life to his fantasies? He should have just brought her a volume of Shakespeare's sonnets. Something mundane and over used. *Shall I compare thee to a summer's day? Thou are more lovely and more temperate.* No doubt she had heard that one a time or two before. Hell, even that Tynemouth pup had probably uttered it to her, right before he'd presented her with his handful of daisies.

He had wanted to laugh when he'd seen them lying atop the table, perfectly appropriate, perfectly innocuous. *Innocence.* If only the man knew what she'd been up to the evening before. If only Tynemouth knew that it was *his* flowers that scented her hair, his lips that had been the ones to touch hers--his mouth she'd moaned into.

But, he'd had to bring Byron, to tempt her with forbidden places and forbidden passions. He'd had to tempt himself. He had to kiss her, to feel his tongue deep inside, possessing her, feeling at one with her. He'd been a bloody, reckless fool and he'd vowed to himself as he prowled around his room that morning that he would never give in to temptation again. And yet here he was, bloody well tempted by just the thought of seeing her.

Voices from the hall thankfully gave him reprieve from his thoughts and he turned to study the figures that entered the room. He knew the names of most of the elegantly dressed guests, but as he had never felt fit to seek or oblige introductions, he knew none of them personally. With a sigh and a glance at his watch fob, he maintained his position of holding up the wall and waited for Madeline to make her grand appearance.

He knew the second she entered the room. He didn't have to see her to know she was there, her breathtaking green eyes scouring the room for him. He felt the strange prickles race down his back, felt his hair begin to rise on his nape. He'd heard his married friends talk of such phenomena but he'd never gave it any credit, always dismissing their outlandish reports as too many hours spent with females and a dangerous level of lust. But tonight he was a faithful disciple, a reformed cynic who now believed that there was some higher plane in which souls could communicate upon.

He looked up in time to see her enter, her hand resting lightly on her father's arm. His breath left him and for one frightening, horrifying moment, he felt as though he would succumb to one of his fits. But when he should have been smelling burning bread and feeling his body shake and tighten, he felt only a burning in his chest.

She was beautiful. Resplendent. Magnificent. Hell, he thought, as he watched her glide into the room, there was not one adequate word in all of the six languages he spoke to convey how absolutely breathtaking she was in her crimson gown.

The color reminded him of blood trickling from a fresh wound. It was rich and deep, burgundy almost, but with an iridescence that made it shimmer more red than burgundy as she walked beneath the chandelier. It was a bold statement, the kind of gown that grabbed and held a person's attention. The color was daring with her flame colored hair and translucent skin. The richness of it only magnified the red in her hair and made her green eyes more turquoise. She looked brazen and confident, a woman comfortable in her own skin. Yet the endearing freckles smattering the bridge of her nose kept her from looking untouchable. There was something about them that made her accessible and infinitely more attainable.

She was careful to keep her eyes trained ahead of her, smiling when someone would speak and feigning interest in conversation. Occasionally she would slip and he would catch her looking out of the corner of her eye, searching for someone--*for him*.

Her father led her to the front of the room and he in turn made his way through the crowd. Taking a program from a passing footman, he took a chair one row back and immediately to her right. She had only to peer over her shoulder and she would see him, no doubt staring adoringly back at her.

The music started and the crowd began to quiet as the musicians began to warm up their instruments. He wondered how long musicales lasted and almost asked the young lady to his left when he recalled that he didn't have the slightest clue who she was. It left him feeling decidedly unbalanced, aware of how inept he was in society.

Clearing his throat, he sat back, forcing himself to forget his dark secret and willing Madeline to look back at him.

He sat there for what seemed like a painful length of time before the Thorndale's eldest took the bench before the pianoforte, giving her harrowing rendition of Beethoven's *Fur Elise*. At least, he presumed it to be the famous sonata.

As he made a conscious effort to listen to the music, he used the opportunity to study Madeline. She had a lovely profile. Strong chin and full lips. High cheekbones and forehead, with delightfully arched brows. From where he was sitting he could see that her lips were red and full, reminding him of ripe, succulent cherries. And her eyes, those glorious lagoon green eyes with their flame fringe--damn, but he could drown staring into those eyes. If only she would turn to look at him he could drown in them now.

And then the heat in the room seemed to send him into a sweat. The music suddenly faded to a distant hum and all the other guests surrounding them melted into the woodwork, leaving just him and Madeline alone together. And then he saw it. That slight tilt of her head, the way her chin brushed her collarbone as she raised her shoulder to look back at him. Her eyes, those amazing eyes peeked up at him, her lips beckoning him, enticing him with memories of last night.

He didn't give a damn who was around, didn't care if all and sundry were staring at them, deciphering their heated gazes. This moment was too great to waste worrying about others. This moment--right now, right here, was between them, and only them. Right then, he had eyes only for her, and she for him and there was no where, *no where*, he would have rather been than there, with her staring back at him, her beautiful lips curving in a secret smile.

He was falling hard. He knew it, yet was helpless to stop it. He didn't know if he could even cease these feelings. He sure as hell hadn't been able to stop thinking of her, stop dreaming of her, naked and flushed beneath him. He'd tried. For the past year, in fact, he'd tried to banish her from his brain, and he tried last night to banish the taste of her from his mouth and the heat of her from his blood. He couldn't.

It was dangerous. It was madness.

This would have to be it, he decided. He couldn't continue on in this vein. His passions were too strong, his feelings much too frightening. Tonight had to be the end, but that did not mean the end had to be anything but spectacular.

* * * *

"I think I'll step outside for a breath of fresh air," Madeline said as she clutched her father's arm. "It's a trifle warm, don't you think?"

"Hmmm," her father mumbled absently, looking about the room. "What's that, m'dear?"

"Outside," she said, grinning. "I'm going to go outside. I'm warm."

"Oh right, right," he grumbled before nodding to Lord Waverley. "I'll just stroll about here. I see a few members of my club I wouldn't mind having a word with."

"I'll meet you back here in a few minutes?"

"Fine." Her father was clearly already lost in thought over the prospect of talking politics. "Take all the time you need."

Madeline strolled unhurriedly to the terrace doors, stopping to talk politely with acquaintances. It wouldn't do to look eager to get outside. She had to look as though she were merely strolling about, passing the time until the musicians started again.

When she was certain no one was paying her any particular attention, she slipped out into the night, picked up her skirts in one hand and walked toward the gardens. She wished she could call out his name, but she didn't dare, who knew what other assignations had been planned for the intermission.

"Here," came a gruff whisper.

She turned in time to see a hand motioning to her from the maze. With a quick glimpse at her surroundings, she assured herself no one was about, then slipped into the maze, coming breast to breast with Blaine.

"My lor-" her breath was cut off as he cupped her face and brought his mouth down against hers, tasting and nipping before sliding his tongue inside and devouring her.

"I have been aching to do that all night," he said gruffly, kissing her between words. "I thought the Thorndale chit would never cease playing."

"It *was* a rather long drawn out rendition of the *Appassionata Sonata.*"

"I thought it was *Fur Elise*," he said, kissing her neck and bringing her tighter against him.

"Poor Hortense." She whimpered when she felt his hands slide to her bottom, cupping and squeezing. "I thought she played terribly."

"Do you know what you do to me in this gown?" he asked, taking her off guard with his question. "I couldn't breathe when you walked into the room this evening. I could only stare, only marvel at the sight of you in this crimson silk."

"Oh," she breathed, shocked at the feel of his hardness against her belly. His embrace was positively scandalous and the heat of his strong fingers squeezing her bottom was deliciously wicked.

"I sat in that damn chair and watched you, studied you as you fanned yourself. And all I could think about was seeing this red silk slide along your skin, revealing you to my eyes, inch by excruciating inch. God, how I want to see you, how I want to touch every inch of you."

"Blaine," she sighed as he kissed her neck. His fingers drew enticing lines over the tops of her breasts before sliding down to her thighs.

"Let me touch you," he whispered against her mouth. "I want to know how wet you are for me. I want to feel your honey this time against my skin."

Madeline gasped as he brought her closer to him, resting her against his knee as his hand found its way beneath her gown. His fingers slid up her thigh only to rest on that part of her that was aching to be stroked by him. And then he parted her and she gasped again, her eyes widening in wonder and fear as his fingers caressed the length of her, wetting them in her slickness before sliding inside her.

"Very wet," he said against the swell of her breast. "Very accommodating," he groaned, sliding another finger inside her so that she was stretched full. She whimpered, arching her back so that her breasts were closer to his mouth, and his hand was cupping her firmer, making his fingers more insistent.

"Do you feel how hard I am for you, Maddy? You make me feel

alive, you make me-" his words were cut off his by his groan and the wetness that suddenly pooled inside her. "Bloody hell, you're just as ready as I, aren't you my little *Houri*?"

Her body begin to shake and quiver as he increased the rhythm of his fingers. It was like nothing she ever thought to experience. She had no idea Blaine's fingers would feel this wondrous inside her or that she would burn with such longing. But she did long for this--for him.

"I just want to give you pleasure, Maddy. I want to see your eyes light up for me, only me."

"We mustn't, not here. We can't-"

"I understand far more than you that this cannot happen."

"No," she shook her head, trying to right her fuzzy head. There could be something between them. They could be married, could have children and enjoy this every night of their lives. It could happen, just not here, in Lady Thorndale's maze.

"Kiss me once more, Maddy," he breathed against her mouth. "I want to know what it is like to be consumed--to be lured to my doom."

She kissed him then, not because she wanted to lure him, but because she heard something in his voice, a need, a vulnerability that reached out to her. She sensed in that moment he was asking her for far more than a kiss.

"Just another finger," he purred, slipping a third finger deep inside her. "Just so that you are totally full of me."

She gasped and he caught her mouth with his. His lips were demanding and rough, taking and devouring, yet savoring her too. His tongue was insistent, matching the rhythm of his fingers and she met his demands, whimpering as she met his eyes as they studied her. There was a need there, a desperation shining in them. He didn't hide it, didn't shade it with his infamous hauteur or mocking humor. Instead he let her see it, moaning deep in his throat when she closed her eyes, giving herself up to an earth shattering experience.

And then the sound of a violin bow, screeching against its strings reached them, shattering the passion surrounding them. It was faint at first, then becoming louder, more audible.

Blaine pulled away, fixing her skirts and bringing her into his arms, circling her tightly and resting his forehead against hers. "You'll never know what these past weeks have meant to me, Madeline. I'll never forget them, or the way you looked tonight in my arms, finding your release."

"You talk as if there will be no more nights such as this," she smiled, stroking his jaw, delighting in the rough feel of his stubble against her finger.

"Our nights of forbidden pleasures end tonight. If it could be anyone, Madeline, it would be you. I hope you realize that."

"You can't just leave," she cried, when he pulled away from her. "What do you mean? What has happened that we must never see each other again?"

He had to get away. Maybe he should go to Derbyshire and try to forget her. Maybe a month spent in the country would cure his blood of her. Lord knew that staying in the same city as her, coming across her in the park with Tynemouth would only destroy what was left of his heart.

Damn it, he shouldn't have done it. He should have just stayed home, should never have fallen for Celeste's tears and agreed to squire Miranda about for the Season. Had he not agreed, he could have stayed in his self-imposed prison and not had to confront his desires. He could have damn well continued to use his hand to ease the ache in his body.

He'd been quite content to visualize Madeline, imagining her doing all sorts of wicked things to him while he tended to his needs. But now that was impossible. It didn't satisfy. He'd ruined it for himself. He'd lived the fantasy and nothing, no matter how tempting the vision, how risqué the position, nothing could make him feel like he did when he had her in his arms. He had thrown caution to the wind when he had decided to kiss Madeline and now, not even his visions of her were enough.

It didn't bode well for his future. If he couldn't even pleasure himself, how the hell was he ever going to slake his desires? He sure as hell couldn't go to a brothel, or keep a mistress. Not after having the flesh and blood Madeline in his arms. No, she'd bloody well destroyed him. In more ways than one.

* * * *

"Lady Madeline has to find herself a husband before the season is out."

Blaine choked on his coffee as he listened to Miranda blurt her shocking statement. With an oath he had never before uttered in front of females, he slammed his cup down, then viscously started wiping the remains of coffee from his trousers. "It was hot," he grumbled when he saw Celeste arch a knowing brow in his direction.

"And how do you know this about Lady Madeleine?" Celeste

asked, turning her attention from him.

"Georgiana Longbottom told me. Her father has flatly refused to give her another pound unless she finds herself a reputable husband."

"What the devil do I care about Georgiana Longbottom and her father?" Blaine bit out, tossing his napkin back onto the table.

"Not Georgiana," Miranda sighed, rolling her eyes. "Lady Madeline. She's the one on the hunt for a husband. I thought you would like to know."

"Well I don't," he muttered, flicking open *The Times*, effectively shielding himself from Celeste's all too knowing gaze.

"You don't?" Miranda asked. "But I thought you liked Lady Madeline."

"She's tolerable. But that doesn't mean I had thought to marry her. If you must know the truth, I do not want a wife who will do nothing but get in my way and be privy to my personal affliction. Nor do I want screaming infants keeping me awake half the night. I'm quite prepared to see the title pass on to Henry, he's more than capable of being the next Earl of Hardcastle as well as the Marquis Greenwood."

Flipping the page of his newssheet, he suppressed a groan. He'd known Madeline would have to marry at some point, but what he didn't know was how much the thought of her being another man's wife angered him. He didn't want to marry Madeline, didn't even want to continue on with their secret assignations no matter how delightful they were. And yet, he couldn't bear the thought of someone like Tynemouth having her all to himself. The pup would be able to awaken to her smiling face, to go to bed with her at night and feel her soft body melded against his. *Damn it!* He didn't like it one bit. And yet, he knew that she would marry--she would have to.

"Surely she doesn't expect a husband to support the financial backing for such a venture?" Celeste asked, munching on a triangle of toast. "A husband could hardly be expected to pay for such a thing as Montgomery House."

"Georgiana told me that Lady Madeline and her mother started the house together and that Lord Penrick contributes the lion's share of money to keep it afloat. He's all but forced Lady Madeline to find herself a suitable mate, or he's cutting off funds to the house indefinitely."

"And has Lady Madeline settled on a candidate?" Celeste asked, her eyes casting furtive glances his way.

"I believe so," Miranda said around a sausage. "Georgiana told me that she's had him in her sights for some time now."

Blaine felt his mouth go dry, as if it were full of wool. She'd been searching for a husband--for months, if Miranda was to be believed. Had he been in her sights all these months? Was she thinking of him as a suitable candidate?

Sweat began to bead on his brow and the prickles of heat and anger scratched at his neck. Had she bloody well thought she could seduce him into marriage? Or was Tynemouth the man she had fixed on? Was *he* just a diversion to amuse her, to keep Tynemouth nipping at her skirts while she waited for an offer?

Confusion and rage filled him and before he could think straight he'd tossed his paper on the table and was making his excuses.

"You won't forget about this afternoon?" Celeste called after him. "Henry has been anxious to see you."

"I'll be here. I must leave, I have an appointment."

"Do keep track of the time."

With a muffled oath he accepted his hat and walking stick from the butler and hurried down the steps. Bedlam was where he needed to go. A visit with Jenkinson always cured him of his fanciful ideas. Visiting the poor souls of Bethlehem Hospital never failed to remind him of what he truly was.

Chapter Ten

"Now then, ladies, shall we begin?"

Madeline munched on a lemon biscuit and watched as Lady Brookehaven, resplendent in a mauve hat with matching ostrich plum conducted the meeting.

"Rebecca, give that child to the nurse this instant. You've spent enough time clucking over her booties and red curls."

Madeline couldn't help but grin. Lady Bronley's baby girl was the sweetest thing.

"I say," Lady Brookehaven scowled, "in my day the children stayed indoors where they belonged and their nurses in attendance as they should be."

"I like taking care of my children," Rebecca murmured, kissing little Anna Maria's plump cheek. "Bronley and I have no wish to live separate lives from our children."

"Hmmph," the dowager huffed as she swatted away a bee. "I daresay all this fresh air will be the death of me. You mark my words, before this afternoon is over I'll be bit by one of these ghastly creatures. Now then," she grunted, tapping her fingers against the table. "Let us begin. This year's charity weekend is to benefit Montgomery House. As we all know, I was extremely disappointed with last years proceeds to the Foundling Hospital, not to mention the poor turnout of guests."

"Lord Carmichael held his *Infamous Lords* party last year," Lady Bathurst reminded the dowager. "The blackheart purposely timed it to coincide with your yearly event."

"I'm fully aware that I've got Carmichael and his cronies to thank for that, but I tell you now, and you may mark my words, that this year will be different. This year's success will rival that of the years when Old Q and Hellgate attended. Those were the days, ladies," the dowager said with a gleam in her eyes. "Those were the times of wild parties and huge donations. I want it to be that way again. I want the Brookehaven charity weekend to be what it was when my dear Clarence was alive and presiding over the title."

"What you need then," Lady Bronley said, handing Anna Maria off to her nurse, "is a theme. Something that will catch the attention and imagination of the jades of the *ton*."

"A theme, eh?" the dowager said, tapping her arthritic finger against her chin.

"Oh, I know," Lady Bathurst cried, "a medieval theme with knights and ladies, and … what?"

"No, no, no," Lady Brookehaven said, shaking her head, the ostrich plume waving vicariously in the breeze. "The ton is tired of that, my dear. What with that King Arthur find of Roth's and the constant chatter about chivalry and such at all the balls and soirees, well, it's only a matter of time before the topic is unfashionable."

"I suppose," Lady Bathurst grumbled, reaching for a cream cake. "Although I shall never tire of it. It'll never be unfashionable for me."

"There, there," Lady Brookehaven smiled, patting her hand benevolently. "You've got your knight waiting for you at home, my dear. He'd rescue you from any evil without batting an eye."

"True," Lady Bathurst smiled, a faint blush creeping into her cheeks. "Bathurst is very good at playing the knight errant."

With a sigh, Madeline reached for another biscuit. She was tired of listening to stories of domestic harmony, especially when her plans had taken a wrong turn last night. And if this meeting to plan the charity weekend was any indication, her life was not about to get back on track any time soon.

Damn Hardcastle for confusing her. One minute she was being swept off her feet, and the next she was chasing after him in the maze, pleading with him to talk with her. She didn't understand him, not for a minute. She'd been so certain she knew what he was about, that she could help him speak of his secrets, that she could heal him of whatever hurt he had suffered in his life. But he refused to let her in.

How in the world could he have come to Montgomery House, read her the most passionate, most exotic tale of desire, proceed to kiss her witless, only to toss her aside with a *'if it could be anyone, it would be you'*.

He'd tempted her in all sorts of wicked ways only to discard her after he was finished kissing her. What was she to make of him for Heavens sakes, he'd actually talked of Harems!

"What?" she said, suddenly aware that three sets of eyes were trained on her and one very wrinkled mouth was parted on a gasp. "Did I," she licked her lips and tried again, "have I done something?"

"What were you saying over there, gel?"

Heavens, had she been talking aloud? Had she said Blaine's name? Oh God, had they heard her say he'd kissed her senseless?

"I thought I just heard the word, *harem,* exit your mouth."

"Well," Madeline looked between Lady Bronley and Lady Bathurst for support. "Well, harem is Arabic for Forbidden Places," she began. "It's sort of ... ah ... er ... a place to start, don't you think?"

Lady Brookehaven continued to stare at her as if she were a candidate for Bedlam. She didn't say a word, didn't even close her mouth, she just kept staring as if she were in utter shock.

"A wonderful idea," Lady Bathurst said, her blue eyes dancing mischievously. "An Arabian Nights theme. Perfectly acceptable for the debs and the old tabbies, but something delightfully enticing for the jaded. What do you think Lady B? It's perfect."

"Arabian Nights," the dowager muttered, her eyes raking over Madeline for the hundredth time. "I suppose it could be considered perfectly benign, but it does have a deeper, more evocative implication."

"Perhaps we can hire gypsies to dance and play music," Lady Bronley suggested.

"And we can set up tents with pillows and food," Lady Bathurst proposed. "And we can dress up too."

"Hmm." Lady Brookehaven hummed, continuing her studying of Madeline with her far too intelligent eyes. "A masked ball perhaps--in Arabian costume. You will have to be properly chaperoned, of course. I will not have Penrick knocking down my door, charging me with neglecting you, or exposing you to wicked behavior."

"Of course," Madeline nodded.

"Perhaps your father would find the company of Lady Bronley, Lady Bathurst, and their friend Lady Reanleigh agreeable. Surely with three refined ladies of the ton, your father could have no argument. Mayhap," Lady Brookehaven suggested, "I should pen your father a note now, requesting your presence and advising him that I've procured appropriate chaperones for you?"

"That would be very beneficial." Her father could not refuse her now. Not when Lady Brookehaven had secured her chaperones. To deny the request would be to insult Lady Brookehaven and her grandson's wife. Her father would never do it. Would never risk the chance of alienating someone as powerful as Lady Brookehaven and her clan. No, she thought with barely concealed glee, her father wouldn't fail to let her go.

"Do you think we can procure a fortune teller?" Lady Bronley asked. "I rather fancy the idea of learning what's in my future."

"Oh, yes," Madeline smiled, thinking how smashing it would be to sit before a jeweled gypsy and have her fortune laid out before her. "I would love to discover what my future holds."

"I daresay, Lady Madeline," Lady Brookehaven said with a grin, "that your future will be altered and quite shortly, I do believe. Why, it might even be at my ball, by some dark and mysterious sultan."

"Do you think so?" Madeline whispered, thinking of the way Blaine looked beneath the moonlight, his dark hair shining and blowing in the breeze. She could imagine him as her sultan.

* * * *

"Your Lordship," Jenkinson puffed behind him, his white handkerchief coming out to wipe the beads of sweat on his balding head. "I have to remind you that it has been only three weeks since your last visit. Progress has been slow."

"Is that your way of telling me that nothing has changed since you received my draft for five thousand pounds?" Blaine continued along the dark corridor, steeling himself against the foul odor of the approaching cells. "You'll find, Jenkinson I'm a generous man, and that I have no end of gifts to dispose of, but," he stopped abruptly and wheeled around to confront the superintendent. "I'm not a man to be trifled with. You'll discover I'm nothing like the dilettante members of the ton."

"No ... I ... er, that is I have no intention of diverting your donations, my lord. I'm simply asking that you not be disappointed when you see the work that's been done."

"I'm not a fool, Jenkinson. I know that one cannot turn a sow's ear into a silk purse within weeks. However, I do believe that it's possible to add some creature comforts, and that is what I expect to find today."

"Of course," Jenkinson huffed behind him. "You'll find a vast improvement in that area."

"I see you've done nothing about the stench in this place," he growled, feeling his stomach roll with nausea. Damn it, he shouldn't have eaten. The suffocating foulness of the air was thick and virulent and it always left him struggling to stem the rise of bile in his throat.

"Here we are, my lord," Jenkinson's voice was muffled from behind his kerchief. "James, unlock the door for us."

The ancient and rusting door opened, the iron scraping along stone, the echoing sound sending the patients into a cacophony of shrieks, cries and howls.

Stepping into the celled area, Blaine fought the automatic impulse to gag at the stench and the sight of the poor souls caged behind iron bars. One man, nothing but sagging skin over bones was actually crawling up the bars, shaking them and howling as if he were a caged primate.

"That's John Smith," Jenkinson nodded towards the man. "A dependence upon gin is his diagnosis. Poor fellow. He arrived but three days ago. He was relatively well up until yesterday when his mood turned rather violent and he began to have the shakes. I'm afraid we were forced to have him dunked under water many times before he could be subdued."

"His body is crying out for the alcohol, is it not?" Blaine asked, watching in amazement as the man, who looked so weak and frail continued his strenuous climb up the bars.

"It's always this way with the gin swillers. I'm afraid they're rather hopeless."

Blaine looked down the long row of cells. Hopeless was a word he was well acquainted with. "I see you've provided them with blankets and pillows."

"Indeed," Jenkinson nodded, "And we've taken the liberty of hiring more guards."

"Why would you hire more men? These patients are locked behind bars, they cannot get out. What purpose do guards serve?"

"Well," Jenkinson mumbled, motioning a burly guard to subdue a derelict inmate. "Safety."

"Safety for the inmates, or safety for you?"

"Well, that is…." Jenkinson trailed off as he nervously looked about the dank surroundings.

"If you've more men on hand, then these patients can be released from their cells. At least once a day, after they've become more stable. They need exercise to clear their minds."

"You don't mean to have these lunatics running on the loose, do you? Milord, I must insist-"

"I assure you, Jenkinson that is exactly what I mean. You've hired these men to work, not play at hazard and empty their tankards of ale. You've hired them, make them earn their wages."

"Of course," he said, benevolently bowing. "As you wish, milord."

"I do not wish it, Jenkinson," he said, strolling along the bank of cells. "I demand it."

Jenkinson said nothing as he followed in his wake while he surveyed the stone cubicles and the patients inside them. The cells were all in dreadful repair and repulsively filthy. His stomach lurched at the sight, and Blaine had to look away more than once in order to right his reeling senses. When he finally looked up, he found himself face to face with Gertrude, her filthy shift hanging in tatters from her frail body. He tensed as he took in her in her dirty fingers with black fingernails as they tightened and clenched around the bars. He looked into her face then and stared into a pair of blue eyes, clear and intelligent and free of any of madness.

This woman didn't belong here anymore than he did. Yet the fates had not been as kind to her as they were to him. She was but a woman, born of the working class, while he'd been born into the peerage, a selfish, corrupt society that cared only for themselves. He was fortunate in the fact that his father had been too full of himself, too ashamed to admit that a son such as he had sprung from his loins. That had been the only thing to have saved him from such a fate. Had it not been for his father's pride, it might very well have been him standing there instead of Gertrude.

"Th … thank you," she mumbled hoarsely, as if it had been some time since she'd last spoken. "The blankets are most welcome. It's cold here at nights."

His spine stiffened as he realized she was talking to him. He'd never had any interaction with the patients. He was merely an observer, a voyeur in fact, as he watched them act out in their madness. He didn't know what to say to her, didn't know if he could even make his mouth work to say any words.

"I'm Gertrude Wilkinson," she said, her fingers tightening once more on the bars, her body coming closer to the cell door. "My husband is a rector in Shropshire."

A rector's wife. No wonder he'd had her committed. The bastard probably believed her to be possessed. How could a man just leave his wife here to just whither and die?

"What is your name?" she asked shyly.

Jenkinson stepped in then, rapping the woman's hands with a stick as she tried to reach out to him. "Back, Gertrude. You know the rules, you musn't stick your hands out of your cage."

"Enough!" Blaine tore the stick from Jenkinson's hands and broke it in half. "You will not hurt her, nor will you do so to any other patient. They are already behind bars. What could they possibly do to you?"

He turned his attention to Gertrude then and tried, tried with every fiber of his being to be the polite and charming gentleman he'd been raised to be. He tried to forget the image of her stained and filthy shift, tried to pretend that her breasts didn't peek out of the tattered neckline. He so wanted to act as though the image of her, her filthy hands and black nails reaching out to him didn't discompose him, but it did. He didn't want to touch her, to go near her. He didn't want to catch her disease and yet he knew damn well the same wretchedness lurked within him.

To touch her was to confront the horrors inside him, to fear that he too might one day find himself in similar circumstances. One day it might be him stretching his hands through the bars, reaching out to another human being, wishing for a small taste of the milk of human kindness from another soul.

With a fortifying breath, he braced himself against the sight and the stench of her, and bowed gracefully before her blackened feet. "Lord Hardcastle, ma'am. A pleasure."

"*Lordship!*" she exclaimed, furiously trying to cover herself. "Oh, my Heavens. I had not thought."

"Do not trouble yourself," he said, glancing away as she tried to bring the shredded corners of her shift together, inadvertently exposing more of herself. "Pray, do not make yourself uneasy."

"Forgive me," she said, her voice cracking on a sob. "But I've no other clothes."

He looked up then, amazed by her pride, the normalcy of her. It terrified him. If someone like Gertrude could be locked up, then why couldn't he? What if someone found out about *him,* feared that demonic possession had taken over his soul as the rector did his wife? What would happen then? Would he find himself in the same sort of cell, filthy and unrecognizable?

He licked his lips and swallowed his fear, trying to fight for outward control. "Would you like something new to wear? I can arrange it."

"Oh, no," she cried, shaking her head. "I couldn't ask it of you. It's not right."

It was right. It was a basic human right to expect to be clean and clothed and fed. My God, they were already reduced to having to live with the rats, could this poor soul not expect to be clothed as well?

"Besides," she said sadly, "why put on clean clothes when you're body is covered in filth?"

He scoured her from head to toe, then looked behind her to study her tiny cell. It was neat and tidy, the bed made and the chamber pot discreetly placed in the corner. She hated being dirty.

"Would you care for a bath?" he asked, not quite able to believe he was talking about such intimate things as bathing and clothing with a strange woman. But he understood her needs. He felt filthy after his fits. Bathing was always the first thing he wanted to do as soon as he was able. Why should it be any different for Gertrude? Why should she have to suffer her attacks alone, then pay for them by having to lay in her own filth?

"Jenkinson," he said, unable to tear his gaze from her. "Mrs. Wilkinson is to have a bath whenever she requests it, is that understood?"

"A bath?" Jenkinson asked, clearly confused. "I don't see-"

"She wishes to be clean, and she shall. See to it that a female helps her. I'll tolerate nothing less. And I'll be back to enquire. Mrs. Wilkinson will tell me if anything untoward occurs."

"My lord," she cried, grasping his hand with lightening speed and strength, bringing it to her lips. "Thank you. A thousand times, thank you."

He felt himself stiffen and his lips twitched in what he hoped was not disgust, but feared it might be. He masked it quickly, struggling to hide his uneasiness.

It was not the dirt or the black nails, or even the odor that disturbed him, rather it was what the grime represented. Waste, hopelessness, despair. He didn't want to touch her and feel her pain, he didn't want to have to understand her and internalize her plight and put himself behind these very bars. And yet, he stood there, his hand clasped in hers until Jenkinson shoved her away, waving his kerchief before him.

"Here, milord. You'll want to wash."

"No," he gritted between clenched teeth, before removing his hat and bowing politely again, trying in vain to make up for Jenkinson's deplorable behavior. She shrank back into her cell, despite his attempts, the darkness quickly engulfing her.

He felt ashamed of his own behavior, worried that she might have glimpsed his true feelings, then almost as suddenly he became curiously consumed with thoughts of himself, wondering if he too would have to suffer the same as Gertrude. Would there come a time in his life when he was so desperate for the touch of someone that he would reach through bars with filthy hands and plead for their kindness? Would that stranger in turn retch and draw back from him?

He imagined himself in this very cell, Madeline on the opposite side, staring at him in horror and repulsion. He saw himself reaching out, his hands covered in filth as he grasped her pale fingers in his, bringing them to his lips. Saw her cringe from him, and knew then that he'd never be able to expose himself to her. His secrets would die with him, and he would have to resign himself to a life without her, because there was no way in hell he was going to suffer in the same way Jenkinson had just made Gertrude suffer.

Chapter Eleven

Blaine stomped up the steps of Celeste's townhouse and let himself in. He was in a foul mood, more foul than he had been in years. He was being an uncaring, selfish prig.

His treatment of Gertrude only firmed his belief that he was behaving without honor towards both her and Madeline. But damn it to hell, what was a man supposed to do when he was faced with human misery--when he was forced to confront his own worst fears?

He'd crumpled in the face of them, that's what he'd done. He'd acted like the simpering aristocrats who spent their Sunday afternoons laughing at the lunatics. He despised them, hated them with every ounce of his being and yet he had stood there, struggling to mask his distaste as Gertrude risked what was left of her soul to reach out to him.

Damn it, if only he hadn't been still reeling from the shock of hearing that Madeline was searching for a husband. Surely if he hadn't already been discomposed he wouldn't have acted so offensive toward Gertrude. He had tried to hide it and he hoped he had. He couldn't bear the thought of harming Gertrude. She wasn't deserving of his repulsion, she wasn't responsible for her present condition.

It was all *her* fault, the Maddening Madeline Brydges. If she had never thought to stroll into his life with her mesmerizing eyes and lithe form he never would have found himself feeling this way.

Damn her and her alluring eyes.

"Shall I announce you, milord?" Celeste's butler asked. With a shake of his head, he refused the offer and strolled into the salon, freezing in horror and disbelief as he looked at the tall, thin woman seated at Celeste's table. It was, he thought, gritting his teeth, just like looking in the mirror.

"Ah, here he is at last," Celeste smiled. "Henry, look who has arrived."

"Uncle Blaine," little Henry cried, running towards him and leaping into his arms. "I just opened the soldiers you sent. Will you come upstairs and play war with me? Will you?" he asked, throwing his arms about his neck. "And you can be the master spy and I'll be the evil spy and you can try to capture me."

"In a moment, old chap," Blaine whispered, ruffling Henry's hair. "I'll have to stay a while with the ladies."

"Awe," Henry whined, looking longingly at the soldier in his hand. "Do you have to? All they want to do is talk about clothes and balls and Miranda keeps bringing up that Renfrew fellow. I'm tired of hearing those stories."

"I'm afraid," Blaine whispered again, catching his mother's cool, yet observant gaze, "that it must be done. We're gentlemen, right, old chap?"

"Yes," Henry sighed.

"And gentlemen don't leave ladies at tea without at least a proper hello. It is our duty to see that they are happy and entertained."

"All right," Henry grumbled as Blaine lowered him to the floor. "But only because we're gentlemen. *Not* because I wish to take tea with them."

"Absolutely," he said, capturing Henry's hand in his and walking with him toward the table. "A self respecting gentlemen never *wishes* to take tea with ladies, but he doesn't shirk his duties, correct?"

"I guess," Henry sighed, scrunching up his face. "How long does a gentleman have to pretend he's enjoying their company?"

Blaine grinned then. "When can we leave, do you mean?" Hell, if the truth were known, he'd rather be tarred and feathered as opposed to being forced to endure his mother's company. "We may leave," he whispered to Henry, "after we've had at least one cup of tea, a sandwich and a slice of cake. Mother," he murmured, standing before her, and bowing civilly. He didn't take her hand and she didn't offer it. Instead, she sat before him, her spine rigid and stiff, looking up into his face with the same cool hauteur he practiced.

"My lord," she demurred, inclining her head. "I trust you are well?"

He bristled at the words, at the sound of his title on her lips and he refused to be baited. He wanted to lash out and let loose his feelings, but he refused to give in to the weakness. Instead he met her eyes, matching her in coldness and detachment. "I believe I am the same as the last time you enquired after my health."

"That was a year ago. Much can change in that length of time."

"Has it already been a year?" he asked, looking away from her, wishing he could erase the sight of her and the horrifying memories from his mind. "Your visit is early this year, Madam. Usually you arrive in the fall, when the season is over and you can spare the time to spend with us."

"You wouldn't have me miss Miranda's coming out, would you? Surely you do not think me capable of that?"

His fists clenched at his sides and he tamped down the urge to yell that he did think her cold and heartless. What mother who was anything but would leave her son to live with such a man and suffer as he had suffered under his father's care while she went blindly about her business, unaware and unconcerned?

"Lovely weather," Miranda said nervously, shooing Henry over to her side. "Grandmama, was just remarking how warm it is."

"There's a distinct chill in the air that I did not perceive when I left here this morning," he said, his gaze wandering to the window.

"I feel it too," his mother said, her accent a mixture of English and French. "It is frighteningly cool. Why, it seems to have just blown in through the door."

"Tea?" Celeste asked, holding up the teapot. "You must have a cup. Mother brought us her special blend."

He nodded, continuing to stare out the window. Control, he vowed. Surely he could drain a cup of tea and devour a sandwich without causing a scene. Five minutes, he thought, five minutes and he could leave, run upstairs with Henry and forget about his mother. Five minutes in her company and he would be safe for another year. He just had to gather his self-control.

With a hefty breath, he turned, prepared to snatch the teacup out of Celeste's hand when he froze, his eyes landing not on his mother, but on a pair of exquisite turquoise eyes peeking up at him.

God damn it, this was the last thing he needed.

He was looking at her as though he'd like to strangle her, Madeline thought, gazing up into his cold gray eyes. She'd never seen him so discomposed, so uncertain of himself. He was pale, far more pale than she had ever seen him. He stood before her for a long time, his eyes staring unblinkingly down at her, his lips firming and thinning into a grim line.

"Lady Madeline has joined us for tea," Miranda said jubilantly.

"Lady Madeline," he said, taking his cup from Celeste. "What a surprise."

"I met Miranda at the glove makers. She invited me to come and meet your mother."

"I am astonished you were able to attend," he said, his eyes flickering along her face. "No other duties to tend to? No suitors to find, no souls to save this afternoon?"

She gasped and she thought she heard his mother do the same. He was being perfectly horrid. She'd never seen him quite so arrogant. He was lashing out, nearly prowling about the room in his agitation and if she hadn't known him, she would have thought him nothing but a haughty aristocrat.

His behavior was scandalous and it was not in keeping with what she had discovered about him. While he was secretive and subdued, he'd never really lost his temper. Those emotions had shown themselves in the form of cutting wit and a razor edged tongue. He'd been haughty and pompous, but never angry, never seething as he now was.

She could see it in his eyes, the way his jaw clenched and tightened. She had detected it the instant he strode into the room and noticed his mother. He had frozen, his face, already pinched and tight, turning into a fierce scowl. She had been privy to the whole thing, witnessed it all as she sat concealed beside Miranda.

"I understand Lady Madeline runs a home for women," Lady Hardcastle said imperiously. "It behooves us all to learn from her example."

"Yes," he said, setting his cup down on his saucer and pacing before the window, his back insolently turned to them. "One must be ever conscious of those less fortunate. Family is, of course, left to their own devices; but the less fortunate, well, *we must* spare them all of our generosity."

"Cream cake?" Celeste asked, passing a plate around.

"And what do you mean by that, my lord?" Madeline asked, feeling the color rise in her cheeks. "Are you saying that these poor unfortunates are not worth your time, or your generosity? Are you saying that you are able to pass these people in the street and think of them with nothing but contempt and ridicule?"

He turned around then, he's eyes blazing and his voice menacingly low. "I meant nothing of the kind. Do not presume to know what I'm about, Lady Madeline. I assure you, I'm quite beyond your understanding."

"I assure *you*," she said, rising from her chair "I have spent years making out those who would try to evade understanding."

He looked at her with such ferociousness that she couldn't for the life of her understand what thoughts were going on his head.

"One could say your time would have been better spent

searching for a husband. You could spend your days dissecting and understanding him and leaving me the hell alone."

She did shut up then. She didn't know what to say. In fact, she didn't think she could utter a word. Not with him looking at her like that. Not with the way he'd said husband as if it were a blasphemy.

"Pray excuse me, your ladyship. But there is a young lad at the door, desirous to speak with Lady Madeline."

"Send him in," Blaine commanded, before Celeste could speak.

"Really, Blaine," Celeste said archly. "I think you had better sit down and get yourself something to eat, you at least need another cup of tea to improve your humor."

"My lady," Daniel came in, his woolen hat hanging between his fingers. "Mrs. Noland sent me to fetch ye. It's Helen. She's callin' for ye," he said, nervously looking from person to person. "Forgive the intrusion," he nodded awkwardly. "But I've searched everywhere for ye. Helen needs you, Miss."

"I'm coming." Madeline reached for her reticule. "Lady Greenwood, I must excuse myself. I hope I do not offend you by leaving?"

"Of course not. But let me have my carriage brought around."

"That's not necessary," she said, tying the strings of her bonnet. "I'll fetch a hack. Daniel will be with me. I'll be perfectly safe. Miranda," she smiled, reaching to clasp her hands. "Thank you so much for your offer of tea. I enjoyed myself immensely. And Lady Hardcastle, a pleasure, madam."

"No, Lady Madeline," Blaine's mother murmured, rising elegantly from her chair and taking her hands in hers. "The pleasure has been all mine. I hope we shall meet frequently while I'm here in London. I would like to get to know you better."

"I would like that as well," she said, curtseying. "Please stop in any time at my father's house. Miranda knows the number. You're always welcome. *Milord*," she said as she breezed passed him. "Good day."

He clasped her wrist in his hand. "You don't think I'd let you leave without a proper escort?"

"A hack is fine, my lord," she said, anger welling up inside her. She was angry with him, furious in fact, at the way he'd talked to her. What right had he to speak to her in such a fashion and in front of his family? He'd all but mocked her and her generosity for those less fortunate then themselves.

"My carriage is out front. I'll take you. Ladies," he said, bowing.

"If you'll excuse me, I'll see that Lady Madeline gets to Montgomery House safely."

And then he was ushering her out of the house, his hand locked about her elbow as he steered her towards the carriage.

"I really do not need an escort, my lord. I'm perfectly capable-"

"Get in," he commanded, giving her a gentle nudge up the steps.

"Really sir, you do try my patience. What do you think you're about?"

He ignored her, directing Daniel to sit up top with the coachman, then he climbed in, slamming the door behind him. The carriage rocked then lurched forward, the horse's harness jingling in the quiet.

"You should have told me." he said, his eyes focused outside the window.

"Told you what?"

"That you're hunting for a husband."

She looked up at him then, clearly speechless. He met her eyes and she shivered. They were empty, cold spheres with not even the slightest flickering of emotion. Clearly, the journey to Montgomery House was going to be most unpleasant.

* * * *

The journey was unpleasant, but as neither of them had deigned to speak, it was rather quiet. Throughout the ride, she had kept her eyes focused on the passing scenery, pretending to watch servants bustling up the street with baskets laden with fresh fruit and vegetables, or watching as young girls sold flowers from carts. Occasionally, when Madeline was certain he wasn't looking, she would steal peeks at him from the corner of her eye, disturbed by the fact that he was still an emotionless rock sitting across from her.

Would she ever understand him? Would he ever *let* her understand him? With each meeting he became more and more difficult to decipher and with each meeting her need to help him increased, and her heart--well, a little bit more of it was lost to him every day.

"We're here," Daniel called out. He opened the door and Madeleine got out, lifted her skirts and turned to thank Blaine for his escort, when she bumped into his chest.

"Oh-" she said, righting her bonnet. "I had thought you'd be off, you did request that I leave you alone."

"I'm staying. I have something I wish to discuss with you."

"Right," she nodded, trying to hide her surprise and trepidation.

His voice, deep and barely controlled did not make her desirous for his company. "You may have a seat in my study. Once I see to whatever is needing my attention I shall come and fetch you and we can discuss whatever it is you wish."

"Fine," he said, holding the door open for her. "I'll wait for you in the study."

"Oh, Luvy," Maggie cried as they stepped into the foyer. "Come quick, Helen is beside herself. Your lordship-" Maggie said, stopping mid-sentence. "I had no idea…."

A loud female cry splintered the air and Madeline saw Blaine wince, then step back, as if he wished to flee. "Perhaps, my lord, it would be best if you left. It seems that it might be Helen's time."

"I'm staying." He removed his coat and hung it on a nearby hook. "I assure you, the devil himself could not make me leave."

"As you wish. Maggie, take me to Helen."

"Wait, Luvy." Maggie reached for her hand, preventing her from going up the stairs. "I think you'd better come in here. Milord," Maggie whispered, "you might wish to wait in the study."

"What's this about?" Madeline asked, letting Maggie lead her into a sitting room they rarely used.

"It's Helen's babe," Maggie said, her voice cracking. "It … it didn't survive."

"No!" Madeline cried, tears immediately welling in her eyes. They'd never lost a babe at Montgomery House. She'd never had to deal with this.

"I'm afraid so. And the babe," Maggie said sadly, looking to the settee where a bassinet was placed. "The babe isn't pretty."

"What do you mean?" Madeline rushed to the settee and cried out as she looked at the baby. "Oh my God," she whispered, covering her mouth with trembling fingers. Tears, hot and fat streamed down her face.

"What is the meaning-" Blaine broke off his speech as he looked at Madeline, tears of grief trickling down her cheeks, her slender shoulders shaking uncontrollably.

He walked slowly to her, as if in a trance, unable to stop, unable to bear the sight of her consumed with grief. Not Madeline, not Maddy the Savior who was always smiling, always seeing the good in people. He didn't want to remember her this way--grief stricken and crying.

He arrived beside her and sucked in his breath. In a bassinette lay a babe with beautiful golden hair and long lashes resting against pale cheeks. She was a perfect babe, a beautiful little girl. She could have made any parent proud, but to those that wished perfection in their child, she would have been a disgrace. What would a parent and society think or say of a babe born with a harelip?

Madeline choked on a sob as she stared down into the babe's lifeless face. Emotions, some new, some old, assailed him and he found himself not knowing what to say to comfort her and not knowing what to make of his own tender feelings towards the babe.

"This isn't fair," she said between gasps of breaths and sobs.

"Life isn't always fair," he said automatically, thinking of the hell the child would have had to go through if she had survived. He knew all too well the pain she would have suffered, the taunts and the stares. Hell, he suffered and his disease was hidden inside. This babe would have had to live her life with the stigma of bastardy, not to mention the deformity of her mouth and nose. It might be cruel of him to think this, but he couldn't bring himself to summon the regret. She was better off in her seat in Heaven then suffering through life feeling like a monster, wishing she wasn't alive.

"It is a blessing," he whispered, twining his fingers between Madeline's, willing her to understand, to see through her grief and visualize the realities of what the child's life would have been like.

"A blessing?" she cried, tearing her hand from his, her eyes a tempestuous green. "I cannot believe you could be so cruel, so uncaring in a time like this. This child has had her life snatched from her and you're telling me that this is a blessing?"

"Yes," he said, looking once more at the babe.

"How dare you! Nothing about death is a blessing."

"Because one is merely alive--eating, sleeping and breathing does not mean they are living," he said, feeling the old wounds once again open up, remembering Gertrude confined to her cell, thinking of himself and the way he lived, or rather, existed.

"God spared her a grueling fate. Surely, you must see that."

"I do not see that!" she stormed, stamping her foot in anger. "I will never see that. We will never know what Fate had in store for this poor innocent. Who is to say she would have suffered, that mankind would have been cruel to her? There is nothing more disturbing or horrifying to me than losing faith in humanity."

"To me," he said, looking at the babe. "There are some fates worse than death."

Chapter Twelve

"Just what the devil did you mean by that?" Madeline stormed, slamming her study door. "And don't you dare cross your arms and look at me like that. I won't stand for it. I see through your hauteur and your brooding masks. I know there is more to you than you would have me believe."

"You profess to understand me so well, why would you need me to explain myself?"

It had been a mistake, a mistake of monumental proportions to let it slip that there were worse fates than dying. She'd picked right up on it, refused to let it go, physically forced him into her study to confront him and learn his secrets.

"Do not think you can cut me to the quick so easily this time, my lord. I'm wise to your ways and I won't be so easily swayed."

She was the only person who had ever been able to look past the façade and see his tortured soul. He had wanted to trust her with his secrets, had wanted to believe that a life full of love awaited him, but seeing Gertrude, feeling her pain, seeing her wretchedness confirmed that those beliefs were a fantasy. They belonged in his dreams, not in reality.

"What did you mean, 'there are fates worse than death'?" she asked again, pacing before her desk. "I've spent my whole life saving those from that exact fate and then you waltz in here and proclaim it be nothing. To claim that there are things in life that make dying a more palatable substitute."

He couldn't tell her of course, she couldn't know that he had the falling sickness. She wouldn't disclose his secret, he knew that, but he couldn't bear to see pity mar her face. He didn't want her to look at him like she did the babe, or the way he stared at Gertrude. It was far better that she think him an overbearing prig than to think of him as one of her 'poor unfortunates' in need of saving. He didn't want her pity and sympathy.

"Am I to assume the reason you're staring at your fingernails is so that you may avoid my question and give the appearance of boredom?"

"Your intelligence is highly acute, madam."

"You mock me at every possible turn," she blurted, wheeling to confront him. "You take me out to the garden and read to me, you send me letters inscribed with beautiful words. You sweep me off my feet and then you mock me. For what purpose? To humiliate me or to vindicate your own vulnerability?"

"I thought you dragged me in here to talk about life and death and our varying attitudes about it."

"*Damn you,*" she hissed. "I came in here to find out what is wrong with you. Why do you act as though you care one minute, only to turn into a cold, unfeeling bastard the next?"

He felt as though he'd been run through with a sword. He'd had any number of insults hurled at his head, but never before by someone he cared this much about. He didn't want to hear her anger, didn't want to see the hurt in her eyes. All she wanted from him was the truth, not some flippant comment, but the truth. The key to his soul, the meaning of his dark existence. But he was too afraid, to weak to tell her, and expose himself to her charity.

"I do not mock you," he began carefully. "I enjoyed our interludes and regret they are over. I have no designs to marry, so you can hardly expect that our association would linger past the most earliest of stages."

"I'm not talking about that. I'm talking about the way you push everyone away. How you're afraid to let anyone get close to you."

"You should have told me you were hunting for a mate," he barked back, moving to the window and raising his arm against the frame. God damn her, her arrows were perfectly aimed--his bloody heart was taking a direct hit. How had she gotten to know him so well in such a short period of time?

"What did you think *this* what about?" she asked incredulously. "Did you think I was nothing but a lightskirt to trifle with? Do you think I always go about risking my reputation by kissing men in museums and meeting them at midnight in gardens? *Did you actually think that I let other men do what you did to me?*"

He shut his eyes against the pain in her voice. It tore him apart to hear her like this, but he could say nothing. To admit part of him knew that she would have to marry, that he knew he was courting disaster would only fuel the flames of her anger.

On some primitive level he had heard the warnings, only to ruthlessly shove them aside and continue on with her. He knew one day she would have to marry, that she would become someone else's wife, mother to some other man's children, and yet he had pushed all those thoughts aside so he could satisfy his craving for her.

"What did you think I was up to if not looking for a husband?"

"You should have told me," he growled. "I had no wish to be caught and trapped with no choice but to marry you."

"No choice?" she asked, fisting her hands on her hips, "My lord, this life is filled with choices. Do not presume to pretend you had no choice when you decided to woo me and kiss me."

"Some choices in life are unavoidable."

"Choices are consciously made, do not think me ignorant of that. You will never convince me that we do not choose our own paths in life. We choose to think a certain way, do certain things and make decisions based on our ability to choose."

"Is that what you think?" he roared, finally confronting her. "Jesus, you're a naïve little chit. Is that what you tell the women who cross your threshold? 'Sorry you got yourself with child but you *chose* to let his lordship up your skirt'?"

She gasped and stepped back and he followed her, his eyes burning into hers. Willing her to understand, to force the innocence, the gullibility from her eyes. "What about the whores? Do you tell them they had a choice? That they *choose* to sell their bodies for men's pleasures? No? What do you tell the little street urchins who pinch an apple from a fruit vendor? Do you remind them they had a choice? Because," he said, following her, his face very close to hers. "They really don't, do they? The maid who denies the lord finds herself packed off to live in the streets. The whore who won't sell her body and her morals finds herself freezing to death in the same street as the cast off servant." Her face paled then, but he recklessly continued on, forcing her to see that not everything in life was as cut and dry as she would like to believe. The world was a vile, nasty place and she hadn't an inkling of what lurked outside the doors of her own little world.

"And your urchins. What choice do they have? Pinch an apple or starve? Or better yet, choose not to steal the apple and let his siblings and possibly his mother starve. So, *Lady Madeline*," he sneered, "what do you think of those God damned choices? Are those not fates worse than death?"

Almost instantly he regretted what he'd said. But she'd pushed and pushed until all he saw was red, till all he felt was impotence at the injustice in the world and in his own life.

"What secret do you carry that makes you feel this angry, that makes you this cynical and jaded?"

"We are not talking about me," he spat, feeling regret suddenly turn to something menacing.

"We are," she suddenly cried, reaching for him. "When you said that in the drawing room, you were referring to yourself. Don't deny it," she begged. "I saw it your eyes. I've seen the way it haunts you and I can't bear to see it. Let me help you."

"What makes you think I want to be saved? *What makes you think you even can?"*

She stared at him then, her face turning into a mask of pity and it made it made him furious. This was what he'd feared, that she would see him as a cause to be saved. That he would never be more to her than someone in need of saving and redemption. He wanted more than that from her. He wanted her passion, her body writhing beneath him. When she looked at him he wanted it to be full of love, not goddamn pity.

"When I set out to seduce you, I was not in want of a mother, but a lover," he bit out, wishing to hide his hurt behind cruel words. "I don't want a mother, I have one of those, and I find them rather a nuisance. Nor do I want a wife. They wear out their usefulness once you've worked them and tired of them in bed, and quite frankly I've discovered that virgins are more time consuming than their worth."

She gasped, her fingers bit into his shoulders as she looked up into his eyes. But she would not crumple beneath his anger. Her chin came up and she stared at him with her stormy green eyes. "You seek to hurt me with your words and I admit they do, but I know you do not really mean them. You wish to hide behind this mask because you still refuse to let me in, to let me understand what it is you're really trying to hide from me."

"Christ, Madeline, don't you understand? I don't *want* to marry you. I don't want a house filled with a wife and brats. I'm perfectly willing to see the title pass on to Henry. I just wanted to bed you. Why can't you believe it?"

"Because I have seen the way you look at your friends when they're with their wives. I have seen you with your niece and your nephew and I know that you wish for children of your own, but something makes you fear having them. I know you're honorable, you did not set out to seduce me and leave me dishonored. You're not that sort of man. Please, if you would only trust me, just-"

"Why won't you listen?" he said, grabbing her about the shoulders, wishing he could shake some sense into her. "When are you going to understand that there is a darkness in me you will never comprehend?"

"When will you understand that I want to help you? That I want to be with you?"

"Be with me?" he asked incredulously. "I'd only make you miserable. Let Tynemouth be your husband. He'll dote on you and smile and let you into his heart. I never will. I won't give you children like Tynemouth will. I won't love you. I don't know how to love."

"You do, I've seen it."

"It was nothing but a façade, Madeline. Just a ruse to get my hand up your skirt."

"And that's it?" she said, her fingers rubbing where his hands had gripped her arms. "This is all you have to say? You tell me you cannot love, that you have a darkness in you that you will not speak of? That there are fates in life worse than dying? What secret is so terrible that you do not want what has been developing between us? What do you fear that keeps you from living your life? Tell me," she said, looking up at him. "What about me, what I want?"

"What you want, is something I could never give you. You may as well understand that what *I* wanted from you was nothing more than a good tumble in bed."

And with that, he closed the door, striding out of her life forever.

* * * *

"Who's next?" Blaine swiped his practice foil through the air while he studied his friends as they stood against the wall of the empty ballroom, their chests heaving with exertion. "Don't tell me I've bested you lot with that bit of an exchange? You've all grown soft."

"Soft?" Bronley panted, holding his side. "You were like a man possessed out there."

"I am possessed," he drawled, studying the point of his foil, "remember?"

"Devil take it," Reanleigh grunted, "you're not possessed. You use that condition of yours as a bloody crutch."

"That condition of mine could have me thrown into Bedlam if the right people found out about it."

"Well, the right people aren't going to find out," Stanfield said, tossing his rapier onto a chair. "And that condition doesn't give you the right to run your friends through."

"I'm here." Bathurst called, striding into the room, his coat dangling from one hand, his practice foil from the other.

"You're late."

Bathurst merely lifted a brow and tossed his jacket across an empty chair. "Isabella and a sleeping baby, suffice?"

"It's the middle of the afternoon," Blaine groaned, sending the other three grinning like simpletons. "Surely you have enough of that during the night."

"You'll understand once you find yourself wed. What in blazes happened to you three?" Bathurst asked, staring in amazement.

"I say," Bronley huffed, "while you were occupied frolicking about with your wife, Hardcastle took a notion to kill us."

"Fighting like a madman," Stanfield grunted, wiping the sweat from his brow.

"If he wanted to exhaust someone, he should have damn well gone to Angelo's. When I came over for some friendly sparring, I didn't think I'd have to prepare myself for full warfare." Reanleigh muttered.

"Ah," Bathurst said, pulling his sword from his scabbard, "frustrations are mounting, are they?"

"Just fight," Blaine said, positioning himself before Bathurst.

Bathurst was a master at the art of fencing. His sword and the way he wielded it had been what kept him alive on the battlefield. He'd have to be on his toes if he were to best his friend. All the better, Blaine thought as he heard Bathurst murmur *en garde.* If all his senses were focused on beating Bathurst, then they couldn't be concentrated on other things. Namely a pair of turquoise eyes and cherry red lips.

"Good parry," Bathurst said, deftly advancing with another thrust. "Your technique improves."

"Improves?" Bronley called, "he damn near skewered me."

"Ah," Bathurst drawled, lunging forward, nearly hitting his mark. "But he won't skewer me, will you?"

Blaine didn't say a word. Instead he focused all his energy on deflecting Bathurst's skillful blows and advancing his own position. The others had not been easy to defeat, but Bathurst would be nigh on impossible. He'd never defeated Bathurst and he wouldn't if thoughts of Madeline and her anguished face kept creeping into his consciousness.

"Nearly had you," Bathurst taunted. "You stepped out of measure. Your emotions are engaged. One can never expect to win when one's emotions lead the sword arm. First thing I learned on the battlefield."

Gritting his teeth, Blaine took a deep breath and lunged forward, cutting and thrusting, the clanging of clashing steel echoed off the walls of the empty room. He didn't like that he was wearing his heart on his sleeve for all to see, but damn him, he couldn't put Madeline out of his thoughts. Every time he closed his eyes he remembered the way she'd look at him, her eyes shimmering with tears, her lips trembling with the pain of his hurtful words.

"You should be doing this to Tynemouth, you know, not us. Isabella will have your head if you wear me out this afternoon."

"Shut up and fight," Blaine spat, refusing to be baited. He didn't want to think about Tynemouth. He didn't want to recall this past week's sightings of Madeline together with the insolent pup. It had been a week since he'd walked out of Montgomery House and Madeline's life. And he'd never felt more out of control in his life. It was if he was some sort of animal, snarling and snapping, caged and confined to a solitary life like a lion in a traveling show.

He hated that he missed her. Hated how he had to watch her with Tynemouth dancing around ballrooms, listening to the hushed whispers that the pup was soon going to offer for her. But what he despised the most was the knowledge that his emotions only continued to spiral more out of control as the days passed without speaking to her, without having her close to him. He'd told her in no uncertain terms to stay away from him. He had purposely tried to frighten her, to give her a glimpse of the darkness inside him. He'd wanted to drive her away, and he had succeeded. He'd gotten his wish, and now he was more miserable than ever.

She truly was lost to him--he felt it, in what was left of his soul.

"You should just admit it," Bathurst said, his voice harshening with exertion. "It only gets more painful the longer you deny it, my friend."

"I don't know what you're talking about," Blaine hissed, gulping in air, refusing to acknowledge the burning in his chest as he advanced once again.

"The Brydges chit. You want her and yet you watch from the other side of the room as someone else courts her. How can you be content with that?"

"You don't know what you're talking about."

"I know a damn bit more than you," Bathurst huffed, struggling against him as their swords clashed together. "You forget I was in this exact same position as you last year."

"We're nothing alike," he grunted, pushing Bathurst back and lunging forward. "A hit," he called, striking Bathurst's middle.

"Acknowledged," Bathurst grinned, saluting him with his rapier. "You admit that you're a snarling bull because of Madeline

Brydges, and we'll call it a truce."

He really should just own up to it. Lord knew everyone in the room already knew of his demons, what would it hurt to have them know he was pining after Madeline as well?

"Fine," his chest heaved as he gulped large amounts of air. "I admit it, I find her attractive."

"Attractive?" Bronley snorted. "You mean to say you nearly killed us all because you're *attracted* to the girl? Come now, old boy, you're not that much smarter than us."

He flung his sword to the floor and watched it spin down the length of the marble floor. "I fancy her, all right? I've thought it might be nice to have her in my bed. Satisfied?"

"No," came Bathurst's reply. "This isn't about a simple case of lust or desire. This is love. Welcome aboard, my friend."

"Love?" His mind froze, and for a minute he thought he might suffer a seizure just from the very thought of having fallen in love with her. He couldn't have, it was impossible. He barely even knew her, she certainly didn't know him. "It's merely lust, nothing more. I can't be in love with her, for God's sake, I haven't even bedded her."

"Bedding and love have nothing to do with the other," Reanleigh announced. "Hell, Chloe didn't allow me my husbandly rights till we'd been married a week and I had been in love with her for at least," he shrugged his shoulders, "a month, I think."

"I was in love with Rebecca before I even knew Rebecca's name," Bronley drawled. "For the better part of six months I was in love with a woman I couldn't find, who actually hid from me. The only bedding that was done was what occurred in my dreams."

"Yes but," Blaine mumbled, reeling from the notion that he might have actually let himself fall in love with Madeline.

"But nothing," Bathurst said. "We've all fallen under the spell. Love has a way of sneaking up and catching you unaware like that. It's like being blindsided by a blow to the head."

"No," Blaine started to shake his head. "I don't love her. I can't. I won't-"

"Oh, we've all said that. If I had a pound for every time I said I would never find myself leg shackled I would be as rich as Croesus," Bronley laughed.

"I don't deserve her, I'd only make her miserable."

"Do you think I deserved Isabella when I set out to seduce her for her fortune?" Bathurst asked, raking his hand through his hair.

"Do you think Bronley deserved Rebecca when he purposely lured her out into the gardens to be discovered by the *ton's* most notorious gossiper?"

"I take exception to that. I didn't *lure* her, I enticed her. A vast difference. And what about Reanleigh?" Bronley accused.

"What I think they're trying to say," Stanfield said dryly, "is that if they can find women to love them despite their dastardly deeds, then you'll have no problem convincing Madeline that you're a superior choice to Tynemouth."

"Tynemouth is normal. He won't be weak and fall to the floor in a fit. He'll make her a good husband, he'll give her children, for God's sake."

"Who's to say you won't give her children?"

"Because I won't," he snarled, whirling around to confront Stanfield. "You know I won't have children. I will not pass this curse on to my own flesh and blood. I won't bring innocent children into this world to suffer as I have suffered. To…." he almost said the words, almost admitted to his friends his deepest fear. But he stopped himself in time. He couldn't admit that he never wanted a woman--his wife to look at him, or his children the way his mother had looked at him--like a hideous monster that needed to be closeted away. No child of his would suffer that cruelty.

"Why don't you just talk to Madeline," Reanleigh suggested. "I've learned honesty is the best policy."

"Women are amazing creatures," Bathurst said. "They have a capacity for forgiveness and understanding that is quite extraordinary. You might be amazed at what Madeline will say.

"I cannot risk it. I have Miranda to think about and Henry, too. I can't have them worrying about my secret getting out. I can't run the chance."

"If you thought she would give away your secret you would never have let her into your heart," Stanfield reasoned. "On some level you trust Madeline, if only just a little. Tell her about your fears for your children and let her decide."

"No. Never. I'd rather never have her in my life than for her to know what lurks within me."

"Well, then," Bathurst said, striding across the room to retrieve his jacket. "I do not envy you. I can't imagine a torture worse than having to watch the only woman I've ever loved marry another a man."

He stiffened at the thought of Madeline becoming Lady

Tynemouth. Refused to envision her round with Tynemouth's babe.

"Think on it, old boy," Bronley said, clasping him about the shoulder. "A lifetime without her. It's a thought I couldn't bear."

"For you, perhaps. What would be insufferable to me, would be to have her disgust, her horror. Or worse yet, her pity. I know I could not bear *that*. I have suffered many things in my life," he mumbled, staring out the rain-splattered window, "what is one more trial? I'll simply add her to my long list of regrets."

Chapter Thirteen

'I'll expect an answer from you upon your return from Kent, my dear. Use this weekend to think on Tyenmouth's offer. He'll make you a good husband.'

Madeline forced her father's words from her mind and busied herself with reading the agenda Lady Bathurst had placed before her.

Everything seemed to be in order. The tents were set up, the food delivered, and the gypsies they'd hired to provide the entertainment were already ensconced in their camp along the periphery of Lady Brookehaven's grand estate. The Arabian Nights charity weekend would officially be underway tomorrow evening, culminating in the masked ball the next night.

Madeline could hardly wait to don her gypsy costume. Lady Bathurst's modiste had done a stunning job creating the jeweled colored veils and skirts. The outfits looked like they could have walked straight out of the pages from the Arabian Nights, right down to the gold tassels and linked coin belts that would wrap around their bare midriffs. They were deliciously scandalous and while she was eager to try hers on, she was thankful at least that she would have the protection of her veil and mask. No one would discover her identity.

"Gypsy auction," Lady Bronley cried as she skimmed the agenda. "What the devil is that?"

"Calm yourself, Rebecca," the dowager soothed. "You needn't get your sensibilities all riled, it's not as sinful as it sounds. It is merely a diversion for the gentlemen."

"Gentlemen," Isabella snorted, "what gentleman would attend such an event?"

"You young ones don't know how to have fun," the dowager grunted. "Why, back in my day, Old Q and Hellgate would have had a field day with such an event. And don't look at me like that, Rebecca, I am indeed in control of my faculties. It is not as though it is an auction for slaves," she emphasized. "Merely gypsies."

"Gypsies?" they cried.

"Well of course, gypsies," the dowager said, seemingly exasperated. "You didn't think I'd have all these women milling about without putting them to good use, do you? Bah," the dowager waved away their shocked gasps. "The girls are going to perform their wicked dances, that is all. The men will bid on these gypsies--and before you look at me as if I have bats in the attic--I will tell you that the gentleman are bidding on nothing more than a dance. They may lie back on cushions like the pasha's of old and watch their chosen gypsy perform the dance of the seven veils for their pleasure. Nothing more devious than that."

"And what if some of these gentlemen wish to take it further?" Lady Bathurst asked. "This sort of thing could get out of control quickly."

"The gypsies have brought their male counterparts to see to their safety. These women are professionals, my dear, they will refuse what offers they don't want, and accept those they wish. The instructions will be a bid on one dance, nothing more. Whatever else occurs is none of my business, nor our concern."

"But-" Rebecca said, clearly wary of the idea.

"No buts, gel. I'll have you know nothing untoward has ever happened in all the long years that my charity weekend has been taking place. Sure there is a little mischief that goes on, I needn't remind you of that," the dowager said pointedly, continuing on when Lady Bronley flushed a bright red. "But it is between consenting adults, and no innocents are involved," she looked then at Madeline, who gulped the rest of her tea. "The money goes towards charity and for that I'm willing to turn a blind eye to a few shenanigans. I always have, only to turn into the Dowager Dragon after the weekend is over. That is the draw, you see, everyone comes because for one scandalous weekend I thwart convention and let the ton see how very improper I can be, and all in the name of charity."

"Well, I think this whole auction idea is very clever," Lady Reanleigh said. "If we wish to have the guests open their purses to charity, what better way to encourage the men to spend freely than to have scantily clad women running about swishing their hips and baring their torso's."

"And what of the activities for the women? I suppose we'll have to endure a day of archery and Pall Mall while the men are having fun bidding on these women," Lady Bathurst asked, her voice conveying her boredom with the idea.

"Don't be absurd, gel. I have something interesting planned for the ladies. Of course there will be a Pall Mall course set up, and I suppose whoever wants to have a go at archery could, but I was thinking of something much more adventuresome and useful too."

"Well," they asked, waiting for the dowager to enlighten them. She cleared her throat and took a genteel sip of her tea, acting every inch the tyrannical marchioness she was. "Lessons," she murmured, her voice cracking. "Dance lessons."

"You must be jesting."

"You mean, learn to dance like they do in Harems?" Madeline said, clearly astonished at the idea, but finding it rather exciting.

"Indeed, my girl," the dowager smiled over the rim of her tea cup. "I think the ladies will be tripping over their slippers to learn some new steps, don't you? Leya, one of the girls of the dance troupe has agreed to teach them."

"Brilliant," Madeline clapped, "Oh, this is going to be such a wonderful weekend. I can hardly wait for it to begin."

"I thought you might think so," the dowager murmured. "You've taken a fancy to this notion from the beginning. I wonder why."

"Oh, it's just so different," Madeline said, hoping the dowager missed the wistfulness in her voice. Ever since Blaine had sent her Byron's poems, and read to her in the gardens of Montgomery House she had nothing but the thoughts of harems and Turkish tents in her head. Her dreams had been filled with exotic colors and silk and velvet pillows strewn about the floor. She'd imagined herself sprawled out on them, Blaine beside her, kissing her as he had the night in the garden.

All too soon the illusion of romance had died with Blaine's hurtful words. *'All I wanted from you was a good tumble.'* The words had haunted her for the past week, had hurt her so deeply that she had barely slept or eaten. He had lashed out, giving vent to everything inside him, forcing her to admit that he wasn't what he seemed.

Beyond that haughty mask, even beneath the romantic poetic side of him lurked something so deep and painful that not even she had been able to reach him. He was tortured, beyond allowing her into his heart let alone his life. He had cast her aside without batting an eye. He had walked out of Montgomery House that day and never looked at her again, despite the fact they had seen each other at numerous balls. They had even been forced to stand beside the other while her new chaperones chatted on about plans for the charity weekend. He had said nothing; he hadn't even acknowledged her and that fact stung most of all.

Even if he didn't wish to marry her, or didn't want to waste the effort it took to 'woo a virgin', he still could have acknowledged her. She liked to think that after what they had shared, they at least had a friendship. Damnation, she had actually shed tears in front of the man, had kissed him, too. Had let him touch her intimately, a fact she could not stop thinking about. It meant everything to her, and nothing to him.

"What is that ungodly noise," the dowager grunted, rising from her chair and hobbling to the window, her cane striking the marble floor with every step. "Well, I say-"

"What?" Lady Bronley asked, jumping up from her seat. Madeline followed closely behind Lady Bathurst and Lady Reanleigh. They arrived at the window just as a loud shout reached them through the open window.

"Whatever are they doing?" Lady Bronley asked, clearly bemused at the sight before her.

"They're filthy," Lady Reanleigh declared, "just look at Reanleigh, he looks as though he's been writhing in the mud."

"Ohh," Lady Bathurst cried, "did you see that? Stanfield just tried to knock Bathurst to the ground. And what are they doing using their heads to butt that ball?"

Madeline looked down at the five men, all filthy and in a state of dishabille. Not one of them had a cravat or waistcoat on; in fact, their cravats were tied to the trunks of trees. Four trees, each marking some sort of passage in which they were trying to steer the ball through with their feet.

Madeline watched with growing fascination as Lord Stanfield shouted a command and Blaine moved forward, kicking the ball into the air, forcing Lord Bathrust to run backwards, only to be tackled by Reanleigh.

"An interesting move," the dowager smiled. "I haven't seen that particular style of play before. Must be making up new rules this year."

"You've seen this," Lady Bronley asked. "They've done this before?"

"Why, yes." The dowager smiled, moving away from the window and leaning heavily on her cane. "They've done it since they were boys. Learned it at Eton, I believe. Used to enjoy watching them, but I expect," she winked before leaving, "not as much you're enjoying it now."

When the dowager left, Lady Bronley burst into giggles. "It is rather silly isn't it? Grown men shouting and tackling each other to the ground."

Lady Reanleigh nodded in agreement. "It's almost like some sort of male passage. Like peacocks strutting about with their feathers displayed."

"Well, they certainly are displaying an indecent amount of flesh," Lady Bathurst gasped. "I cannot believe my husband has removed his shirt."

Lady Reanleigh gasped, "he has a tattoo? Bella, you never once told me of that."

"Quite spectacular, isn't it?" Lady Bathurst smirked.

Madeline didn't notice who was wearing what, or who was doing what to whom. She only had eyes for one man and he was, she thought breathlessly, unfastening his shirt, revealing an extraordinary amount of taut muscle on his chest and belly. The black line of hair that disappeared beneath the waistband of his trousers held her attention for an indecent length of time.

She watched, mesmerized by the beauty of him as he ran, moving the ball between his feet, the tails of his shirt blowing behind him as he struggled to make it to the tree, while Bathurst and Bronley were hard on his heels trying to trip him.

She looked at his face, smiling and laughing as he pushed and shoved his way through his friends, obviously having the time of his life. He looked carefree and happy, the haughty mask and the guarded stance was all but gone as he sported about with his friends. It was almost as if nothing was amiss, Madeline thought, catching herself smiling as Blaine picked himself up from the ground and wiped his hands through his hair. Standing there, watching him laugh and jest, nearly lulled her into believing that he was nothing more than a carefree gentlemen.

But she knew better. He wasn't carefree, he was tortured, and he was, she feared, quite beyond reach.

"You're awfully quiet, Madeline, are you unwell?"

"No, Lady Bathurst." She forced her eyes away from Blaine. "I'm quite well."

"You must call us by our Christian names," she said. "I think I can speak for all of us when I say that this 'lady' business is quite droll."

Her chaperones laughed and nodded their heads. "Please," Lady Bathurst smiled, taking her hand. "Call me Isabella,"

"And me, Rebecca," Lady Bronley said.

"And Chloe," Lady Reanleigh joined in.

She was grateful to them for their warmth and their offer of friendship. Over the past couple of weeks they had grown closer, and they were now more like dear friends than chaperones.

"You must forgive our husbands. When they get together they sometimes forget they are grown men. They enjoy these schoolboy antics far too often, I'm afraid."

"Ugh," Rebecca groaned. "Do you remember last Christmas, that snowball fight Blaine started? Why, he had us soaked to the bone, the devil, and had even cajoled our husbands into pummeling us with the dreaded stuff."

"Fiendish devil." Chloe grinned. "He's too clever by half. Always into some sort of mischief."

"I have never seen that side of him," Madeline murmured before she could stop herself. She felt her cheeks flame as her friends turned back to her, mysterious grins on their faces.

"You have no doubt seen a much different side of Blaine than even we have," Chloe said softly.

Why hadn't she kept her mouth shut? How had she let her guard down? She wasn't back at Montgomery House with Phoebe, or Maggie, she was with his friends. She shouldn't have breathed a word of what thoughts were going on inside her head. She shouldn't be standing here now, ogling the man.

"Why don't you just admit it," Isabella said with a sigh. "You're in love with Hardcastle."

She truly did blush then. Unable to think of what to say, Madeline looked down at her folded hands.

"Oh, come now," Isabella teased. "You don't think we haven't noticed, do you? We're not blind, we've seen the way you look at him when you think no one is watching. And furthermore, we've taken note of the way he watches you."

"He only looks at me as he does everyone else--with contempt."

"He doesn't," Chloe said, wrapping an arm about her shoulder. "He wants everyone to think that, but to those who know him, he is clearly smitten with you. We know, we've been watching for some time now."

"We have talked," she said awkwardly, blushing, knowing they knew more than talking had gone on between them. "It does not signify what my feelings are. I must marry and he is not inclined to, so I must bury my feelings and look elsewhere."

"Nonsense," Isabella scolded. "You simply cannot bury feelings of love. Absolutely impossible. Once you've given your heart you can never take it back. I am correct in assuming you've given him your heart?"

She had given him her heart long before they'd been introduced;

she'd loved him secretly for nearly a year. But sometimes love wasn't enough.

"He said a darkness lurks within him. Do you know what he speaks of?"

"Do you love him enough to risk everything?" Isabella asked, her eyes scouring her face.

"Yes," she whispered, unable to help herself from staring at him longingly through the glass. "God help me, but I do. I don't care what lurks inside him. I can live with whatever secrets he wishes to hide, but I don't think I can live without him. I've thought so much about it, you see, and I don't think I can marry Tynemouth, not even for the sake of Montgomery House." She looked at her friends then, desperate to know if they knew the path to Blaine's heart. "I love him so much that I'm willing to sacrifice all that has been important to me up until now. Montgomery House has been my life, it has meant more to me than anything, and yet I'd give it all up to just have him."

It was a terribly selfish thing to say, but she had come to grips with what was in her heart. She could not marry another just to save the house, she could not stand by and wish for Blaine every day for the rest of her life. She couldn't--and if that made her selfish than so be it. She could not make her heart feel otherwise.

"Well, then," Isabella said, her eyes shimmering in the light. "He deserves you. And my friends and I would love nothing more than for you to marry him. He is a good man, Madeline, but he is indeed carrying around a heavy burden. You have seen through it and still love him. Now, all you have to do is make him see that you will stop at nothing to have him."

"And we will help you," Rebecca said, enfolding her in a warm, friendly embrace. "The four of us will come up with a plan to sweep him off his stubborn feet. And you needn't worry about resistance from them," she said, pointing to where Bathurst and Reanleigh and Bronley where huddled in a circle, "they'd love nothing more than for you to marry their friend."

"Welcome to the family, Madeline," Chloe said, hugging her tightly, "You'll make a most excellent addition to our little group."

* * * *

"I say," Bronley called, "Faversham was out of bounds."

"I wasn't," Faversham barked, wiping his mud-caked hands on his britches. "You need a pair of spectacles, Bronley."

"I bloody well saw you," Bronley spat, "you stepped beyond that line of trees to get the ball. That's out of bounds."

"Get on with it, Dev," Bathurst demanded. "We're winning, don't worry about Faversham, just set the ball and kick it."

Blaine watched with increasing moodiness as Bronley set the ball before Faversham and ordered him to kick it. He and his friends had been enjoying their game until Faversham and the *pup* showed up, interrupting their free spirited play.

What the hell had brought them here anyway? The guests were arriving tomorrow, only family and close friends were accepted this evening. And he was quite certain that the Tynemouth pup was no friend of the Dowager Dragon.

Blaine raced down the length of grass, attempting to take possession of the ball from Bathurst. It wasn't so much Faversham's company that bothered him, although, it could be a little uncomfortable if he were to fall down and succumb to a fit before him. But as he had been feeling fit for the past few weeks and none of the signs of impending doom were palpable, Blaine felt fairly confident his secret would be safe.

So, if it wasn't Faversham, or his fear of an impending seizure, it must be the golden-haired Adonis currently running beside him that was making him more than a little irritated.

He'd been heartily angered when he saw Tynemouth strolling across the lawn with Faversham, his golden hair shining like a beacon in the sunlight. Tynemouth was immaculately dressed in fawn britches and a blue woolen jacket. He was every inch the polite gentleman and the pup made him feel every inch the snarling beast.

This man, he thought, shoving Tynemouth aside and taking great pleasure in it, was going to be Madeline's husband. The man who would take her virginity, who would sleep with her and make a life with her. The thought enraged him and feeling more than a little angry, Blaine viscously kicked the ball, sending it flying between the trees.

"Good shot!" Reanleigh clapped Blaine on the back. "Thought Tyenmouth might get the better of you. All the better for our team that he sets a fire under yer arse."

"Hey," Bathurst drawled running up behind Blaine, "little bit hard on the fellow, don't you think? He's half your size."

"He'll be a third once I pummel him into the ground."

Bathurst merely arched his brows and sauntered off to his side of the makeshift pitch. Holding the ball above his head, Blaine checked the position of his team mates, noting who was free and who was not, and very nearly dropped the ball when he noticed a group of women sauntering across the lawn, Madeline leading the charge.

"Throw the ball," Reanleigh taunted, "we haven't got all day."

Forcing himself to pay attention and forget about the sight of Madeline, resplendent in a yellow walking dress with matching parasol, Blaine tossed the ball, and ran into the fray.

What the devil was she doing here? Virgins and innocents were always excluded from the Dowager Dragon's invitation list. The country party was nothing but a gratuitous way to spend a weekend, all made clean and proper by the emptying of ones pockets to charity.

It could only mean one thing, he thought with disgust, belatedly noting how the game had stopped mid play. The bastard had offered for her and she had accepted. It was the only reasonable explanation for her presence. Damn it, he swore, kicking the ball in frustration, the bloody bastard was going to take her.

"Umph,"

The grunt was emitted from Tynemouth as the ball connected hard between his shoulders. He was in the process of bowing over Madeline's hand, her fingers were nearly to his lips when the ball made contact. It was an accident, but Blaine suddenly took perverse pleasure in it. The way Tynemouth stood, his face awash with shock and embarrassment, delighted him. It was something a beardless boy would do, certainly nothing a gentleman would even think of in the presence of ladies, but who the hell cared? No one had ever made the mistake of thinking he was a gentleman.

"What," Tynemouth enunciated, "was the meaning of that?"

"You stopped in the middle of play, what did you expect?"

"There are ladies present." Tyenmouth was glaring at him, his eyes narrowing sharply. "You will do well to remember that."

"You would do well to remember who you are speaking to," Blaine murmured with a dangerous hint to his voice, the same hint that usually sent his servants and rational people scurrying to run from him. With a look of pure disgust, Tynemouth turned back to Madeline and pressed her palm to his mouth.

"Excuse me, my lady, some *gentlemen* do tend to get carried away in their manly pursuits."

"No need to make excuses for me, Tynemouth, Lady Madeline is very familiar with my manly pursuits, are you not Lady Madeline?"

Her eyes finally met his, and he did nothing to mask his fury. How could the little minx give herself so willingly to him, wish to marry him and save his blasted soul only to turn and give herself to another within a sennight?

"One could never accuse you of being anything but in complete control," she said, holding her magnificent turquoise gaze on him, pinning him with her intelligence and scrutiny. Blaine had the unsavory urge to squirm under that steady gaze.

"I'm surprised to see you here," he announced, fastening his shirt, trying in vain to appear as though he were a proper gentleman, but there was something about Madeline that made him forget his manners, made him want to push aside the dictates of good breeding and shock her with his baseness. She did something to his brain that he could not understand nor control.

"Why should you be surprised?" she asked, straightening her spine, readying herself for a challenge. "I'm the proprietor of Montgomery House. The money from this charity weekend is to benefit my cause. Why, pray tell, would I not be here?"

She was goading him, far more than she realized. He'd love to tell her just what he thought she meant by coming this weekend, longed to tell her what he thought of her ability to give her heart to someone new in such a short length of time, but he refused. Not when his friends and their wives were around to hear him, not with Tynemouth grinning at him as Madeline attempted to put him in his place. No, he would not lower himself in such a fashion. He would act the part of the God damned gentleman, no matter how much he wished to be otherwise.

"Well," Isabella said as she reached for her husband's arm, "you all look as though you need a good long soak in the bath."

"I suppose," Bathurst drawled, settling his arm around his wife's shoulders, "that is our wives way of delicately putting an end to our sporting match."

"I wish to have a word with Lord Hardcastle," Madeline stated when Tynemouth offered her his arm. "I'm afraid we've had a misunderstanding and I fear I cannot let it go on."

"If you wish," Tynemouth bowed, "I'll wait for you by the bench."

"Alone, if you please," Madeline commanded, her gaze firmly fixed upon him. "I shall meet up with you shortly. This won't take more than a minute."

The group left and after a few moments they were completely alone, standing opposite one another, each measuring the depths of the other's emotions.

He arched his brows in response to her challenging stance.

"Allow me to congratulate you on your forthcoming nuptials. I'm sure Tynemouth will make you an infinitely proper husband."

"I have accepted no offer of marriage."

"You being seen here with him will be taken as such. Since innocents are normally excluded from such events, one must concur that you are either engaged, or no longer innocent."

Her chin tilted defiantly, her eyes flared briefly before she masked it. "I'm neither engaged nor defiled."

"Is that so?" he asked, "never defiled? Funny, I distinctly recall having some sport with you not more than a week ago. But, perhaps you have forgotten."

"I have not forgotten," she said tightly, "and furthermore I do not consider myself defiled."

"True, I certainly did not take all your innocence. You are indeed not defiled at my hands. Perhaps then, you're here this weekend so that you may partake of more of the delights offered by Forbidden Places?"

"I have no plans to discuss this with you."

"Rumors are circulating that you are to be the next Lady Tynemouth. Are you here this weekend to see what awaits you in the matrimonial chamber?"

He didn't like her this way, cool and aloof. He wanted the Maddy of a week ago, the Maddy who wanted him, who wanted to save him and be with him. Not this cool creature who was looking at him with distaste.

"I told you, I have accepted no offers."

"He plans to have you," he said, resisting the urge to go to her and bring his lips down hard against hers. "I'm certain he plans to help himself to your charms this very weekend."

"Even if I allowed him, it is no concern of yours."

"You should have been mine," he hissed, unable to stop himself from moving toward her. Something inside him snapped when he thought of Madeline crushed beneath Tynemouth. She was his. God help him, he couldn't deny it. She belonged to him.

"You did not want me, nor wished to accept what I had to offer. You have no right to accuse me of anything, much less marrying Tynemouth. You knew what I was about. I told you I needed to marry."

He tilted her chin up and looked down into her eyes, wishing to hell they didn't have that effect on him. He was losing the battle to kiss her, he wanted to feel her mouth against his. He'd been unable to get the taste of her out of his mind.

"My lord," she said, licking her cherry red lips, tempting him beyond what he could endure. "I will have something understood between us. First, you may as well come to understand that I will no longer be a doormat for you to stomp upon. I'm through with wishing to save you, as you are quite beyond my skills. And second, you did not want nor welcome my feelings or attentions when I gave them, therefore you no longer have a say in what I do or whose company I seek. You told me you wanted nothing more from me than a good tumble. Well, my lord," she said, pulling her chin away from his hand. "I have no intention of being just a *good tumble*. From where I stand our lines are clearly drawn. We now completely understand each other, do we not?"

Her words were lost on him, so too was the cryptic message in them. Was she going to marry Tynemouth or not? Was she here to dally with some other member of the ton or did she mean to infuriate him, to get back at him for his venomous words that he had just spoken to her, and perhaps for the afternoon he'd said those cruel words to her. Lord, he couldn't think straight.

"I'm finding myself a husband this weekend, my lord, I suggest you stand aside and let me secure him."

Bloody hell, he swore as he watched her march away. The matter was far from finished.

Chapter Fourteen

The dreadful but undeniable fact was, he wanted her. Desperately, completely--forever.

Blaine prowled around Lady Brookehaven's drawing room with growing frustration. Damn it, why couldn't he just leave well enough alone? He'd already told her he wouldn't marry, that he refused to sire children. That should have been it--the end to all these foolish desires. She was an innocent, not someone he could dally with then turn over when he wished. Her station demanded a marriage proposal, hell, his own honor demanded he marry the girl before defiling her.

It had taken the better part of two weeks to finally admit that what he was doing with Madeline Brydges was more than a mere flirtation. She was creeping into his heart and he was succumbing to frightening dreams--all revolving around martial bliss.

When he had decided his infatuation with Madeline had gone too far, he'd taken steps to halt it, to put her in her place and make her understand he would never marry her. It had been painful, of course, but it had all worked out. That was, until she stood before him that very afternoon and announced her plans to 'secure herself a husband'.

The chit would never understand what her words had done to him. He'd been in a towering rage, wavering between taking her by the shoulders, shaking her till her teeth rattled, and kissing her senseless in an attempt to make her realize she needn't look further than him.

Damn it to hell, he couldn't marry her. It was too dangerous, she would discover his secret and then where would he be? And yet part of his brain whispered she might not be like the others. That she might accept him as he was, love him despite his dark secret. A part of him ached to ask her to marry him, to tempt fate and his demons and risk living with her. But the risk to both his pride and his heart was so great.

And that was the reason for his damnable mood. He couldn't decide which path to take. Did he leave her be? Stand helplessly by as she was married off to some other man? Or should he take a chance and offer for her?

He stole a look over his shoulder and found her sitting on a settee, looking far too beautiful and seductive. She'd worn that damn crimson gown to dinner. The one she'd worn to the Thorndale musicale, the one that made him catch his breath, that made him envision doing very ungentlemanly things to her. Just seeing her made him ache to possess her.

He had watched her all through dinner, laughing and talking with his friends. Smiling at Tynemouth, and not bothering to even so much as glimpse his way. Damn her, she had him tied in knots. He was as lost as a ship adrift without benefit of a map or compass.

"You'll wear out my carpet, Hardcastle." Lady Brookehaven stamped her cane to get his attention. "Sit and have a brandy."

He stopped before the window, his hands fisted against the sill as he looked out into the black night. He needed to get himself under control. He couldn't be having everyone suspect what was troubling him. He couldn't have Madeline thinking she could so easily discompose him.

"Thank you." He took the snifter of brandy from Bronley while ignoring his friend's inquiring look.

"Come, sit down," the dowager commanded. "There is an empty spot beside Lady Madeline."

Her eyes met his from across the room and he felt his insides clench. It was dangerous to sit that close to her, to have her warm body touching his. It was more than threatening, but nevertheless he found himself taking the cushion beside her, the crimson silk of her gown spilling onto his knee, contrasting sensually with his black trousers.

"Now then, what does everyone think of the preparations thus far? Was it not ingenious of us to come up with an Arabian Nights theme?"

"Yes," Tynemouth announced from the chair across the room. "It has been the talk of the ton for weeks. Whoever thought of the idea?"

"Lady Madeline, of course."

"Lady Madeline?" Tynemouth couldn't keep his astonishment from his voice. "Rubbish. Where ever would Lady Madeline have come across those tales? No, I refuse to credit it."

"I say, Tynemouth, you're not suggesting that I'm lying, are you?"

"No, no." Tynemouth hurried to correct himself. "It's just that Lady Madeline is so pure of heart, one wonders how she could have intimate knowledge of those scandalous tales."

Blaine felt Madeline tense beside him and he watched her smile give way to a strained expression. *He* knew exactly where lady Madeline had acquired her knowledge. Memories of just how intimately she was acquainted with the Arabian tales had kept him awake for the better part of two weeks.

"Come," Tynemouth continued, "did you really suggest the idea, Lady Madeline, or is the dowager having a laugh at my expense?"

"I'm afraid, my lord, Lady Brookehaven is indeed correct. I suggested the theme."

"I had no idea you were acquainted with the works. Where on earth did you get your hands on them?" Tynemouth grumbled, clearly displeased with Madeline's admission. Blaine turned his head in time to see her flush, no doubt wondering if he would speak up and tell the insolent pup just how she had become familiar with Arabic themes. The temptation was so very great, he wished nothing more than to put Tynemouth in his bloody place, but he refused to bring censure upon Madeline. He would not make what they had shared that night sordid and dirty. It was between them and no one else. The memories were theirs and theirs alone.

"I read the Tales of a Thousand and One Nights when I was still in the schoolroom," Isabella said saucily. "I trust you do not think my moral character in question, Lord Tynemouth."

"Who could ever think you immoral, my love?" Bathurst grinned, raising her hand to his mouth.

"I never meant to imply such a thing, Lady Bathurst," Tynemouth stammered, tripping over himself to right the perceived slight. "I only meant that Lady Madeline seems so very…." he paused, trying to think of some plausible excuse.

"Saintly?" Blaine supplied, feeling Madeline tense further, he could almost hear her spine snapping as she sat ram-rod straight against the cushions. "Why would you find it astonishing that Lady Madeline has not acquainted herself with the tales? She is, after all, *very* much acquainted with Byron's Turkish tales, is that not right, Lady Madeline?"

Madeline flushed further, gripping her skirts so tightly her knuckles were now a pasty white.

"Byron, good God, you don't go in for that sort of thing, do you, Lady Madeline?" Bronley asked. "The man has a startling penchant for the dramatic."

"I do indeed, Lord Bronley. I think he has written some of the most beautiful words ever penned. He has a way of elevating the senses."

"I think the man is a melodramatic fool," Bathurst grunted, tossing back the contents of his brandy. "Can't see why all the women wish to flock about him."

"He has a way with words, my lord," Madeline countered, moving restlessly in her seat. Dear God he could feel her thigh against his, could smell the scent of lemon verbena as it clung to the air between them. She was so close to him, *so temptingly close.*

"Have you never read anything of his? I vow, I've never been so moved as I am when I read his works."

"Good God, no," Bathurst grimaced, "I don't go in for pretty words and sacrificing of souls. I'm a man of action, not subtlety."

"I can attest to that," Isabella smiled. "My husband has never subscribed to such notions. He's always very blunt in his wishes."

"Damn right," he mumbled, confirming Isabella's statement. "Why the hell should I cover up perfectly normal desires with pretty metaphors and melodrama?"

"I don't believe Byron is a suitable reading choice for young ladies," Tynemouth pronounced. "I fear it gives them an unrealistic view of the world and what to expect in regards to love and marriage."

"You're not saying you would restrict your wife or daughter's reading choices, are you, Lord Tynemouth?" Madeline asked, her voice rising with barely controlled irritation. Blaine could literally feel the tension flowing from her. It was impossible to credit, but he thought he might have seen her straighten further.

He was enjoying this little discussion, relishing the fact that maybe the Tynemouth pup would not make her all that suitable a husband. He clearly saw it would have its drawbacks, but did Madeline?

"I do not think of it as restriction, my dear, merely guidance. It would be my wish to instruct the females of my household in their choice of reading material. One must be ever cautious of what one puts into their minds. Am I not correct, gentlemen?"

"Wouldn't presume to tell Rebecca what she could or could not read," Bronley groaned.

"I find the reading of certain material vastly useful--for the purpose of discussion, of course," Bathurst said, arching his brows knowingly at his wife.

"I believe," Tynemouth stated, getting up from his chair to pace the length of the room. "Females who read appropriate material have a cool head about them. They do not live with their minds in the sky. They're aware of their duties to their husbands and home. In short, they are faithful and loyal, while providing their husband with heirs."

"Rather like a favored hound," Madeline said, while artfully arranging her skirts and brushing his knee in the process. "I'm certain those are the same qualities you would choose when deciding which bitch to add to your kennels."

Tynemouth gaped in astonishment as a ripple of female and male chuckles erupted in the room.

"Touché," Bathurst saluted. "I believe the lady has hit her mark."

"The topic is becoming rather tedious," Blaine announced, rising from the settee. He felt Madeline's discomfort and wished nothing more than to set her at ease. Tynemouth deserved her cool reproof, but she did not deserve the pup's censure, of which, Blaine was certain would be forthcoming.

"Shall we not all have a game of whist?" he asked, offering Madeline his hand and assisting her to stand. "I'm certain his lordship would not deny a lady a hand of cards amongst friends."

Tynemouth had the grace to blush, but nodded his head in agreement. When the tables were all set and they were seating themselves, Blaine took the opportunity to graze past Madeline. She looked up at him, but he resisted the urge to drown in her hypnotizing eyes. He still wasn't certain what was going on his mind, but he was damn sure he couldn't let the lady see his indecision.

"I'm afraid," he began, his voice low as he tilted his head to whisper in her ear, "it'll be a somewhat cold marriage, won't it, my sweet? No midnight readings of Byron, or Harems beneath trees. Just political duties, perfunctory conjugal visits, and the raising of offspring. One does wonder if you've got your line drawn in the correct place."

* * * *

Oh, the odious man! Madeline ranted as she trudged through the damp grass. He was insufferably arrogant and utterly confusing. One minute Blaine was cold and uncaring, insinuating she had let Tynemouth have his wicked way with her, while the next supporting her in her choice of reading material and hinting that he might be a superior choice for the role of husband.

What the devil did the man want? Did he truly wish to be rid of her, or was he someone like Faversham, unable to stand for not getting what he wanted?

Madeline wrapped her shawl about her shoulders in an attempt to protect herself from the cool breeze. Although it was June the breeze was brisk and a touch cooler than she liked. Nevertheless the reprieve from the stuffy drawing room had been most welcome.

Tynemouth had partnered her first in whist, then Blaine. It had been an uncomfortable affair and she had to ask more than once what was trump. The devilish man had occupied her thoughts and prevented her from paying attention to the game. She had felt his cool gray eyes on her, watching her, studying her through his black veil of lashes. What did the man want from her? He had made it clear in no uncertain terms that he desired to be left alone. And yet tonight he had done his best to stay close to her, to take advantage of every opportunity to brush alongside her, or murmur in her ear. He had looked at her with unmistakable carnal interest. She could almost read what thoughts were in his mind.

She wanted to take that as a sign he was interested, that perhaps he might have reconsidered his stance. But Madeline had the sinking feeling he didn't like to lose, and therefore his damnable male pride was the true reason behind his attentions.

Sighing, she trudged up the slope toward the house. She'd been outside for nearly an hour, trying to clear her head. It had been a fruitless venture, her thoughts and feelings remained jumbled and confused and her desire for Blaine stronger than ever.

Seeing the glow of the lanterns flickering in the distance, she hurried forward, forcing herself to forget the image of Blaine looking devastatingly handsome in a silver waistcoat, the color a perfect match for his eyes. She attempted to push aside the vision of his fingers raking through his hair, leaving it artfully tousled and almost too irresistible to avoid touching. She was fighting so hard to ignore the desire that flooded her veins every time she thought of him that she didn't see the large tree roots protruding out of the ground before she nearly tripped over them.

"Bloody hell."

Madeline froze at the familiar sound of Blaine's voice. Whirling around, she peered into the black night searching for him. "My lord?"

"What are you doing out here?"

She looked down, only to see him sitting on the ground, one leg stretched out, the other bent at the knee. He was clutching a bottle of brandy in one hand while his other contained a snifter filled with the golden liquid. On the ground beside him was his jacket and cravat, carelessly discarded in a heap.

"I'm taking a stroll," she said, choosing her words carefully, sensing he was in one of his brooding moods. "I assume it was your feet I tripped over and not some overgrown tree root."

"Hmph," he grunted, swallowing the liquid, only to refill the balloon once again. "Surprised you even saw me down here. It's the first you've noticed me all bloody day."

There was something in his voice that alerted Madeline to the fact that he was angry. His voice was quiet, measured, yet held a current of cold contempt that made her shiver.

"Cold?" he asked. "Don't doubt it, you're damn near falling out of that dress."

Her shiver had nothing to do with the chilly breeze or the deep cut of her gown, but it did have everything to do with the way he was looking up at her through half closed lids. He reminded her of a black panther waiting to pounce on a helpless gazelle.

"Cat got your tongue? Not like you to have nothing to say. Perhaps you've lost your zest for sermonizing." He took a drink then wiped his mouth on the back of his hand, before refilling his glass. "Although I rather doubt you've given up your saintly ways. I'm certain you're itching to lecture me on the danger of too much drink. But do you know," he said sardonically, drinking the contents of his glass while holding her gaze. "I *choose* to drink myself into oblivion tonight. And I'm choosing to wake up with one hell of a headache on the morrow. What think you of those choices, my lady?"

"I think you're choosing to hide behind a brandy bottle, that is what I think."

"And what do you propose I'm hiding from?"

"Your feelings, my lord."

She hated how he looked at her with cool reproof, his gray eyes glinting up at her in the pale moonlight. He was more than just brooding, there was an edge to him that she had never seen before.

"By feelings, do you mean desires?" He took another swallow of his brandy then tossed his glass onto the grass. "Because I can assure you, I have a healthy measure of those. My cock is as hard as it's ever been before. But feelings, well, I don't believe myself capable of feeling much of anything."

"You're foxed," she snapped, taken aback by his common talk.

"Hmm," he murmured, as he stood up, wavering briefly before straightening himself. "Not nearly drunk enough, I'll wager. If you're afraid I can't perform, let me assure you now, my cock is up and ready, my Mistress of the Night. Come, you've teased it enough, don't you think?"

"Why are you doing this?" She winced at the commanding sound of her voice, but she couldn't help it, he looked utterly menacing as he towered above her, glaring at her. It wasn't like him to drink too much. It meant losing control and he never lost control.

"Ah, the lecturing begins."

"I mean it, what the devil are you doing out here alone, drinking yourself unconscious."

"I'm always alone, or have you not noticed?"

"Rubbish, you have your friends. You're obviously all very close."

"Have you never been in a room, surrounded by people, hearing their voices and laughter and still felt alone?"

"No I have not."

"You're fortunate then," he said, raising the bottle to his lips and taking a gulp, his eyes trained on her as he drank from it. "I've felt this way most of my life."

"I think you've had enough," she whispered, taking the bottle and tossing it onto the ground.

"Not nearly enough," he drawled with more than a hint of mockery in his voice. "I'm still awake and aware of my surroundings. I can still see you, smell you. I'm still on fire for you."

Madeline closed her eyes against the despair she heard in his voice. "My lord-"

"We're back to that are we? That night in the maze, when you found your release, you whispered my name with such passion that the memory of it has haunted me for weeks."

"You told me you did not want me. That you don't need a wife. I don't understand what you're saying or what you want from me."

"Neither do I, apparently."

"What is it you want?"

"What I can't have."

Suddenly she felt overwhelmed by the torment of the past few weeks. She could no longer go on feeling this way, wondering what was in his heart, wondering if she'd meant anything more to him than a good romp.

"Why did you say those things to me? What made you wish to

hurt me in such a fashion?"

"I wanted to make you understand that I could never marry you."

"And yet, you become insolent and derogatory when I tell you that I'm searching for a husband. You accuse me of allowing others to have their way with me, when in fact you have been the only one to come close to my ruination. I told you that afternoon at Montgomery House that I wished to marry you. You informed me you wanted nothing but a tumble in bed."

His eyes narrowed, and he crossed his arms defiantly against his chest. He was about to speak when she interrupted him. "Do not deny you spoke those words to me. You made it perfectly clear you do not wish to wed, nor have children. Since I must wed to save the House, I must search elsewhere. Kindly explain why now you're taking an active interest in who I wish to marry, when you have clearly stated that you are opposed to marriage."

"How is it so very easy for you to forget about what we've shared and set your sights on someone else? *Kindly tell me that.*"

Madeline stepped back as if she had been slapped. The violence of his words caught her unawares, leaving her feeling confused and helpless.

"Do you know what it is like to lie awake at nights and dream of something you can never have?" he growled, taking one threatening step toward her. "Can you have any idea what it is like to face a life full of nothing but loneliness?"

"You choose-"

"Do not *dare* to presume to tell me that I choose to live this way," he roared. "My fate was chosen for me, do not ever forget that. Any choices I have made in my life have been out of necessity, not desire."

The raw pain she heard in his voice twisted her heart, making her feel a sick, gnawing sensation in the pit of her stomach. He needed someone so desperately in his life. *He needed her.*

"You cannot even begin to fathom the depths of my loneliness, madam. You've never been where I have been, you will never feel what I feel. Therefore you will *kindly* refrain from questioning my choices."

She took a step back as he advanced toward her, his eyes dangerously narrowed. "Do you think it is easy to stay away from you? Do you think it was easy for me to look at you and say those things? I am a monster, Madeline, but upon my honor, I hated having to hurt you."

"You're not a monster," she whispered, reaching for his hand. "I could never think that of you."

His eyes met hers then and the sadness in them made her forget her anger. At that moment she didn't care what his reasons were for treating her this way. All she could think of was reaching out to him. Letting him know she had not forsaken him for another. He truly thought he was alone, she realized that now, and she wanted nothing more than to make him understand that he wasn't.

"I know I must stay away from you and yet I cannot stop myself from thinking about you. I cannot bear the thought of seeing you with Tynemouth. The pain of always wanting and never having is more than I can bear. I thought I could-"

"Blaine," she murmured, stepping closer to him, seeing that his chest was rising and falling much too rapidly. "I haven't stopped wanting you, or hoping you would change your mind."

"Maddy," he groaned, before bringing her tight against the length of him. "I don't know if I can make you happy or be the husband you need."

"I'm sure," she whispered, feeling his lips seeking her pulse. "I'm not asking for perfection, just you, my lord. I just want you."

"Oh, God, Maddy," he said huskily as he nuzzled her neck, his hands roaming frantically along her breasts, cupping and squeezing with an urgency that frightened, yet excited her. "You don't know what you're getting yourself into."

She framed his face in her hands and forced him to meet her gaze. "I know I want you, Blaine, I'll sacrifice what I have to in order to have you."

"What about a family, Maddy? Would you sacrifice never having children in order to marry me?"

Her mouth gaped open despite her resolve not to show him her shock. Could she live her life without children?

He took in her expression and with a sharp breath he drew away from her. "I think we have our answers." He stepped away from her only to bend down to retrieve his jacket and the brandy bottle.

"I have not yet given you my answer, Blaine."

He turned slowly, his face once again a blank mask. "I could not ask it of you, Madeline. You're made to be a mother. I could never deprive you of the right."

"Yet you would deprive me of my right to decide?"

"I fear that in this case, I'm choosing for you. I know far better than you what such a commitment will cost you. And I'm not prepared for you to pay the price."

"What if I'm prepared?"

"This night's business has already cost me what is left of my soul, let me not have the burden of knowing that this bargain would cost you yours. Good night, Madeline. I'll stand in your way no longer."

Madeline watched him stalk off into the night, his coat tossed over his shoulder, the brandy bottle swinging from one hand. He had wanted to reach out to her, had all but admitted that he would wed her. And that was all she had needed from him. An affirmation of his desires. She would risk it--all of it. Nothing was as important to her as saving Blaine from his demons and loving him for the rest of his life.

It would work, she vowed, and the cost would most definitely not be her soul. He wouldn't let that happen. She knew he wouldn't.

Chapter Fifteen

"Time to get up, old boy."

"Bugger off, Ringwald," Blaine mumbled into his pillow, wincing as a bright shaft of orange light filtered through the bed curtains.

"Get up."

"You can damn well find yourself another post, Ringwald. Consider yourself dismissed," he snarled, only to moan as a wave of nausea washed over him. Good God, how much had he drunk last night?

Blaine fought through the thick mental fog, trying to ignore the pounding of his head, only to remember that he'd stopped counting at two decanters of brandy. The urge to retch was strong as he recalled sitting beneath the stars, brooding over Madeline and drinking himself into a stupor.

"Pass him that chamber pot, Dev. I think he's about to cast up his accounts."

Bathurst? The deep, commanding voice sounded like his. And Bronley? What in the world were they doing in his bedchamber?

"Where's Ringwald?" he asked after belching loudly, only to grimace as he tasted acidic bile.

"With the staff, taking supper."

"Supper? I bloody well just got to bed."

"You've slept the day away," Bathurst drawled, flinging back the covers. "It's past time you got up."

Raising his head from the pillow, Blaine glared at Bathurst while he reached for the blankets. "Sod off, and leave me the hell alone. I wish to die in peace."

Bronley's chuckle set off the drums in his head. "Come now, old boy. You don't want to miss all the festivities. You should see the grounds; it's a veritable Harem out there."

The last bloody thing he wanted to think of was Harems. He'd thought of nothing else last night and look at where it'd got him.

"Look," Bathurst commanded. "Get up and get yourself presentable. You've spent enough time wallowing in self pity and God knows what else."

"Brandy, by the smell of it."

Blaine cracked open one eye to see his friends standing beside his bed, both grinning at him like a pair of fools. What the devil had he been thinking to have drunk so much? He knew better, he bloody well *knew* that over imbibing was something that triggered his seizures. How could he have placed himself in jeopardy? And then he groaned, closing his eyes, remembering that he'd chosen the brandy instead of going to Madeline.

He'd discovered in the course of the day which room was hers and he stood outside it last evening, listening to the sounds of her preparing for bed, imagining her naked body beneath the virginal white gown, remembering the feel of her wetness on his fingers as he coaxed the honey from her. He'd had to physically force himself not to barge in and take her. He'd been so hard, so hungry for her. But instead, he'd taken a bottle outside, drank himself into oblivion and still he couldn't get her out of his mind. He wanted her, so much in fact that he was willing to forsake his vow and marry her, just so he could spend a night between her thighs.

"Come on." Bronley tossed him his shirt before striding to the door. "You need some fresh air."

He didn't need fresh air, he bloody well needed Madeline, right here. This minute, in fact, if the stirring in his trousers was any indication. He needed her to ease the ache in his groin, to fill the emptiness in his heart. He just plain needed *her*.

"You know, Isabella heard an interesting tidbit today," Bathurst drawled, sauntering after Bronley. "She overheard Tynemouth speaking with your grandmother, Dev. He was requesting a special waltz to be played after his impending nuptials were announced."

"Really?" Bronley reached for the door. "And when is the big announcement to take place?"

"Tonight."

"Anybody we know?"

The door suddenly closed, Bathurst's murmured and inaudible answer drowned by the thick wood. Blast it all, Blaine swore, struggling to fight the dizziness as he sat at the side of the bed. He was going to kill the pair of them, but not before he got his hands on Tynemouth. The pup, Blaine thought, suddenly reaching for the chamber pot, was going to learn that he would not stand idly by and watch him take Madeline away. He'd put the insolent dog in his place. It was going to be his first order of business. Right after he was through casting up his accounts.

* * * *

Two hours later, after a hot bath, a shave and fresh clothing, not to mention a cup of strong coffee and a slice of much needed toast, Blaine made his way with his friends through the grounds of the Brookehaven estate.

Everywhere he looked, gypsies traversed the lawn, their brightly colored costumes matched the striped tents that lined the park. Music sounded through the hum of activity as the gypsy men played the dombek and the darabukka in the characteristic sultry beat of Turkey and Morocco.

"Say," Bronley asked, halting before a black tent. "Ever fancy having your fortune told?"

"Not really," Bathurst grumbled. "Never was a believer in that hocus pocus stuff."

"I'm a believer," Stanfield said, staring at the black canvas billowing in the breeze. "My mother visits a lady with the sight. Always has."

"Well, that's different," Bathurst groaned. "Your mother isn't English."

"She's part English," Stanfield corrected. "And there is much to be learned in Middle Eastern culture. Don't put it down until you've had a taste of it."

"Well, I personally don't care to know what Fate has in store for me." Blaine shuddered at the thought. He had no wish to hear of the loneliness he no doubt had to look forward to.

"C'mon," Bronley grinned, waving them toward the tent. "It'll be good for a laugh."

"We'll have to compare fortunes, I'm certain they only have a handful to go around," Bathurst smirked as he followed Bronley along the grass path to the tent, where two blazing torches stood on either side of the entrance. "She'll probably tell us we'll find ourselves spending the night with a beautiful gypsy," Bathurst snorted.

"Gennlemen," the old gypsy said with a smile she looked up from her glass ball that sat atop an ornate gilt base. "Come in, come in," she waved, her bracelets tinkling together with the motion. "You have come to see what Madame Sefika sees for you, yes?"

She had a thick Turkish accent which leant an air of authenticity to the otherwise gaudy interior of the tent. They were surrounded by black and red beaded scarves, artfully draped along the makeshift walls and ceiling, imitating a sultan's tent. Numerous candles, all burnt to varying heights, were scattered amongst her table. Madame Sefika, well past the first blush of youth, held court in the center of the tent wearing an elaborate purple head veil, from which gold coins fringed her forehead, dancing and shimmering in the flickering candlelight. Her be-ringed fingers started to roam along the glass as her kohl-lined eyes surveyed them through smoking tendrils of jasmine scented incense.

"So, English Lords, what is it you seek?"

"Our futures," Stanfield said when it was apparent no one would speak. "What do you see for us?"

"Happiness," she said, closing her eyes while her leather-like hands traced the shape of the ball. "Great love. Everlasting love." Her brown eyes opened and immediately fixed on Blaine. "Painful secrets."

Blaine fought the urge to shrink back into the shadows. She had a queer, disembodied look about her, as if she truly could see inside him. It was a disturbing feeling, and when she curled her lips at him in a mysterious half smile he felt a tingle of apprehension snake down his spine.

Bloody hell, he was still drunk, he thought with disgust. The brandy combined with the atmosphere inside the tent was what was making him fall for her outlandish act.

"You," she pointed to Stanfield. "You believe, yes? You are different from these English lords. I see it in your eyes. I know what it is you seek. It is not time for you. Go, now."

Blaine watched as Stanfield stiffened before reaching into his vest pocket, pulling out some coins. "Thank you, Madame," he murmured as he bowed to her.

"Soon, lordling, soon you will find what you so seek."

Stanfield made his way to the entrance. Their eyes met through the incense smoke and Blaine was surprised by the emotion in them. Stanfield truly did believe the nonsense the old crone was touting.

"You," Madame Sefika's voice sliced through the air. "You will spend the night with a beautiful gypsy."

Bathurst snorted and shot him an 'I told you so' expression.

"This night," Sefika whispered, her dark eyes shining black in the glow of the candles. "This night you will give her your babe."

"I'm a married man," Bathurst scoffed, clearly astonished by the implications of such a thing. The teller merely shrugged and gazed back into her glass.

"You will not be able to help yourself. You will want her with a hunger that belies all thought. That is all I see."

Bathurst tossed his payment onto her table. "Bloody hell, I can't believe I've come in here and paid to find out I'm an adulterer."

Sefika grinned as she watched Bathurst stomp out of the tent. "Two lordlings left," she mumbled, peering once more into the glass. "I see betrayal, deceit. A woman crying."

Blaine felt his stomach knot as he looked to Bronley, whose eyes were now giant spheres.

"I see love, too. But it will not be easy."

"Well, I'm not listening to this drivel," Bronley snapped, replacing his hat. "I'm utterly devoted and completely in love with my wife, and I have no intention whatsoever of betraying her or making her so unhappy that she weeps. So, *Madame*, I bid you farewell."

Blaine tried to follow him, but for some strange reason his feet seemed planted firmly to the ground.

"Wise, he is," Sefika murmured, meeting his gaze above the glistening glass globe. "I was not speaking of his future, English lord. I was seeing yours."

"I do not subscribe to such nonsense," he said, feeling himself return to his normal mental state.

"Ah, you are, how to say? A scetich?"

"A skeptic, do you mean? A non-believer?"

Her dark eyes lit up as she reached her hand out to him. "Yes. That is the word I search for you. You do not believe, do you?"

Ignoring her outstretched hand, Blaine snorted in disgust. "I doubt very much, madam, that you are able to see a blasted thing in that glass sphere of yours."

"No, English lord? Then let me show you another way. Give me your hand."

"I think not. This has been an amusing way to spend a few minutes, but I believe I've heard all I wish to know. Here," he said, placing a sovereign in her hand. "My thanks for an entertaining performance."

Her wrinkled hand seized his, surprising him with her strength as she turned his hand in hers, revealing his palm. "I see a babe--near death, not breathing. I hear the quiet of the room and I see the shaking of the babe. I see the child slowly come to life. I see *you*, English lord."

His breath froze in his chest as he struggled to snatch his hand away from hers. He felt a strange tingle down his back as her mysterious eyes traversed his face, felt his hand shake as her wrinkled fingers traced the lines on his palm.

"I see great love, lordling. I see that you fear that love. I sense the loneliness in you."

"You don't see a bloody damn thing."

"Ah, but I do. I see the woman you love. I know that you want her, but that you fear being with her. I feel that fear." She looked up at him, her painted lips glimmering in humorless amusement. "I see that your fear nearly overshadows your love."

"I haven't a clue what you speak of, Madam, and furthermore-"

"You will not see her go to the other," Sefika carried on, ignoring his protests. "You will marry her, but the road to love will not be easy. You will know great pain before love will prevail."

"I have no wish to listen-"

"You cannot stop it, English lord. The wheels of Fate are in motion. It *will* happen."

"Who the devil do you think-"

"Fate will hand you a gift tonight. Do not make the mistake of letting that gift slip between your fingers, for if you do, you will never have another chance. Go," she said, dropping his hand. "For I see nothing else. You control your future now."

He looked away from the penetrating gaze of the gypsy, only to stare in amazement at his hand.

"Lordling," she called as he was about to pull back the flap of the tent. "You must give a piece of yourself this night if you are to have what you truly desire."

Blaine nodded, unable to believe that the woman had peered into his soul and guessed his fears--and his desires.

* * * *

"I think your modiste may have miscalculated, Isabella," Rebecca sighed, pulling at the beaded garment covering her breasts.

"I agree," Chloe grimaced, staring at her reflection in the mirror. "It doesn't seem to fit."

"Nonsense," Isabella muttered as she tied the strings of Madeline's bodice. "It's supposed to fit as such. Haven't you seen those gypsies walking about?"

With a sigh, Chloe finally admitted defeat and ceased trying to attempt to cover her exposed bosom. "Well they weren't wearing anything as scandalous as this."

Madeline finally turned and looked in the mirror, gasping at the reflection that looked back at her. She truly looked like one of the Harem woman she'd glimpsed in books. The bodice, all beaded and sparkling cupped her breasts, pushing them together until they were in high mounds. The lush fringe that sparkled in the light hung nearly to her waist from the bodice, shimmering and grazing her exposed midriff. The skirt, made of a filmy, translucent material whirled around her thighs and legs while the coin belt around her waist jingled in the quiet room.

"You look beautiful in green," Isabella said to her as she covered her hair with a green veil edged in gold thread. "It brings out your eyes."

Madeline swallowed hard, forcing the knot of tension aside. The dress was as risqué as it was beautiful, and she wasn't certain she could go through with her plans to enter the ballroom wearing such a garment.

"There," Isabella announced, securing Madeline's face veil. "Perfect. No one will know it is you, Madeline. Your identity, as well as your reputation will be safe. You do know that you must stay with us at all times, correct?"

"You aren't to go wandering off," Rebecca added, "unless it's with us, or one our husbands."

"Or Blaine for that matter," Chloe muttered, back to fixing her bodice. "He won't allow you to get yourself into trouble."

"I think I should go with the peasant garb," Madeline blurted. "I'm not sure I can wear this."

"Nonsense," Isabella scolded and reached for her hand, "the room will be packed with nothing but peasants and gypsies. No one will have dared to dress as Harem girls."

"That is what I'm afraid of," Madeline sighed, allowing herself to be whisked out of the room and down to the ballroom where the ball was to be held.

"It is always good to stand out in a room," Chloe whispered behind her. "You never know whose attention you might attract."

Let's hope it's the right person's, Madeline thought, suppressing a shiver.

Chapter Sixteen

Blaine stared in open-mouthed shock as he looked around lady Brookehaven's transformed ballroom. The room, which had only yesterday been a study in all that was refined and elegant, was now looking like the inside of a Sultan's tented Harem. Everywhere he looked were silks, all jeweled colored, billowing in the breeze from the open terrace doors. Glass lanterns, decorated in the Moroccan style hung from the ceiling, replacing the blazing chandeliers with a softer, more intimate glow. Incense burned on braziers, the scent exotic and alluring. Already, numerous gentlemen had piled into the room, some wearing elaborate costumes, or plain evening clothes as he'd chosen to do. Whether they were in costume or not, they were all assembled waiting for the gypsies to begin their dancing, signaling the beginning of the ball.

"Well, looks like the Dowager Dragon has gone all out this year," Bathurst drawled, settling himself against the wall and sipping his champagne. "I feel like a bloody Pasha awaiting my Odalesque."

"Looks like that sitting room of your mother's," Blaine murmured to Stanfield.

"Indeed," Stanfield grinned, his white teeth flashing in the dimly lit room. "Although I'm quite certain Mama doesn't have any beautiful gypsies on hand to dance for me."

"Ah," Bronley muttered, coming up to stand beside them. "I see Grandmamma was successful in making everyone bend to her wishes."

"I tried to give her a thousand pounds to get out of it," Stanfield smirked. "She ushered me into the room with a flick of that damn cane of hers."

"Well, I'm only here due to threats on my physical well being," Bathurst grunted, finishing off his champagne.

"The dowager?" Blaine asked.

"Isabella," Bathurst grinned.

"The Dowager Dragon surely has outdone herself," Reanleigh murmured looking about the ballroom. "She's never done anything quite as risqué as this."

"Oh, this is nothing," Bronley quipped, waving the comment aside. "From what I understand the days when my grandfather was alive, and Old Q and Hellgate attended, this charity event was nothing short of scandalous."

"It's still considered nothing short of scandalous."

"Yes, but it does bring in the pound notes, does it not?"

"Ladies and gentlemen," Lady Brookehaven announced, ending the deep rumbling humming through the room. "Let us begin with the masked ball." The dowager hobbled with the aide of her cane as she circled the dance floor. "Leya and her troupe have agreed to dance for you this evening."

Numerous male shouts and whistles erupted, all but drowning out the restrained feminine clapping. Blaine noticed numerous un-amused glares on more then one wife's face as her husband took to jubilantly welcoming Leya and her gypsies.

Amidst the raucous applause, numerous gypsies ran into the room, their shawls billowing out like clouds behind them, their finger cymbals clicking in a frenzied manner.

"Where have the women got to?" Blaine heard Reanleigh ask.

Bathurst gazed about the room looking for them. "Don't know why Isabella felt she needed to get dressed with the others. How different can one peasant costume look from the next?"

The dombekka sounded, its sultry beat carried on the breeze from the terrace. The gypsies swirled in circles, their hips moving to the rhythm of the music. A lavishly rounded figure pulled out of the circle, shimmying and shaking, causing a frenzy of loud whistles and shouts to erupt throughout the room.

Despite the tension he felt swimming in his veins and the lingering effects of the alcohol he'd consumed last evening, Blaine caught himself grinning as a group of young men in front of them began to shoulder each other out of the way to get a better glimpse of the dancer.

"Quite lovely," Stanfield murmured beside him, "wouldn't you say?"

"I suppose," Blaine said, not really paying attention to the woman and instead scanning the room for any sign of Madeline. The dancer was voluptuous and well endowed and he might have been drawn to her at one time, but his bent these days seemed to lean toward red haired imps with lagoon green eyes and cherry lips.

"Damn it to hell," Bathurst suddenly grunted, sounding as if he'd been punched in the gut. "What the bloody hell is *she* wearing?"

"My God," Reanleigh breathed.

"What?" Blaine asked above the increasingly appreciative shrieks and whistles.

"I'm gonna murder her," Bathurst grumbled, unable to tear his eyes from the staircase.

"What is it, old boy?" Bronley laughed. "You look as if you're in need of a vingarette."

"It would seem that our wives have taken a fancy to dress as Harem girls and not as peasant gypsies."

Good God, could it be true, Blaine asked himself, snapping his head in the direction of Bathurst's gaze. On the bottom riser stood four beaded and draped Odalisques, all dressed in a myriad of colors and all of varying heights and forms. The one common denominator he thought, suddenly realizing that there was one extra woman gathered with them, was that the costumes where scanty, visually stunning, and very arousing.

Blaine straightened against the wall, a strange awareness flickered within him as a pair of arresting kohl-lined eyes locked with his in the candle light. His spine tingled and his mouth went dry knowing that the nameless beauty gathered with the women was Madeline. No one made his body tighten, his nerves taught with awareness like Madeline did.

"Just what the bloody hell are they about?" Bronley slammed his champagne flute down onto an unsuspecting footman's tray.

"I say we escort them onto the dance floor," Bathurst muttered, pushing away from the wall. "It'll only be a matter of seconds before every libertine in the room is racing to get their hands on them."

Jesus, Blaine thought, his breathing ragged and short, he was going to suffer an apoplexy before this night was through. If he had to stay beside Madeline dressed like that, her navel enticingly exposed, he was going to go mad.

"I think I'll leave you to entertain your wives," Stanfield smiled rakishly, staring back at the dancers. "I have the uncontrollable urge to introduce myself to Leya."

"What the devil has gotten into him?" Bathurst asked as they watched Stanfield weave his way through the crowd, making his way to where the gypsies danced.

"Hell if I know," Blaine muttered, feeling heat flare in his veins, knowing that Madeline's gaze had once again settled on him. "We were supposed to spend the night getting foxed."

"C'mon," Reanleigh motioned for them to follow, "Ashton and

Huxley are closing in on our wives."

Blaine followed his friends, trailing in their wake despite the fact he knew he was tempting Fate. Hell, he thought, Fate had been tempted since he first set eyes on her.

"Good evening, ladies," Bathurst drawled as he reached for Isabella's hand. "Let's take a turn about the gardens, shall we?"

"My lord," Isabella cooed, the veil covering her nose and mouth puffed out with her breath. "I'm afraid we are married women."

"I'm quite certain your husband won't mind," Bathurst grinned, pulling her towards him. "In fact, I think he'd rather approve."

Lagoon green eyes suddenly met his, and Blaine started at the intensity of them. He was unaware of the fact that his friends were now departing for the garden, their wives in tow, until it was only he and Madeline, alone, gazing at each other.

His eyes scoured every inch of her, familiarizing himself with the rise of her breasts, the way her waist indented above her hips, the way her coin belt dipped below her naval, drawing his eyes to territory that should be forbidden to him. And Lord he was hard, so damn aroused he could have taken her right there on the stairs.

"I fear I should go," Madeline whispered, her green face veil whispering softly against her chin.

He reached for her arm, which was bare and warm. He ignored the protestations of his brain, no matter how weak they were. "Not so fast, gypsy."

"Sir?" she said, imitating a Turkish accent. "Where are you taking me?"

"Do you tell fortunes, gypsy?" he asked, pulling her behind him to the terrace and into the night.

"No," she said, her voice nothing but a breathless whisper that called to his quickly slipping self-control.

He was practically running now, dragging Madeline behind him, the sound of her belt and anklets tinkling behind him, arousing his lust to a fever pitch. God, he was on fire for her. All rational thought had left him the minute he'd seen her standing on the stairs, her eyes beckoning to him.

"My lord, I don't think-"

"You're losing your accent, gypsy," he warned, making his way to the edge of the lawn where numerous tents had been set up.

"Where are you taking me?"

"I do believe you're not a gypsy at all," he said, pulling her to a stop before the entrance of a tent, far removed from the others. "You seem to have a London accent. Have you ever been to

London, my lovely gypsy?"

Blaine watched her eyes widen as he ushered her into the tent. He followed her, closing the flaps and meeting her gaze through the candlelight.

"So, tell me, gypsy," he murmured, helping her to sit on the silk pallet that lay on the floor. "What do you see for my future?"

"Really, sir," she huffed, her veil billowing out with the action. "I'm certain that we shouldn't be here. Someone is likely to be quite perturbed to find us making free with their lodgings."

"What if I were to tell you this tent belongs to me?" he said, unable to resist stroking his hands along her bare arms. "What if I told you it was my intent to you bring you here all along? What if I were to tell you I've fantasized about making love to you in a tent such as this? What if I were to share with you that I've dreamed of having you as my willing *Houri*, pleasuring me as I wish?"

"But how-" she broke off, her breathing heavy and her lined eyes wide as he let his fingers stroke her waist, then her hips.

"How did I know?" he asked, sliding the veil from her hair, slowly revealing the mass of red curls that burned like fire in the candlelight. "I would know you anywhere, gypsy," he whispered, bringing the head covering to his face and inhaling the familiar scent of her.

"Blaine," she whispered, running her hands through his hair. "This isn't the place for this."

"Then where is the right place?" he asked, lowering her face veil so that her nose, then her full, red lips were revealed in the candlelight. He studied her then, his gaze focused on the soft, succulent flesh of her mouth. He was so hungry for her, so damn tired of wanting and denying himself--of fearing his demons. "Tell me, *Rat Ki Rani*," he whispered against her lips, "tell me, and I will take you there."

He didn't give her time to answer him. He covered her mouth with his soft one and his tongue entered her in one swift move. She didn't resist him. Instead, she went soft and willing, her hands groping his hair, tugging him closer to her, her mouth widening, devouring him in a kiss that made him hunger more.

In a moment of despair, and perhaps absolute madness, he'd purchased the tent from one of the male gypsies. He'd been walking mindlessly around the grounds, that damn fortune teller's prophetic words ringing in his ears. He'd known on some level that tonight would be his only chance to have Madeline, to make her his. If he failed to let go of his fears and his demons this night, she would be lost to him forever. He knew that--believed that now, even as he'd tossed the gypsy a money pouch worth five times that of the tent's value.

His mouth slanted deeper on hers, and his fingers raked through her curls, dispelling pins to the ground as he shook her hair free. He wanted her. She was willing. And she was his. The tent was theirs, he'd planned to bring her there--somehow. He'd imagined it in his mind, making love to her in the tent, amongst the pillows and the silks and the incense. The time was right and he refused to listen to her pleas to the contrary or his demons that told him he was mad to be doing this.

Madeline felt her bones melt as Blaine pushed her back onto the pallet, her head and shoulders cushioned by the numerous pillows beneath her.

"This is our Harem, Madeline," he whispered against the swells of her breasts. "And you're my Mistress of the Night."

She nodded, her lips unable to utter one word save for a soft sigh as Blaine's fingers traced her body. Her skin tingled with unfamiliar longing. She felt restless somehow, as if his teasing touch only enflamed her desire instead of slaking it.

"Dear God, how I want you," he said, his voice nothing but a harsh groan. "You can have no idea."

"If it is anything like how I want you, my lord, it is very great, indeed."

His eyes met hers, burning a warm gray that she'd never seen before. His hands stilled on her belly, his finger tracing the outline of her navel.

"You know what I desire, do you not?" he asked, wetting his mouth, making her wish he'd stop talking and kiss her as he had earlier. "You know that I mean to make you mine tonight. That I shall never give you up once I have you."

"Yes," she said, closing her eyes as his hands cupped her breasts, then reached around to untie the bodice of her costume. "I will agree to anything, Blaine. I'll do whatever it takes to experience this with you. I want you."

"Do you want me enough to marry me, Madeline?" he asked, his eyes glowing almost blue as he revealed her breasts which were already full, the nipples straining for his touch.

"Yes."

"But will give up having children? Can you agree to that? I will not go further if you cannot. I will not sully you and leave you if it is a promise you cannot fulfill."

She stared into his eyes which dulled, the passion obviously lessening, giving way to the haunted coolness that so frequently flickered in his gaze. He was asking her to give up her dreams of being a mother. A dream she'd had since she was a young child herself. It was an enormous promise and one he would never dismiss. It would always be between them and yet, she couldn't imagine having to lay with Tynemouth--to make love with him in such a way in order to have children. Not when Blaine was here with her, making her feel alive and wanton. Madeline knew then that she had arrived at her answer. "I'll promise you anything if you'll only make love to me."

To her surprise, his fingers shook as he reached out and traced her nipple with the tip of his finger, the steeliness of his eyes slowly melted away. "I'll make you happy, Maddy. I swear it."

"I know," she moaned, feeling him suckle her as his hand skimmed her belly. His mouth was hot and insistent as he lowered himself atop her, his body hard and warm against her.

"You're beautiful, Maddy," he whispered, tracing her belly. Feeling something cool against her, she looked down in time to see him place the green gem that had been on her bodice into her navel. A wicked and satisfied smile came to his mouth as he traced her navel with a reverent finger. "Every Houri needs jewels," he whispered, before lowering his head to her belly. His breath was hot and soothing and arousing on her skin. His tongue came out to trace the circle of her navel and Madeline whimpered, raking her hands through his hair.

The candles continued to flicker, casting shadows on the canvas. The sounds of the gypsies playing their instruments wafted on the night air, the breeze, heavily scented with jasmine and anise drifted into the tent, making Madeline feel as if she were floating. The feel of Blaine's lips on her skin, his strong hands tugging at her skirts as the breeze whispered along her skin, made her feel light as a feather, as if she were disembodied somehow.

"Lovely," Blaine whispered as he revealed the thatch of red curls he'd only ever dreamed of seeing. His gaze lowered, taking in the firm white thighs and delicate ankle encircled with charms.

He looked up into Madeline's face and smiled, male satisfaction coursing within him as he realized she was giving herself up to his lovemaking. She'd agreed to his terms with only the briefest of hesitation. She'd freely, almost thoughtlessly given up her dreams in order to feel him inside her. She wanted him, and Lord how he wanted her.

He parted her thighs then, seeing that she was ready for him. Stroking his finger along her wetness, he peered into her face, grinning as her lips parted on a silent moan.

"You do not know how long I've waited for this--for you," he said, sliding his finger inside her, closing his eyes, he felt her tighten around his finger. "So many nights I've thought of you, and what it would be like to have you all to myself."

"I'm yours," she murmured, raking her nails along his shoulders. "And I think I've waited my lifetime for you, Blaine."

Shrugging out of his shirt and trousers, Blaine tossed the garments aside and rested his body along the length of Madeline. She gasped as his skin covered hers and moaned, fueling his desire further.

"Maddy, open for me."

She did as he commanded, and he settled himself between her thighs, taking her breast into his mouth, suckling her with all the desire he'd kept pent up for so many weeks--no, so many months.

"Blaine," Madeline purred, arching her back when he sucked and tugged at her nipple, before laving in it in soothing circles. "I have to feel you."

"Where?" He teased her with his hands. She jumped when she felt his fingers part her, panted in anticipation as he slid down her body, and nearly screamed as his mouth covered her, tasting her arousal.

"Blaine, you mustn't-"

"I must," he purred, licking and laving, driving her to the precipice of desire. "I simply must," he whispered again, before gaining control of her body, making her unable to think, but just simply feel.

He parted her sex with his thumbs and he stared at the pink silk, taking in every inch of her, not wanting to miss anything about this night. She was so wet, her lips swollen with her arousal. He kissed the pouting bud of flesh, then licked the length of her until he reached the narrowing opening of her body. He slipped his tongue inside, thrusting in and out as he swirled his thumb along the sensitive nub.

"Blaine," she cried, grasping a handful of his hair. "Oh, God," she keened, arching beneath him, her ankle bracelet tinkling in the quiet as she lifted her knees and rocked her hips.

He felt her become wetter, and he replaced his tongue with two fingers and began to swirl his tongue with earnest along her clitoris until she was gasping and shaking. "Come for me, Maddy," he encouraged between flicks of his tongue. "Let me taste you in my mouth. Give me all of you."

And then she stiffened beneath him, and her head arched back, and he watched her in the throes of her orgasm as he continued to tongue her sex and finger her opening. And as he watched her, he felt his cock swell further. He was painfully aroused and he needed release, the kind of release only Madeline could give him.

As she writhed and panted beneath him, he slipped his hand from her breast and reached for his cock, stroking it like he always did, with tantalizing slowness. He would come too soon if he went any faster, and he wanted to prolong his pleasure until he built hers back up.

"Blaine," His name was more a question than statement, and her voice full of languid passion aroused him further. "Then her gaze slipped down to his hand and she watched him, unashamed, and curious as he masturbated before her.

"Do you know how many times I've pleasured myself like this and thought of you?" he asked. Her eyes widened and she wet her lip, studying the way he stroked his cock. "Look at it," he commanded, and she did, and he swelled further.

"Is this what you need? You need this inside you? Do you need me?" She nodded, and he felt a dribble of come seep out. "Then take it," he said and she reached between their bodies and wrapped her fingers around his shaft, stroking him as if she were a professional courtesan. Faster and faster, she gripped him and he watched her, getting hotter and hotter with every stroke. He was so close, so close to spilling himself onto her hand. But he didn't want it that way. He wanted to get inside her. To feel her body mold around him.

"I can't wait. I know this won't be as good for you, but I can't wait."

And then he was filling her, sliding into her and stretching her so that all she could feel was him. With a forceful thrust he was inside her, his whispered words soothing her until he began to move. His honeyed words gave way to heated demands that she wrap her legs around him, that she drive her little nails into his shoulders and that she not hide her cries of passion from him, but pant and moan and tell him what she felt and what she wanted.

He felt wonderfully hard, filling her as he moved atop her, his body firmly muscled and warm and powerful as he held her in his arms, his strokes deep and masterful. Soon, any pain she had felt was gone, replaced with a languorous wonder as she found and matched his rhythm, letting herself be free to simply let Blaine make love to her.

When the rhythm became faster, more forceful, she scored his back with her nails and raised her hips, allowing him more control over her body.

"Too soon," he groaned, the veins of his neck full and tight and then she felt him stiffen, felt the jolt of him deep inside, a trickle of heat engulfed her before he could pull out of her body, emptying himself onto her belly. She watched his seed spurt on her flesh, and he groaned, pumping himself onto her. "So damn good," he chanted, until his seed stopped and he collapsed atop her.

"Maddy," he kissed her neck then her breasts as he gathered her close in his arms. "We have to leave tonight."

"Hmm," she murmured, feeling utterly sated and comfortable in the cocoon of his arms.

"I simply cannot go another night without you. We have to leave tonight. I have to make you my wife."

"You're going to miss the Gypsy Auction," she teased, ruffling his hair and kissing his forehead.

"To hell with the auction, Madam. I've found the gypsy I've been looking for and I'm never giving her up."

"Indeed?" she asked, feeling coy and mighty satisfied with herself and the way she was able to arouse Blaine's desires.

"Indeed, Madam," he said, before kissing her soundly. "And I fear that if we do not remove ourselves from this tent, I might have to have my way with you again."

"That doesn't sound so very bad."

"No? Then let me tempt you to stay then, gypsy."

Blaine's last thought as he slid once more into Madeline's welcoming body was that he'd never experienced such a feeling of pure joy while at the same time fearing for what the future may hold.

He'd done it. He'd made Madeline's his, for all time. For better or for worse. It was his dream and yet, it might very well prove to be his worst nightmare.

Chapter Seventeen

Scouring the evening paper, Blaine reached for his valerian tea and grimaced at the taste. He'd let it grow cold in the half hour since Ringwald had brought it to him. In fact, he hadn't read more than a paragraph of the newssheet before him. His thoughts were elsewhere--in particular, on a weeping wife currently barricaded in her room.

With a grunt of disgust he clinked the cup into its saucer and folded the paper. The day had been nothing short of a disaster. He and Madeline had been married less than two days and already the union was rocking on its foundation. It had nothing to do with him, or rather, what lurked within him. No, the problem lay with Penrick, Madeline's furious and indignant father.

The earl was less than happy that his aspirations for a union between Madeline and Tynemouth was over. A union, he had informed Madeline, that he'd spent weeks attempting to bring about. Blaine could still hear the earl's words ringing clearly through the paneled walls of the study.

"Damn me, Madeline, don't tell me you've been so stupid as to cast aside a suitable candidate such as Tynemouth in order to marry a man you know nothing about."

Madeline had argued his case well enough, pleading with her father to understand that this marriage between them was what she had wanted. But the earl clearly hadn't been satisfied with her testimony that she would be happy.

"What do you know of him besides the fact he's considered odd and if I may so, exceedingly rude?"

Blaine had bristled at that. He nearly charged into the study to retrieve his wife and leave Penrick to suffer an apoplexy, but he had thought better of it. Such actions would only confirm Penrick's suspicions about him and one thing he couldn't afford was the influential earl nosing about his private affairs. There was no telling what he would say to Madeline after he learned his lackluster son-in-law was a halfwit idiot.

Shaking himself out of his musing, Blaine tried to forget the sound of Penrick's voice, loud and furious as he'd tossed Madeline out of his study and his life. *"You can damn well make your own way in the world after this business, young lady. And you needn't expect so much as a guinea from me for support of Montgomery House."*

And that had been the end of it. And here *he* was, well past midnight, hiding out in his own study, not knowing how to comfort the woman he'd just married.

Damn it, he truly was a bastard. He'd ruined her, taken her virginity, married her without any thought to her future and without her father's consent. What the devil had gotten into him?

"Blaine?" His breath hitched when he saw Madeline, looking frail and pale faced, gliding into his study. "Aren't you coming to bed?"

He swallowed hard, feeling a suffocating tightening in his chest. God she was beautiful, despite her red-rimmed eyes and tear stained cheeks. He was more fortunate than he ever dared to dream, but his prosperity came with a price--Madeline's happiness.

He watched her near him, wearing nothing but her soft lawn wrapper. She smiled at him, that same welcome smile she'd given him when he'd slipped his ring on her finger. He winced as he thought of all Madeline had given up when she'd agreed to become his countess.

"When did you start to wear spectacles?" she asked, situating her rounded bottom on his desk then running her fingers through his hair. Jesus, her touch set him on fire. He wanted her. But tonight was not the night, she was likely exhausted from their trip home. And if the carriage ride hadn't fatigued her, the hours of endless crying in her room surely had.

"You look pale, Blaine. Are you well?"

He closed his eyes as she raked her fingers once more in his hair. He had a touch of the headache and his eyes did feel tired, but none the worse for wear. No, he was feeling rather fit, nothing to warn him of an impending seizure, just a little unsettled in his thoughts of Madeline.

He'd refused to think of his current situation as he went about his business, but now, with Madeline seated on the edge of his desk, her knee brushing his hand reminding him of what they had shared and the new bond between them, Blaine couldn't help but be reminded of his precarious position and his one nagging question.

Did she regret her hasty agreement to wed him? The thought tore him apart, and he closed his eyes once more, refusing to look into those open and honest green eyes.

"You must forgive me for my depressing display of emotion. Normally I'm not so ... so vocal."

Vocal didn't quite define Madeline in the throws of uninhibited weeping.

"My father-"

He put his finger to her mouth, preventing her from speaking, stopping her from thinking she needed to explain herself. "I had no right to marry you without your father's permission. In that he was correct. What I did was dishonorable, Madeline. I should never have made love to you then whisked you away to get married by special license."

Eyes wide, they immediately started to glimmer with tears. "You regret it so soon?"

"Madeline," he murmured, pulling her off the desk only to sit her atop it once again in front of him. "I do not regret anything, my sweet. But you must see that I was in the wrong. No gentleman wants his daughter to be wed in such a manner."

"Would you make your daughter-" The words froze mid-sentence as she realized what she was saying. "Well the whole matter is terribly old fashioned."

And suddenly he felt even more uncomfortable then he had with just having to hear Madeline weep, for now he was confronted with the true anguish that filled her. He'd made her promise she would not ask him for children. She'd known his stipulation prior to letting him seduce her. It had all been well and good in the darkness, with lust coursing through their veins, but now, in quiet reality--in light of her father's warnings, perhaps she was wavering in her decision.

And could he blame her?

She'd caught herself just as she'd begun to talk of their children, children they would never have. What sort of selfish bastard had he been to make her promise such a thing? She adored children, he knew that. She wanted a house full of them, and he had known that too, but still it hadn't stopped him from taking it away from her.

She kissed his forehead, only to rest her cheek against him. "It won't happen again, I promise you. I was just saying--that is, I haven't forgotten--

"It's all right, Madeline, no harm done. In time it will no longer even matter will it, hmm?"

He looked up at her and felt regret pierce him. The rational part of her understood that he would never father children, the romantic, passionate side was still grappling with the enormity of her promise to him. He really shouldn't have done it and yet if he hadn't made her promise him, he wouldn't have her as his countess. She wouldn't be here in his house, sitting on his desk wearing nothing more then a thin wrapper.

He should be feeling heartily devious, and yet he couldn't summon the feelings of regret. The only thing he felt was the extreme pleasure of having her as his wife and having the soft feel of her body pressed against his.

Reaching for her, he untied the belt of her wrapper. "Let us put this day behind us."

She nodded and sat back, pressing her weight on her wrists as he parted the wrapper and bared her naked body to his gaze. His eyes raked hotly over her heavy, rounded breasts, the coral nipples puckered and hard, waiting for his mouth. His gaze roamed lower, to the mound of her belly and the red curls that lay between her thighs. He spread her legs and ran a finger down the soft thatch of curls, his cock immediately hardening. He lowered his head and inhaled her scent as he kissed the silky patch of skin on the inside of her thigh. "Maddy," he said against her thigh, and she sighed and ran her fingers through his hair. "I want you to know that you needn't worry about Montgomery House. I'll support it. I'll give you whatever it takes to keep it going. You mustn't worry about what your father said."

"Blaine," she moaned when he palmed her other leg and kissed a trail up to her breasts. "You needn't think-" she arched her back and he circled her erect nipple with the tip of his tongue. Her breath hissed between her lips and he felt her shaking fingers rake through his hair, felt her green eyes watching him love her.

He captured his gaze and purposely flicked her nipple with his tongue, it hardened further for him and she stirred restlessly atop the desk. He built her up, and holding her gaze he slipped the nipple into his mouth and suckled her, all the while encouraging her to watch.

"My lord," she panted, trying to speak. But he captured one full breast in his hand and squeezed, shaping her to his palm and he suckled her nipple, making her break off in short panting phrases. "That is to say, you don't have to feel you need to support--that is," she whimpered, "I'll find a way to keep the house. It's only a matter of time before I start seeing profits from the Morning Lane Project."

"Consider it a wedding gift."

She arched further, filling his mouth with her hard nipple. His hand reached between their bodies and he stroked her, feeling the wetness that was between her thighs. Leaving her breast, he continued to hold her gaze while he kissed a trail down her torso and belly to the goal he wanted most of all. With deliberate slowness, he raked his tongue from the bottom of her sex to the top and saw that she was watching him lave her. He licked her slowly, thoroughly, like a cat licking its paw, and he saw that her body was trembling and her arousal was heavier the longer he worked her. As she watched each stroke of his tongue she panted, an erotic mewling sound that sent his desire near the edge.

Close to finding her release, he left her and brought his lips to her neck, below her ear. "Take my cock out and look at it, Madeline."

She did as he asked, and Madeline could not stop thinking how delightfully soft the skin was. He was thick and hard, the head of his phallus dark with blood. The tip was glistening, and she suddenly wanted to do more than feel him, she wanted to taste him, as he had her. She wanted to know if she would like the feel of him in her mouth as much as he liked to taste her. She wanted him to *watch her*.

"Up and down," he commanded and his gaze slipped to where her hand curled around his shaft. "Up and down and tight, as if I were inside you."

She found a rhythm he liked and soon she had him panting and palming her breast in growing passion. His thumb and finger rolled her nipple, sending sharp sparks to her belly, and she arched, tightening her grip on him. He hissed and moved his hips, and she felt a drop trickle onto her finger and before she could guess his intent, he took her hand and brought it to her sex, where he brushed her aching flesh with the tip of his erection.

She arched against the exquisite sensation and she lifted her hips, wanting him to continue his caress. "You look so beautiful, flushed with arousal," he groaned, and she watched him stroke himself against her flesh. "I've never felt this, Madeline. I've never needed a woman as much as I need you." Straightening, he took his erection in his hand. "Put me inside you," he whispered harshly against her mouth. She did and closed her eyes. "No, Madeline. You will watch as I enter you. You will see me become part of you."

Her eyes flew open and she watched his thick shaft slide into her body and she moaned, savoring the feel of her stretching to accommodate him. His gaze was fixed on where their bodies joined and slowly he thrust into her, his pace slow and unhurried, as if he had all the time in the world to make love to her. As if they were on a bed and not atop a desk. His hands skimmed up to her hips, showing her the rhythm he wanted. She learned it and when she was matching his slow thrusts, he captured her breasts in his hands and fondled them, his fingers brushing and rolling over her nipples so that she was mindless with need, begging him to hurry as she watched the erotic dance of his phallus entering and retreating from her.

"I hurried the first time, love, but I won't tonight. Tonight you will learn what it is to shake with need."

"I do need you," she panted, wrapping her hand around his neck and bringing his lips to her mouth. " I need you so much, Blaine."

He kissed her, his tongue mating with hers, his fingers busy arousing her, his phallus sliding teasingly slow in and out of her body. And then she jerked against him, stilling. But he would not let her stop. Instead, he tugged at her nipple and thrust into her. He reached for her hips and brought them hard against him. His kiss turned hungrier, more carnal, and she couldn't keep up the pace. She didn't know what she wanted. She was reaching for something that was so foreign and frightening. She didn't have control over her mind or her body and it terrified her. But he kept her safe and soon she was shaking in his arms and tears were in her eyes and she didn't know why she was crying. She just knew that she felt shattered and desired, and it was the most wonderful, contented feeling ever.

With one last thrust, he surged into her, forcing himself to the hilt inside her. With a savage moan, he pulled out and she watched his essence spurt out of his body as he spilled himself on her. His hot seed splashed beneath her breasts and trickled sensuously down her belly. She felt his finger glide along her nipple and she looked down to see that he was brushing a drop of the white liquid along her erect nipple.

"I've marked you, Madeline. You belong to me now. Whatever happens, you will always belong to me."

"Yes," she murmured against the top of his head. And she brushed her fingers against his and felt his seed against her skin and his hand. He covered her other breast with his essence and she couldn't help but notice how he watched his hands covering her.

"I can bathe you like this every night, and maybe it will be enough," he whispered, and she wasn't certain if she was meant to have heard him. "I can give you life this way," he murmured, nuzzling her neck and rubbing his hand along her wet belly. It will be enough," he said fiercely, clutching her to him. "I will make it so that you will be satisfied and never have a regret."

And then he captured her mouth again and she felt his erection, full and hard again, nudging her opening. He pressed her back so that she was laying flat on her back and he covered her glistening breasts with his hands and thrust into her, taking her hard, and making her body tighten and coil beyond what she thought she could endure.

"Blaine!" she cried, but he kept up the pace, driving her to the brink.

"Say you want this, say you I haven't turned you away from me."

"I want this! *Oh God, Blaine!*" she cried when he began to flick the swollen nub at the crest of her curls. And then he stopped and pulled her up so that she was sitting and staring into his gray eyes that now shone a pale blue.

"Make love to me, Maddy. Show me what it is like."

She didn't know what he wanted, but he showed her. He sat in the chair and brought her down atop him. Cupping her bottom he showed her how to ride him and when she had the right of it, she caught his hands in hers and clutched them tight. She captured his gaze, holding it as she loved him, and she thought she saw his eyes fill with more than desire. She thought she saw love shining back at her, but then he blinked it away and reached for her and slid himself out of her body, emptying his seed on to his own belly. He clutched her to him and he held on to her like a drowning man holds on to a lifeline.

"Mine," he whispered into her hair and she knew then that she was his lifeline in a sense. Something profound had happened. It had been more than sex or making love. He had given everything to her this night, and she would hold the memories close to her heart forever.

* * * *

"Blaine?"

Madeline sat up in bed and brushed her hair from her face. It was still dark outside, but she could see the pale blue streak of light in the distance, heralding the dawn.

"Blaine?" she asked again, peering through the murky darkness in her room. "Are you unwell?" She thought she'd heard him pacing the floor a while ago, but she'd been so languorously sated that she hadn't been able to open one eyelid. Blaine's lovemaking had that effect on her. It always filled her with warmth and comfort. He was so kind and gentle, always concerned for her. She smiled as she thought of him. *Am I too rough? Do you like this, my sweet? I'm going to come....* Her face flamed when she thought of that, and what she had been doing when he'd said it. How savagely beautiful he had looked as she brought him to climax with her mouth. How he panted and writhed as she captured his erection between her breasts and allowed him, in his words, 'to come all over you'. The memory sent a ripple of heat and desire through her. She had never thought to desire such things, she had not even known such passion could be found with a man.

Straightening in the bed, she reached out a hand and instantly met with something cold and sticky. Her spirits sunk as she recalled what it was.

She wasn't such a simpleton to not understand how children were conceived. For heavens sake, she ran a home for women who'd gotten with child--several of whom had been prostitutes. She knew perfectly well that a man had to spend his seed inside a woman for a child to grow. Blaine *had* given her his seed. He had poured it over her body, laving her with it and giving her soft, arousing, titillating words as he did it. He was very inventive with his seed and she was not averse to what he had done. In fact, it had been highly arousing, the feel of his seed, hot and thick coating her skin. And there was no denying that he always looked lethally sexy as he'd done it. But he had not given her his seed as a man does woman, or a husband does a wife. He'd given it her body, but not inside her. It was a stark reminder he didn't want children.

Contentment soon gave way to frustration as she thought of the promise she'd given her husband. She'd promised not to beg him for children--promised not to plead with him to change his mind-- in fact, she'd vowed not to even mention them. She had wanted him so desperately that night at Lady Brookehaven's that she would have promised the devil her soul for but one night in Blaine's arms, and she did not regret it, not a bit. But she did wonder at his steadfastness to avoid fatherhood. She questioned his motives even as she thought of ways to make him change his mind. Surely as an earl he had no wish to see his title pass on to his nephew. He must want a child of his own--a child with her.

The stomping on the stairs pulled her from her thoughts and she slid out of bed, donned her wrapper and reached for the connecting door of their chambers. It was locked.

"Blaine?" she asked, hastily tying the sash around her waist before shimmying the latch. "Are you in there? Open the door."

No answer came, but she heard more stomping and what she thought was Blaine's valet, Ringwald, in the hall. Padding over to the door, Madeline opened it and peered into the hall. It was dark and devoid of activity. Straightening, she took a step forward, shrieking as she met the stony face of Blaine's valet.

"May I be of some service, my lady?"

Madeline licked her lips and grasped the collar of her wrapper while she smoothed her disheveled curls with her hand. "I, er, that is I thought I heard some commotion in the hall. I was searching for his lordship."

Ringwald's eyes blinked slowly, the only part of him to show any outward signs of life. "I'm afraid that his lordship is indisposed, madam."

"Do you mean ill? I must go to him, then. Is he in need of something?"

Ringwald's iron grip grasped her wrist, effectively halting her from taking one step. "His lordship has asked that I see to your comfort, madam. Is there something I may get you?"

"I want to see my husband," she sputtered, not liking the sinking feeling in her stomach. Something was wrong, she knew it--felt it.

"I'm afraid his lordship is feeling under the weather. He is not fit for guests."

"I'm his *wife,*" she spat, attempting to twist her way out of Ringwald's vice-like grip.

"Ringwald," a voice called out from Blaine's chamber. "Here. Now."

"Sterling?" Madeline breathed, unable to credit seeing the butler's head peering out of her husband's bedchamber.

Ringwald nodded to the butler and pushed her back into her room. "Now then, Madam, if you do not require anything at the moment, I'll see to his lordship."

"I want to see my husband," she stated, rubbing the stinging skin of her wrists. "*Now,* Ringwald. I am not a guest in this household, I am his wife." And, she thought silently, she had the marks to prove it.

With a polite bow, the valet backed away and reached for the door. "His lordship has requested that you be kept from his room. He fears this illness might be of the catching kind and he does not want you unwittingly exposed to it. Good night, madam."

With a quiet click, Madeline found herself locked in her room, confused and frightened.

* * * *

"Let me look upon you," Phoebe smiled as she clasped her hands around Madeline's face. "Marriage agrees with you, Dearest, you're positively glowing. I take it his lordship is taking very good care of you?"

Madeline felt her face flame and looked away from Phoebe's all too knowing gaze. "His lordship is very attentive."

"You're looking radiant, but I see something in your eyes. Care to talk about it?"

Madeline shrugged and allowed Phoebe to guide her to the settee. Once she was settled, she accepted a cup of tea and mindlessly stirred the frothy bubbles about the cup.

"Your father was just here," Phoebe murmured around the rim of her cup. "He just left, in fact. He looked terrible, Madeline. When is this feud going to stop between the two of you?"

"I did not start this feud, as you term it. Father did. I have no quarrel with him, but he seems to have taken exception to my husband."

"You must understand the shock your papa must have felt at learning you'd eloped with Hardcastle. You must give him time, Madeline."

Madeline shrugged and sipped her tea. She didn't like what her father had said about her husband and she hadn't liked how he treated her, either. But she did miss him, these past few weeks had been the hardest in that respect. If her father would only concede that she'd done the right thing by marrying Blaine, if he would only realize that Blaine was a good man, that he'd been wrong to accuse Hardcastle of making her a bad husband, she would forgive him completely.

However, she had grudgingly admitted that it would be quite a blow to a father to learn that his responsible, level headed daughter had run off in the middle of the night with the most notoriously mysterious man of the ton.

Phoebe reached for her hand and squeezed it affectionately. "What worries you, Dearest? You're not yourself."

Madeline shrugged off the memories of her father and his hateful words as she stared into her steaming tea. She wasn't herself. She was lost and confused. She didn't know how to make the situation with her father better and now she had to deal with the strange happenings in the house she shared with her husband

and the fact that Blaine was distancing himself from her. The intimacy of their first few days as a married couple were all but gone and in their place was a polite and cordial relationship that lacked the spark and fire of those first few nights.

"You're not going to turn missish on me, are you? I thought you were well passed the green girl stage, even when you were a green girl." Phoebe straightened and tipped Madeline's chin up with her fingers. "He's not mistreated you has he? He hasn't forced you or done anything you haven't wanted."

"No," she shook her head and looked away from Phoebe's gaze.

"But he's demanding in his passion, is he not?" Phoebe asked. "His passionate nature is exerting itself? Does it frighten you, Dearest?"

Madeline grinned, thinking that the last thing she felt around Blaine was fear. She loved his passion, and his desire and urges fueled her own. She had reveled in their passionate, heated couplings and only wondered why their nights of hot loving had fizzled to nothing but polite, chaste kisses before bed. He had desired her. Now, she was no longer certain.

At last she met Phoebe's concerned gaze. "There is a problem," she murmured, wondering where to start. "Hardcastle hasn't been himself for a fortnight. He's very secretive and aloof. Sometimes at night I can hear the servants scurrying about like mice below stairs. I've heard strange noises, like someone is struggling to breath, or a strangled cry that rents through the middle of the night. Whenever I attempt to investigate the matter, Ringwald, Hardcastle's valet refuses to let me out of my room. He says my husband has taken ill. I'm never allowed to comfort him, or see to his needs. In fact, I don't see him for days and then when I do, he's pale and tired and he ushers me out of his study. He refuses to discuss the matter, saying it's a stomach ailment, or some other such nonsense. Phoebe," Madeline reached for her friend's hand. "He doesn't want … er … that is he won't-"

"He is no longer amorous?" Phoebe supplied.

Madeline nodded and hid her blush. It was the truth, her husband no longer wanted her. They hadn't shared a bed in more than a week. In fact, he'd barely even given her more than a cool peck of a kiss before sending her on her way to her bedroom alone.

"Perhaps it is some sort of ailment he's contracted. Men never want to appear weak, Madeline. You've been married such a short time, I'm quite certain Hardcastle has no wish for his new bride to see him in such a state."

"I can understand that part, but how do you explain the fact that he no longer wishes my company in bed? He was so eager before," and then she trailed off and stared out the window of the salon. "He blatantly refuses to discuss children, or the matters between us."

"Is it the lack of your, er … nocturnal activities, or is there something in particular that is bothering you in regards to the matter?"

She hadn't a mother and her friends were too innocent to understand what she was trying to say. Only Phoebe could help her through this murky maze of marital intimacies.

Taking a steadying breath, she blindly plunged in. "My husband refuses to have children, he will not talk of them, nor will he tolerate any discussion of them. He takes precautions when we are intimate, and I'm afraid that my breasts or my belly, and occasionally our bedsheets are the recipient of his seed."

There she said it. She refused to look at Phoebe, she was too afraid and embarrassed to see what her admission had done to her friend. But what else could she do, she simply had no other female acquaintance to talk to about such matters.

" I see," Phoebe said, straightening further in her chair, her mouth pinched into a hard line. "And this … his actions shame and humiliate you. That is the problem, correct? You feel, you feel…." Phoebe swallowed hard and stared down into her lap. "His actions make you feel like a cheap whore, to be used as he wishes."

"Heavens, no!" Madeline protested, reaching for Phoebe's hand. "In truth, I find it … er…." she blushed, but pressed on. "I find it highly arousing. He is very caring and loving during our sessions, and after," Madeline flushed further, remembering how he lovingly covered her with his seed. How he always whispered against her skin that he was bathing her with his life. There was a connection between them when he did this. She longed for it, craved it, but she still worried over the words and the way he held himself back, not truly giving himself to her in the height of his passion.

"You're disturbed about this."

"Well, yes, I'm disturbed," she hissed, feeling impatient and frustrated and confused. "He's an earl for Heaven's sake, he *must* want an heir. But he refuses to discuss the matter, I don't even know why he doesn't want children, all I know is that he won't capitulate on the matter."

"And what is it you seek, Dearest? What is it you want me to tell you?"

Madeline turned teary eyes to her friend. She hadn't meant to cry, but all the frustrations and fears of the past two weeks came to a head, and she needed the release. "How do I please him, Phoebe? How do I get him back into my bed and how do I change his mind and make him love me, when he won't listen to reason?"

"I don't have those answers, Dearest," Phoebe purred, wiping Madeleine's tears from her cheeks. "I can only tell you how to pleasure him, to make him mindless with need so that he might at the very least lose control."

"Tell me," Madeline pled, squeezing Phoebe's hand between hers. "You must tell me."

"It is never wise to start a marriage with deceit. While I do not pretend to know the intricacies of your marriage, I do have the feeling that there is more here then you are telling me. I'm warning you that a man like Hardcastle will not appreciate such tactics. It might make matters worse, Dearest. Can you not try talking to him once more?"

"I've talked till I'm blue in the face, he won't listen," Madeline cried. "Please Phoebe, I know what I'm doing. Please believe me. Help me to seduce my husband."

"Very well," Phoebe sighed, "but never let it be said that I didn't warn you. I've seen what deception can do to a couple. I've come between more husbands and wives then I care to recall. I'd hate to be the reason behind the destruction of your marriage."

"You won't, Phoebe. Hardcastle will never know. And it's worth the risk, it is, I know it. He'll appreciate my efforts in the end."

"Tell me, Dearest, in the end, what will your efforts bring you?"

"A child. And my husband's love."

Chapter Eighteen

The Minx was up to no good.

The thought finally registered in Blaine's heated brain after Madeline 'accidentally' brushed his thigh for the third time in less than half an hour. Each time her delicate fingers had come closer to his stirring, not to mention rampant manhood.

Good God, what was she about teasing him here of all places? There was a sea of people surrounding them. Anyone might notice her hand on his thigh, or the way her slippered foot slid along his shin. No, a public box at Vauxhall Gardens was not the place to have your thigh stroked by your very tempting wife.

"I do believe you're correct, Reanleigh. You bloody well can see through it," Bathurst drawled, holding a slivered piece of ham up to the moonlight.

"We're here for the fireworks and the music, not the table fare," Isabella chided her husband. "Besides, you can't be all that hungry, you had at least three helpings at supper."

"I have large appetites," Bathurst said with a leer, before popping the ham into his mouth.

"As do I," Madeline purred, sliding closer to Blaine, running her fingertips along his thigh. Blaine caught her hand beneath the table before she reached the bulge in his trousers. Good God, he was about to explode. If she licked her lips one more time he was going to toss her over his shoulder and carry her back to the carriage. Did she have any idea what she was doing to him? After nearly two weeks of abstinence, his body was clamoring for release. The release that only came with sinking himself into his wife's soft and welcoming body.

"It's very warm, isn't it?" Madeline asked, fanning her bosom with her hand. Blaine couldn't help but watch that delicate hand as it whispered slowly back and forth and over the exposed mounds of her breasts, of which, the bodice of her French gown did little to hide. "Wouldn't you agree, my lord?"

"Huh?" The word was a strangled huff, torn from his throat when one of her fingers traced the length of him through his trousers. Thank God the table was shielding them and thank God no one but Madeline could see the reaction her boldness was having on him.

"Are you warm, too?" she asked, looking up at him through her veil of copper lashes. *Warm?* Sweet Jesus, he was on fire. When her hand slipped through his and cupped him, he pulled at his cravat, forcing himself not to groan or buck his hips against her palm.

"Perhaps a little stroll might cool me down." Madeline said, rising from her chair. "Would you care to join me?"

It was a blatant invitation. He knew one when he heard it and he was most eager to accept this one. There was something about Madeline seducing him in a public place that stirred his imagination--and his cock. Hell, there was something about Madeline just seducing him that ignited his fantasies. He wasn't about to pass up the opportunity to see what the little minx had in store for him.

A loud crack rent the air then, followed by a red streak through the black sky. Appreciative gasps and whistles from the crowd followed the glittering streak. All eyes immediately became fixated on the horizon. All except Madeline and Blaine's, which stood staring fixedly at each other. Blaine felt his breathing quicken as Madeline pointedly gazed at his erection.

"Well, what say you, my lord, are you game?"

He fairly jumped out of his chair and reached for her hand. "I'm more than game, madam. I'll meet you and best you at any game you've decided upon."

* * * *

"Jesus, Madeline, where the devil are you going?" Blaine fought the crowd in order to reach his wife.

She smiled over her shoulder, hurrying her pace. "Catch me and I'll show you."

"It's black as pitch and you're heading toward the Dark Walk, you know. You can have no idea what sort of devious activities take place there."

"I know of one such activity."

He growled low in his throat and tried to ignore the stirring in his britches. If he was ever going to be fortunate enough to get a hold of his wife, he was going to punish her mercilessly for her teasing. Pleasant visions clouded his mind as to just what sort of punishment he was going to subject to her.

"Are you coming?" she teased, her green eyes flashing at him.

"Oh, I plan to," he drawled, finally reaching out and grasping her about her arm. She had no way of knowing the crudeness of his thoughts. But damn it all he was fired up. There was a dangerous level of lust coursing through his veins and it had nothing to do with tender loving and everything to do with fierce passions. She damn well shouldn't have decided to play the wanton in a public place if she didn't want every wicked thought running through his head.

He pulled her along the walk, away from the crowds. His breathing was fast and Madeline's was coming in short, husky pants that drove him wild. It was the sort of sound she made beneath him when he was thrusting into her.

"My lord, wherever are you taking me?" she asked in feigned ignorance that sent his lust spiraling out of control. "Sir, you must know I'm not that sort of lady."

He pulled her to a stop, leaned against the stone wall and brought her up against him. "I know precisely what sort of lady you are, madam."

"Milord, I fear you've got this all wrong."

"Have I?" He tugged her bodice down, growing painfully hard when her firm breasts bobbed free of the silk. "I think not, my lady. You toyed with me back at our box. You've whipped me to a fever pitch and now you're going to get exactly what you want."

"And what is it you think I wish for, milord?" she purred as he palmed her breast before tweaking her nipple.

"My cock inside you, giving you what you want in a dark alley."

"Blaine," she cried before he took her mouth in his and devoured her with his tongue.

He wanted her with a frantic passion he didn't know he was capable of. Her teasing and taunting had driven him mad and the fact she was participating in this very risky act of loving fueled his desire further. She was every man's dream--the beautiful, adoring wife by day, the fiery courtesan by night. He truly couldn't have found more happiness in another.

"Maddy," he groaned, tearing his mouth from hers, loving the way she pulled his cravat from around his neck before furiously unbuttoning his shirt. "My, God, I want you."

"Do you like this?" she asked against his skin before flicking his nipple with her tongue. "Is this one of the devious activities you were talking about? Or is this?"

He sucked in his breath as she stroked her hand up the front of his bulging trousers before unfastening the flap and freeing him into her hand. She worked him, her tiny hand pumping up and down with just the right amount of pressure--the way he'd shown her. He felt himself swell further, and his hips bucked forward as he took both breasts into his hands. He bent his head to lick each pebbled nipple.

"Mmm," she purred, gripping him harder, stroking him faster so that he could a trickle of come seep out. "I do so love to feel your tongue on me. All over, my lord," she cooed, brushing her breasts along his face, " put your lips and tongue all over me."

Her heated words pushed him on, and he suckled her fiercely, while he palmed her other breast--hard--not giving a damn if someone could hear them or not. He wanted her--right here in the Dark Walk, her back against the stone wall, her thighs surrounding his waist, her cries splintering the quiet.

"Let me feel you," he murmured against her breast, his fingers searching for the hem of skirts. "I have to feel you, Maddy. I want to know how wet you are for me."

"*Very*," she demurred, "I'm drenched with my desire for you. I'm thinking of you hard and hot between my thighs," she teased, sliding her breasts along his chest and belly, her hard nipples tickling him. He could feel the wetness from his tongue clinging to her nipples as she teased them along his skin. It sent a fierce possessiveness coursing through him, reminding him of how she belonged to him, and only him.

She moved lower, her lips nuzzling his bared belly and navel, all the while her delicate little fingers curled around him, making him throb harder, making him want to explode all over her hand.

"Oh God, yes," he cried, stabbing his fingers through her hair as she went to her knees. "Take me into your mouth, minx, and show me how much you want this."

He groaned heavily, feeling the velvety wetness of her mouth engulf him. It was like nothing he'd ever felt before. It was urgent, hot, as if she needed him as much as he needed her. He wanted her--and if the way she sucking him was any indication, she wanted him too.

"You're good," he groaned, raking his fingers through her thick hair. He felt his body start to stiffen, the familiar rush of joy swimming in his veins.

"Do you need to come?" she asked in a throaty whisper, right before taking the length of him in her mouth.

Oh God, yes, his mind shouted as he watched her suck the length of him. He wanted to come, he wanted her to taste him, he wanted to feel himself pulsating in her mouth as he emptied himself.

"Tell me," she whispered again, "tell me where you want to come. My belly?" She licked him and swirled the tip of her around the head of his cock. "My breasts," his gaze lowered to her rounded breasts that were swinging with her movements and he captured them in his hands and let go of them with a small, gentle slap, watching as they swayed faster. She purred as he repeated the motion, this time a little faster, a little harder, and his cock swelled further in her hand. "My throat?" she asked, her hot breath caressing his shaft, forcing his gaze away from her breasts only to see her tongue curl around the rimmed cap of his cock. "My mouth," she teased in a deep, wanton whisper.

He closed his eyes and wrapped his hand in her hair. "Yes," he said, filling her mouth with his cock. "Your pretty mouth."

She took him between her lips, her rhythm slow and erotic, and he watched her, and he wanted it so bad, but he wanted something else, something that kept building deep inside the longer he watched her work him.

"Stop, my sweet. You must. I'm so close and I don't want it like this tonight."

She took him into her mouth again, greedily licking the length of him, laving his shaft in curling licks and gazing up into his eyes so that all he could see was her on her knees before him, loving him like a beautiful, wanton *Houri.*

Their eyes met and held and she smiled, right before flicking her tongue up the length of him and watching his reaction while she did it. Nothing made him quite so aroused as Maddy's jeweled eyes challenging him to lose control. And then she took the whole length of him in her mouth and pumped him with her hand and sucked--hard.

"I have to be inside you, now," he bit out between set teeth. "I want to … I *have* to come inside you."

He lifted her up and braced her against the wall, one leg hooked around his waist. He bared her to his eyes and he stared at her wet sex while he fingered her for a long while, taunting her with teasing slowness. She writhed against him, and he felt her damp skirts brush his hand. She was wanton and hot, and he wanted to take her hard, especially when she mewled softly and pushed her wet sex against his probing fingers.

"Look at me." She did, her beautiful eyes glazed with passion and need. "Watch." And then he sunk himself to the hilt inside her tight, wet sheath in one powerful stroke. Her eyes widened and her lips parted on a silent moan. "So damn beautiful, and you're mine," he whispered, holding her gaze, watching the tremors of pleasure flicker along her face with every one of his thrusts. "You're all mine, aren't you, Maddy? Just mine."

"Yes," she breathed against his neck, her pants matching the rhythm of his strokes.

"Forever, Madeline?" he asked, mindless with need, careless with his words as he forced himself inside her. "Because it has to be forever."

"Blaine," she cried as he thrust faster into her, her nails digging into his shoulder as she moaned into his neck.

With an almost primal cry, he pumped into her, his fingers biting into her bottom as his seed spilled freely into her. He felt as though he were weightless, floating in the darkness. It was earth shattering, yet frightening to have lost all sense, all control over his mind and body.

For once, he'd truly given every ounce of himself.

As he came back to earth, realization slowly infused his thoughts. He'd done the unthinkable--he'd given Madeline his seed, he'd broke his solemn vow and done what he'd promised himself he'd never do.

"Blaine," she mumbled against him. "That was so wonderful. We simply must do that again."

Yes, he thought, holding her close, but he would not loose his self-control to such a depth. *Never again.* He couldn't risk fate. And if it there truly was a God, nothing but sweet memories would be there to remind him of this night's business.

Settling a shaking Madeline to the ground, Blaine pleaded with his maker that no child would be conceived this evening.

* * * *

Three weeks later, Blaine was still grappling with the enormity of what had happened between him and Madeline. *He'd actually spilled his seed inside her.* Not since that first night with her had he lost control, hell, even the first time with her he hadn't been so mindless as to spill himself entirely into her warm body.

Blast it all, what had he been thinking? He hadn't been--obviously, else he would never have done such a thing. And his wife? Just what the devil had she been up to seducing him in such a manner? Had it been her goal to tempt him, to force him to forget himself? She had been more than wanton in the Dark Walk, she had played him like a Cyprian played the men of the ton.

Impossible, he scoffed. His wife was an innocent, a beginner in the art of love. How would Madeline know the art of seduction?

Her whore friends. The thought suddenly crept into his brain and he shook his head, forcing it aside. No, Madeline would never do such a thing. She'd promised him, and she would not break that vow. He knew that. If there was one thing he was certain of, it was Madeline's integrity and honesty.

The carriage slowed to a stop, forcing his thoughts away from that heated night in the Dark Walk to more pressing concerns-- mainly ascertaining his donation to Bedlam was being dispersed appropriately. Reaching for the package beside him, he let himself out, his boots crunching on the gravel drive.

Stalking up the stairs two at a time, Blaine let himself into the entrance of Bethlehem Hospital. It was a deceiving view, he thought, taking in the clean floors and whitewashed walls. One was met with a sense of order and calm when they first stepped into Bedlam. No one knew or could understand the extent of the deception until they'd actually viewed the darkness and filth that filled the corridors beyond the bright and cheery entrance hall.

"Ah, my lord," Jenkinson bowed. "Might I congratulate you on your nuptials?"

"Thank you," Blaine nodded, feeling the familiar suffocating feeling enclose around him. "How are the repairs going?" he asked, not wanting to dwell on his marriage. He didn't want to think of Madeline right now, for it only made him ponder her possible motives for seducing him in the alley.

"When I last visited I believe repairs were just getting under way."

"Indeed," Jenkinson nodded, motioning for him to proceed ahead. "We've started on the east corridor. We've added a solarium and a few chairs and tables. Some of the residents go there to escape for a few hours."

Blaine followed Jenkinson, thankful they would not be starting their tour in the basement of the mad house. He always needed time to mentally steel himself against the sight and smell of those who were most seriously deranged.

"Her, Grace, the Duchess of Newcombe donated numerous boxes of books to the solarium. You do know that we have His Grace, here, do you not? End stages of syphilis. Mad as a March Hare, he is."

"I doubt her grace would be pleased to hear you bandying about tales of her husband."

"Bah," Jenkinson waved, heedless of the reproach in the comment. "Everyone knows that his grace was a philanderer and a wastrel. Only a matter of time before his bad behavior caught up with him. Her grace was more then happy when we took him off her hands. What's that you've got?" Jenkinson asked, motioning him into the new solarium filled with bookcases and a domed ceiling that basked the room with warm, bright sunlight.

"A book," Blaine replied, amazed at the beauty of the room, proud that his donation had gone toward the much needed improvements. "I thought Gertrude might want something new to read."

"Gertrude?" Jenkinson asked, his face tensing slightly. "Well, I suppose since you've been away these past weeks you haven't heard. She's dead."

Blaine tore his gaze from the ceiling and fixed it upon the superintendent. "How?" he asked, feeling himself engulfed in confusion and dread.

"Swallowed her tongue, the physician said. Had one of those events that sometimes occur in those with the falling sickness."

"And what event is that?" he forced himself to ask, refusing to tug at the cravat that was slowly choking him.

"Mister Gibbert had some strange name for it, status something. In any event, she continued to have her fits, one after the other without waking. Died from it, Gibbert said."

"Status Eplipticus," he breathed, fearing the word. Samuel Tissot, a Swiss physician his father had invited to come and 'study' him had spoken of such a condition. A condition where one suffered a series of seizures so violent that it swelled the brain, rendering the person comatose and dead soon after. The condition had been his fear since he was a young man. Every time he had an aura he found himself wondering if this would be the time he'd never wake up.

"My lord," Jenkinson asked, "shall we?"

"Gertrude," he said, ignoring Jenksinson's invitation to continue their stroll. "Did she have a proper burial? Did her family come?"

Jenskinson stared in disbelief and Blaine knew that the superintendent could tell that more than the death of Gertrude was disturbing him.

"No, no mourners, my lord. She's buried in Spitalfields, the cheapest plot of land we could find. We informed her husband, but he was out of the county apparently, visiting with friends."

He nodded, his fingers squeezing around the book he held in his hand. She'd died alone, her demons consuming her as her bastard husband was miles away, forgetting the fact he even had a wife.

Would Madeline forget she had a husband?

"Good day, Jenkinson," he said, shivering away the thoughts of Madeline locking him up in Bedlam and leaving him to die alone, unloved and forgotten.

"But you've not seen the improvements to the cells," Jenkinson called after him. "I think you'll be impressed with those changes as well."

"Another time," he said, quickening his step, trying to outrun the superintendent and the personal demons that clamored after him. "I have a pressing matter of business to attend to."

When he opened the door, sunlight and fresh air greeted him and Blaine breathed deeply, trying to forget what he'd heard, attempting to forget that the same fate might very well befall him someday. He'd never be free of it, he thought, climbing into his carriage and slamming the door. It would always be inside him, lurking, waiting to ruin whatever happiness he had in his life.

He thought of Madeline and he shivered with dread. He'd been a fool to marry her and bring her into his life. He was only going to make her miserable. He was going to be an embarrassment to her, much like the Duke of Newcombe was to his wife. How much bloody longer could he reasonably keep up this charade? It was only a matter of time before his wife discovered his illness.

His gaze went to the package on his lap and he viscously tore open the wrapping. A brown leather volume of the King James Bible greeted him. With an oath he tossed it across the carriage only to have it land unceremoniously by the toe of his boot.

What a fool he was to believe that there was anything but misery in this life.

* * * *

"I'm happy to see you, Papa," Madeline smiled, pouring her father another cup of tea. "I've missed you these past weeks."

"Well," her father colored while he worked to loosen his cravat. "I might have been wrong about Hardcastle. He might be odd, but I can see he's taking good care of you. Not that Tynemouth wouldn't have, mind you. You know the young man was heartbroken, don't you?"

"Papa," she smiled, resting her hand atop his.

"He wanted to challenge Hardcastle, you know." Her father snorted before taking another sip of his tea. "Wanted me for his second, too, by Jove. Had a devil of a time convincing him to turn his anger into something productive."

"I didn't fall in love with Lord Tynemouth."

"So that's the way of it, is it?" he asked "You've given your heart to Hardcastle?"

"Yes. He's truly a good man, Papa. Just give him a chance."

"I suppose I'll have to," her father grunted, gulping his tea. "I suppose I'm stuck with him now, aren't I?"

"He's a good man, Papa. You'll see."

"Your ladyship, the dowager countess is here."

"Let her in, Sterling," Madeline said, excited to introduce her father to Blaine's mother.

"Good day, my dear," the countess smiled, kissing her cheek affectionately. "My, you're looking more beautiful and radiant every time I see you. Marriage becomes you, I think."

Madeline flushed and motioned to her father. "My father, Lady Hardcastle, the Earl of Penrick."

"Delighted, my lady," her father bowed, slightly flustered. It was the first time Madeline had ever seen him waver in a woman's company.

"My lord," the countess murmured, her cheeks equally as flushed. "What a pleasure to make your acquaintance. You've raised a lovely daughter. I'm quite pleased to call her daughter, you know."

"Yes ... well--um, thank you, your ladyship. Madeline," he said, straightening his waistcoat and smoothing his moustache. "I fear I must be running. Business, you know."

"Of course, Papa," delighted in his discomposure. "I will see you soon?"

"Soon," he grunted, rushing from the room. "Don't hesitate to call, my dear."

"I'll tell my husband you stopped by," she said before he could close the door.

"Lovely," her father replied. "That would be lovely."

Madeline grinned as she listened to her father's boots beat a hasty retreat on the marble tiles.

"Where is my son?" the dowager asked, sitting down and helping herself to some tea. "Out again?"

"I'm afraid so, Madam," Madeline sighed, taking her seat. "He spends much of his days busy with his duties."

"Hmm," the countess murmured. "I wonder what keeps him occupied?"

Madeline had wondered the same thing. Ever since the night at Vauxhall, Blaine had been distancing himself from her again. He was forever leaving before she arose, only to climb into bed late at night, too tired to do more then sleep.

"How are you feeling, my dear?" she asked, her gray gaze, so like her son's, flickered over her.

"Quite well, thank you," Madeline said, wondering at the meaning behind the question. "I'm quite fit actually. I enjoy good health."

"Indeed," the countess smiled around the rim of her cup. "But I was not asking about that, now was I?"

"My lady?" Madeline asked, nearly choking on a bit of biscuit. Had the countess realized what she herself had only confirmed a short while ago? Did Blaine's mother know that she was in the family way? Impossible, Madeline scoffed. She barely had any symptoms herself and her body, in her estimation, had not yet begun to show her condition. No, it couldn't be, she reassured herself.

"When are you going to tell my son you're carrying his child?"

"Madeline?"

Madeline realized instantly that the dark voice coming from the opened door was Blaine's. She took in the countess' startled expression and then her husband's enraged visage and promptly starting choking.

"What is the meaning of this?" he asked, bursting into the room, roaring in distemper.

"Your mother," she wheezed, trying to clear her throat. "Has kindly paid us a visit."

"Get out," he spat, glaring at his mother.

"My lord," Madeline cried, recovering from her shock. "You cannot talk to your own mother in such a fashion. I will not have it."

"I will not have her in my house. Out," he said again, his eyes never once straying from Madeline. "It seems that my wife has something of a personal nature to discuss with me."

"As you wish," his mother said, coolly sliding past him only to offer an expression of apology to Madeline behind Blaine's back.

"What is it you wish to discuss, my lord?"

"Did I or did I not just hear my mother say you are carrying my child?"

"Well, that is…." she paused, wincing and twining her fingers, hoping the words she'd practiced so hard would come out as she planned. "Well, there is some possibility-"

Madeline froze when she heard the vicious oath come from her husband's mouth. She hadn't heard the word before, but she knew it wasn't polite, nor was it a good sign--nothing uttered with such violence, such vehemence could be taken as anything but confirmation that her husband was most seriously displeased.

With a glare, and a string of blasphemies, he turned away, leaving Madeline alone, and unsure of how to proceed.

Chapter Nineteen

"Blaine, say something."

He couldn't. He stood transfixed at the window, watching as carriages traveled along the cobbles only to vanish through the mist. His whole world was crashing down around him, his existence as he knew it was fading into nothingness like the carriages on the street and there wasn't a damn thing he could do about it.

Damn it, why had he let his passion get so out of control? He knew, even as he had spilled his seed into her that he was making a grave mistake. He could tell just by the look of her that night, the determination that shone in her eye as she teased him down the path to the Dark Walk that she was seducing him, making him bend to her wishes. She'd damn well been ready to receive him.

She wanted this child, she loved it already, instinctively he knew it. But his young wife didn't know what he did about life and what fate could do to bring you down.

"Blaine-"

"Are you certain? When were your last courses? Surely you cannot be that far along. That night of madness was only, what, three weeks ago?"

"I have not had a cycle since before the weekend at Lady Brookehaven's."

He closed his eyes and pressed his head against the glass, his fingers curling against the frame as he calculated the days in his mind. She was at least two months along if she conceived the night they'd first made love. Two months since life had been stirring and growing inside her.

"How long have you known?" he asked, thinking he must have been a bloody fool not to notice the changes in her body. No, not a fool, just a terrified simpleton, afraid to admit the truth. He'd refused to pay heed to the way her bottom had filled out, the heaviness of her breasts and the way her nipples had turned a shade darker.

He had wanted to believe himself safe. He laughed at the absurdity of it--he hadn't been safe since the moment he laid eyes on her.

"Blaine?"

"I asked how long you've known."

"Blaine," she murmured, her voice nothing but a worried whisper. He stiffened as though he'd been branded when he felt the tentative touch of her fingers on his back.

"How long," he bit out, struggling not to shout at her and the impotence he felt when he thought of his life spinning out of control.

"I wasn't sure till last week. Maggie confirmed it then. I ... I wanted to be certain."

He nodded, his breathing harsh and hard. So nanny had betrayed him, also. She hadn't breathed a word of this to him, hadn't even dropped a hint that Madeline might be breeding. *God damn women and their manipulations.*

"Aren't you pleased? We're going to have a baby."

"Get rid of it."

The air hung heavy, the words of his demand blanketing the already taught atmosphere. It was a deplorable thing to say, but he had uttered it in truth. Perhaps now his wife knew how he truly felt about the prospect of becoming a father.

"My lord, you can't possibly mean ... abort-- " she stopped herself from saying the word, and his hand fisted tighter against the window frame.

"There are ways. Ask Phoebe or another woman at the home. They're the ones who told you how to seduce me into giving you a child, they can damn well tell you how to rid yourself of an unwanted one. I don't care how you do it. Just get rid of it."

"*It?* You talk as if this child is nothing at all," she cried, her voice rising to a fever pitch. *"This is our baby."*

"Is that what you think?" he fumed, whirling around to confront her, his rage spiraling out of control when he saw how she placed a protective hand over her womb. "You think that the life growing inside you will be a perfect babe? You think nothing will go wrong? That all will be well? Well I'm here to tell you, madam that things do go wrong. Babes don't always come out the way we want them to."

"What are you saying?" she asked, stepping away from him and backing up against the bed. "Are you saying you will tolerate nothing less than perfection in our child?"

"We're not talking about me," he hissed, closing in on her. "We're talking about *your* expectations. What you want to see when you hold your child in your arms."

"I will love my child no matter what."

"Is that so? I wonder how many mothers have professed the same thing only to discard their less than perfect offspring? I wonder what you'll do if you find that your beloved infant is not what you desire."

"You're mad," she said, her expression finally giving way to disgust. "I cannot believe I'm hearing that you want me to rid myself of your baby. What sort of monster are you?"

Shadow raised himself onto his haunches then, sniffing the air as tension and fear poured from each of them. With a low growl, he began to pace between them, the throaty snarl slowly giving way to a high pitched whimper.

"Shadow, sit," Madeline commanded, pointing to the spot beside her slippers, but Shadow ignored her and instead thrust his muzzle into Blaine's hand, pushing him into motion.

"I must leave," he groaned, feeling his vision begin to swim before him, knowing that his anger had brought on another aura. He had to leave, it would only be seconds before Madeline learned he truly was a monster. He must flee before she thought of the babe growing inside her--wondering if it too, would be a monster like its father.

"You'll do no such thing," Madeline demanded, digging her sharp nails into his arms. "You always run away whenever something you do not wish to speak of creeps up. I won't have it. You cannot demand I rid myself of your child then leave as if it was not but a request to join you for supper."

The smell of burning bread reached him as well as the piercing bark of Shadow as the animal pranced frantically in circles about them. "Let go," he snapped, shaking her off and pushing her away, refusing to let the shock of her face register in his mind. But it was too late, his mouth clamped shut, then his teeth locked together and he felt himself struggle to draw in air.

"Blaine," she cried, rushing to reach for his sleeve. Her eyes widened and he watched her expression turn from anger to surprise, to shocked horror.

Oh God, he groaned, seeing her face swimming before him as he fell slowly, inexorably to the ground. She was looking at him like his mother had when he was twelve. She despised him, he sickened her. He was no longer able to hide what he was. She knew what he was now and nothing could stop her from remembering how he looked when succumbing to his fit.

His last thought as his body thudded heavily to the floor and his voice gave out it's characteristic strangled cry, was that he could never stand to see the woman he adored, the woman he placed above all others stare at his own child with the same look of horror and repulsion as she was now showing him.

* * * *

Madeline crept into Blaine's chamber after assuring herself that Ringwald and Sterling had taken their leave. He was frightfully pale lying against the white linens, despite the warm glow of candles and firelight. His breathing was deep and harsh, almost as if he were snoring, only much deeper, the sound so much different--almost haunting.

Standing at the foot of the bed, Madeline stared at her husband, his broad shoulders and chiseled chest, naked, contrasting sharply with the weakness she saw in his lax face and the limp hand that rested atop the sheets.

Dear God, why had he never told her? How did he think she was to prepare herself for such a sight when he had kept his falling sickness from her? She'd been terrified as he fell before her. She'd done nothing but helplessly watch him slip into un-consciousness. Had it not been for Ringwald and Sterling, she feared what might have happened to him. Had he told her from what he suffered from, she could have had some training, could have at least been prepared for what it might look like--him, almost dying before her very eyes.

She covered her mouth, smothering the sob that threatened to overwhelm her. Why hadn't he trusted her? Why did he not think enough of her to tell her, to let her share in his affliction, to bloody well let her tend him instead of locking her in her room and pushing her away?

He stirred restlessly then, attempting to push the covers off. Perhaps he was fevered, Madeline thought, wondering if she shouldn't remove the blankets for him. Did one suffer from a fever after a fit?

Standing beside the bed, she placed a trembling hand to his forehead. With a deep moan, he pressed his face into her palm, immediately quieting as she stroked his hair. Cool and clammy-- most definitely not fevered.

He looked lost, defenseless as she watched him rub his stubbled cheek against her hand. He was so in need of love and she did love him--dark secret and all.

She felt the warmth of her tears as they rolled along her cheeks and she kneeled to the floor then, resting her face against his chest.

She needed him and blast him and whatever he thought, he needed her, too.

"I love you," she whispered before kissing his chest and closing her eyes. "I'll love you forever, Blaine and we will get through this. You'll see, my love, you won't ever have to doubt me again."

Madeline had no idea how long she slept, but she came awake with a start, aware that a pair of glacial gray eyes were impaling her with their coldness.

"You saw, didn't you?" She looked up through a veil of hair and met his cold glare. "Are you happy now?" he spat, his eyes flashing in the dim light. "Now you know."

"Blaine," she pleaded, straightening from his chest and reaching to stroke his hair. "You mustn't worry, or tire yourself."

"Don't touch me," he roared, moving his head away from her hand. "Answer me, are you happy now that you've seen me fall to the floor as I flail about like some God damned fish on the beach?"

"Don't do this," she begged, reaching for his hand. "Please, you'll have another ... that is-"

"Is your damn curiosity appeased?" he flung her hand from his face as he struggled to sit up in bed. "I'm sure you watched it all, staring at me in horrified fascination as if I were a freak in a traveling show."

"It wasn't like that."

"Do not lie to me! I've seen it, Madeline. I've gone to Bedlam to watch and learn, to see what I look like, when I succumb to a fit."

"It's not like that, Blaine. You're wrong."

"It bloody well is like that. I'm just like them. I know. I've seen what they look like flopping about on the floor, their spit flying from their mouth as they bite down on their tongues. I've watched them loose control in front of the horrified onlookers. And do you know, you remind me of them--of the polite society who come to snicker and jeer. Oh, they try to look away, but somehow their compulsion keeps making them watch. They like to stare at the animals, terrified, mortified by the sight of it all, yet completely fascinated and absorbed."

She shook her head, trying in vain to make him see that she didn't think like that. She only wanted to help him. God help her, she'd been scared to death by what she'd witnessed. It was as if her husband was dying before her very eyes. She didn't think she'd ever get over the shock or fear of seeing him thus. She'd been unprepared for what she'd seen, by what resided within him.

In her foolishness, she thought Blaine suffered from bouts of melancholy. Some depressive disorder that made him withdraw into his shell. Never had she thought he suffered from something as severe as the falling sickness.

"Your face was the same, you know. I saw your face, saw your repulsion as I fell to the floor, pissing myself. Get out," he growled as he tried to hold her away from him. "I want you out of my house and out of my life."

"Don't push me away. Don't do this."

"Get out and don't ever come back."

"What about our baby?"

"I never wanted the child and furthermore, I no longer want you."

* * * *

Propping his booted feet atop the desk, Blaine pushed aside the valerian tea and reached for the brandy decanter. The tea was of little use now--his secret was out. His wife was completely aware of the evil that lurked within him.

Not bothering with a glass, Blaine drank heavily from the decanter, his lips curved in mock mirth as he stared at the portrait of his father, the bastard's cold eyes staring emotionlessly back at him.

His house was eerily silent. The wind and driving rain against the windowpanes, along with the occasional crack and spark of a log in the hearth, was the only sound to be heard. Even the servants went silently about their duties, fearful of incurring his wrath, or making him glance their way.

It had been a week since Madeline had left. In fact, it had been that long since his house had taken on the aura of a tomb. It was disturbingly quiet, almost as if it were cloaked in a death pall. Perhaps that was what it truly was, he thought, swallowing more of the brandy, noticing that he could no longer taste it. He certainly no longer felt like living--not now, not after he'd thrown Madeline out of his life.

Damn it, he swore, pounding his fist against the desk, he should be furious with the chit. She'd deceived him, betrayed him with tricks her whore friends taught her. He had every right to toss her out on her ear and out of his life. Any husband would have done the same.

So why then, did his rationalizations make him feel less of a man? Why was it whenever he thought of how he'd pushed her away, or how he demanded that she get rid of their child did he feel like slinking into a corner, his tail between his legs? Why did he continue to dream of her? Why did he miss her and why the hell didn't he have the compunction to go to Montgomery House and drag her home where she belonged?

Damn her! Ever since he'd met her his world had been turned upside down. She'd done nothing but confuse him and tie him in knots. Had he never let her into his heart he wouldn't now be sulking in solitude, wishing he could numb the feel of his heart shattering into tiny shards.

Bloody hell, he'd been a fool to fall in love with her.

"Allow me to announce you, madam," Sterling's voice, raised in agitation, called from the other side of the study door. "His lordship has expressly informed staff that he is not at home to visitors."

Madeline? For a heart stopping second, Blaine allowed himself to believe that Madeline had come back to him, prepared to shower him with her love and brave his surly mood. For a fleeting second, hope and anticipation filled his veins that perhaps she had forgiven him.

"He will see me."

The clipped sound of his mother's voice sliced through his drunken haze, making his spine straighten and his nerves tense and alert.

"My lord," Sterling just managed to get the door open before his mother breezed through, resplendent in a rose evening gown and matching shawl. "Your mother, milord."

"Close the door, Sterling," Blaine commanded, refusing to look away from the censure he perceived in his mother's eyes.

"Shall I arrange for tea, milord?"

"Her ladyship will not be staying long enough for the pot to boil. You may return to your post."

"As you wish, milord."

"Well," his mother said at last, pulling her gloves from her hands and slapping them against her palm. "What a pretty picture you make tucked in your study, licking your wounds and drinking yourself to death."

He inclined his head and raised the bottle to his lips, forcing himself to drink more, if only to offend her further. He was in a devilish mood and unfortunately for her, she'd picked the worst possible time to lecture him on his current state--indeed, to lecture him on anything.

"And to what do I owe this great pleasure, Madam?"

"We have business to attend to," she said curtly, her eyes scouring him, silently chastising him as if he were an errant schoolboy and not a man well into his thirties.

"And you left your evening entertainments to what, lecture me on how I've been remiss in my duties as your son?" he asked, wiping his mouth on the back of his hand, hoping he'd disgust and goad her into leaving. Instead, she glared at him with burning, reproachful eyes.

"You're the very picture of your father," she said, sliding into an empty chair and crossing her legs. "I cannot count how many times I found him sitting behind that very desk, brooding and drinking."

"I'm nothing like him," he snarled, slamming the crystal decanter down against the desktop. "Do not ever compare me to him again."

"You think not?" she asked, shooting him a cold look before settling her gaze on his father's portrait. "Perhaps you forget that he threw me out of his life, too, once he'd reasoned that it was all my fault his heir was less then perfect."

Blaine sucked in his breath. "You have some nerve, Madam, strolling into my house and speaking things I have no wish to hear. If you've come to remind me that I'm less than a whole man you could have saved yourself the trip, for I've no need to have my memory refreshed--I live with the fact daily."

Her eyes narrowed, her black brows furrowing tightly together as she scowled back at him. "For years I've treaded carefully around you, fearing that anything I may say or do might set you off, but by God, I'll no longer walk about on tenterhooks. You'll listen to what I have to say before this night is through."

"Treading carefully?" he half laughed, half grunted. "Madam, you fled to France when I was fourteen. You left me with my bastard of a father without so much as a word or backward glance. I assure you, your claim that you walk about on tenterhooks around me is unfounded. You barely deign to spend more than five minutes in my company during your yearly visits."

"Damn you!" she cried, rising from the chair in a rustle of silk and lace.

"I believe I am."

"You take delight in this, do you not," she accused, whirling around to face him. "You enjoy sitting back, being the martyr, the hurt and wronged little boy. Well, I'm going to set you to rights. I'll not go on feeling guilt-ridden because you're too bloody busy indulging yourself in the role of victim."

"If you will but recall, Madam, I am the victim."

"You are not," she cried, her frail fingers shaking with rage. "I would have done anything to save you. Your father, I'm certain of it, is responsible for your condition. Had he not ruthlessly torn you from my body, had he not shook you like a rag doll in order to make you breathe, you might not have had to suffer what you do. But he wanted his heir, and I," she whispered, wringing her hands. "I wanted my baby."

He watched his mother pace before his desk, her face looked weary and old--much older then she had when she first arrived in Town. "You're working yourself into a state, Madam. Might I suggest you cease your pacing."

Suddenly she spun on her heel, her hands planted firmly on the desk, her gray eyes, mirrored his own and he fleetingly wondered if his eyes betrayed him as his mother's were now doing. "You were my baby, and I loved you. I loved you the moment I was aware you were growing inside me. That love only grew as you grew, as you kicked and rolled, letting me know you were a part of me."

He shifted uncomfortably in his chair, unused to the passionate emotion pouring out of his mother.

"I used to lay in bed and run my hand over my stomach, and you would kick and let me know that you felt me, too. I wanted you so desperately and when I could not deliver you, I felt a piece of me dying. When your father held you aloft, I thought you were gone. I would have gladly died for you to live. I loved you so much that I would have done anything to save you. While I feel anger when I think of what your father did to you, I can only feel gratitude that he saved you. You see, I'd much rather have you as you are, then to not have had you at all."

He felt as if he'd been hit with a hammer. What was she saying? She loved him? She wasn't ashamed of him? The implications sent his mind reeling and his hand reaching for the brandy. His mother saw his intent and grasped the decanter before he could reach it, sliding it well out of his grasp.

"The night your episodes turned violent you turned from me. I want to know why. Why did you shut me out of your life?" His eyes met hers and for a long minute each stared at the other. "Why, Blaine? Why did you toss your own mother out of your life?"

He felt like he did when he was twelve, exposed and weak. He didn't like the feeling at all, so he buried it, smothering the emotion. "If you must know, it was because you looked at me as though I were a monster. A freak to be locked away in a closet and forgotten about. I merely made it easy for you to forget me. I simply got rid of you before you could cast me aside."

Her face softened and her gray eyes filled with tears. "I never knew," she whispered, her lips trembling. "All these years you wouldn't let me come close to you. I didn't know what I'd done. I didn't know what to do."

Bitterness threatened to swallow him whole. He didn't want to see her this way, with emotion and feeling in her eyes. He didn't know how to deal with her like this. He hadn't touched her in years, hadn't let her touch him, either, had only ever called her Madam, not the *Mama* of his childhood. And now she was standing before him, his frail, tired, old-looking mother, in need of comfort, and he couldn't--didn't know how to reach out and console her.

"Blaine," she began, "you terrified me that night. I might have looked horrified, but it was not because I was ashamed of you, it was because I thought you were dying. You'll never know the fear of sitting across from your own child, watching as you think he's dying before your very eyes."

Madeline had thought he was dying, too. He recalled her words, remembered the fear he heard in her voice. She thought the very same thing as his mother. Was it possible that he'd mistaken repulsion for fear? Not fear of what lurked within him, but fear for him, for his well being? Could he have been wrong all these years?

"I know what your father was like and I do feel shame that I left you alone with him, but you must see that I did what I thought was best. Your father," she said then stopped to search her reticule for a handkerchief. "Your father was livid with you and he was disappointed with both of us. You for being less then what he wanted in his heir, me for giving him such a son, and my inability to bear him more children. His behavior to you only worsened when he saw me clucking and fawning over you, as he used to say. He became irate whenever he would see me holding you. Don't you see," she asked, her words almost pleading. "Can't you understand that I left to make it easier for you? I thought…. I thought…." she choked, "that I was doing the right thing. I was trying to be a good mother, but then you turned from me and then I no longer knew what the right thing was. I only knew that I had lost my son."

Squirming in his chair, he fought to look away from the tears streaming down his mother's cheek. He didn't know how to soothe the woman he had literally cast aside and purposely forgotten about. How, after so many years was he to console his mother? How could he console anyone?

"Blaine," she sniffed into her handkerchief, "I know that it might be too late for us, but it is not too late for you and Madeline. Go to her, settle this business between you. She loves you, surely you must know that."

He stiffened and any warm feeling he might have had for his mother and her tears froze deep within him. "Did Madeline send you over here? She bloody well must be a fool to think that I'd fall for anything you had to say. You, who haven't been in my life for eighteen years. She must be very desperate, indeed."

His mother straightened, her features once again schooled into an emotionless mask. "Your wife most certainly did not ask me to come to speak to you. And Madeline is not a fool. I'll have you know that you've married a treasure and if you're too bloody blind to see it then you should suffer whatever Fate has in store for you. Here," she said, reaching inside her reticule and tossing a missive at his chest. "The first reason for my coming was to clear the air between us. For some misguided reason I thought you might be receptive to it. But I see now that you are as bitter and lonely as ever. The second reason is that missive. It's from Maggie Noland. I hope what news this letter contains brings you whatever it is you seek in life. I bid you good evening, my lord."

He watched his mother storm out of his study before looking down at the missive. A curious mix of apprehension and fear twisted his gut. There was something about Nanny writing to his mother that boded ill.

Flicking the letter open, he read the words, his heart plummeting to his belly.

My lady,

Fate would once again have us pleading for the life of an innocent babe. The countess has begun to bleed and I fear it might only be a matter of time before she, or the babe, or both, are lost.

The letter dropped between his fingers. Madeline was bleeding? He couldn't credit it, couldn't think of it, could hardly even breathe. Had she tried to abort their child as he asked? Had his demands been the reason she might be now be dying?

The thought of a life spent without Madeline made his insides clench, made him violent and nauseous and terrified. He'd been a fool to act as he had. He'd been cruel and selfish and unthinking when he demanded that she rid herself of his baby. He could not think upon his words without hating himself. He didn't want her dead, he didn't want to spend the rest of his life without her. And furthermore, he couldn't bear the thought of his child being torn from its mother's body in such a vile, cruel fashion. He couldn't stand the notion that it had been his wish that his child not survive at all.

He'd been lying when he said he didn't want her or the babe. He'd been acting the martyr as he mother had accused him of. He was wallowing in embarrassment and self-pity, lashing out like a spoiled child.

It was only when confronted with the very real possibility of losing both his wife and his child, did he admit that he wanted both--more then anything.

"Sterling," he bellowed, making Shadow jump from his spot by the fire. "Have a carriage brought round immediately."

"At once, milord," his butler bowed. "Shall I have a bag packed for you?"

"No, but have my chamber ready for when I arrive home."

"Very good, sir."

"And Sterling," he said, halting the butler. "You may inform staff that I shall be bringing the countess back with me."

The smile that parted the butler's lips momentarily stunned Blaine. He hadn't seen Sterling smile that particular way ... well, ever. "Staff will be happy to have her back, if I may so, milord."

"So will I, Sterling. So will I."

Chapter Twenty

"Rest now, luvy."

Madeline whimpered when another cramp seized her womb and swept around to her back. "The pains," she mumbled, crying once more. "They're back."

"Sssh, now, luvy," Maggie crooned, smoothing back Madeline's hair. "Just lie still. There's a girl. It's what's best for the babe now."

"Maggie," Madeline choked, feeling another cramp tighten her insides, forcing a trickle of fluid to escape and run down her thigh. "I'm losing my baby, aren't I?"

"Now, don't go saying that," Maggie muttered. "There's been many a woman whose body has threatened to lose a babe and they've managed not to. Have faith, Madeline."

"God's punishing me," she cried, rocking on her side, weeping as she felt another rivulet of blood snake down her leg. "He's doing this because I tricked Blaine. Because I deliberately got myself with child when I knew--when I promised I would not."

"Hush, luvy,"

She held herself, attempting to keep the life within her from escaping. This was their child--Blaine's child. The only one they would have. She couldn't allow it to die. She couldn't let what remained of Blaine to leave her, not when she would never have another chance to conceive and bring his son or daughter into the world.

"I shouldn't have done what I did. Phoebe tried to tell me, but I wouldn't listen. I thought I knew what was best for him. I was wrong and I'm so very sorry, but I don't want my baby taken from me."

"Hush now," Maggie demanded. "You'll do naught but get yourself in a state and bring on the pains. You've done too much this week, that is all. You've been upset and preoccupied over your disagreement with his lordship. You've cleaned this place from top to bottom trying to forget your problems and that's the reason for the bleeding and the pains. God is not taking anything away from you, Madeline."

"Why didn't you tell me?" she whimpered, gazing at Maggie

seated beside her, her wrinkled face marred with worry. "You knew his secret and you didn't tell me."

"It wasn't up to me. That was up to his lordship to tell."

"I still love him, Maggie, despite what he thinks. He thinks I despise him, but I only hate myself for betraying him."

"I know, love." Maggie consoled, brushing her hair out of her eyes. "Love has a way of making us do things we shouldn't. I know you meant no harm, luvy. In time his lordship will realize it, too."

"Maggie," Phoebe whispered from the door. "Go downstairs for a bite to eat. I'll stay with her."

Maggie rose from the bed, her hand still clasped tightly in Madeline's. "Phoebe's here, let me go and get you some tea. You need your strength."

"Close your eyes, Dearest." Phoebe sat atop the mattress, her hand, warm and soft, rested lightly atop Madeline's. "The girls say that what you need is rest right now."

"Phoebe," Madeline began to weep again. "You tried to tell me, but I wouldn't listen. I thought I knew, and now … and now…." she choked, racked with uncontrollable sobbing. "Now I've turned him from me forever. I've lost him. He'll never love me. He hates me and our baby."

"He doesn't hate you or the babe," Maggie sighed from the door.

"Then tell me," Madeline cried, tears blinding her. "Make me understand why my husband would wish for me to rid myself of his child. Why would a man wish his wife to commit such a sin?"

Maggie sunk down on the other side of the bed, looking much older and more tired then Madeline had ever seen her. "His fears, I suppose are to blame," Maggie whispered. "For years they've consumed him, eating him alive until he was nothing but an empty shell. No one could reach him, he wouldn't let anyone get close to him. He always swore he'd never let another into his life. His pride, you see. His cursed male pride is to blame."

Maggie let out a long suffering sigh before patting Madeline's hand. "He came breech, you know. He was big and he was the countess' first babe. I couldn't deliver him and the countess was beside herself with pain and exhaustion. She wouldn't push and I watched his wee little limbs turn from pink to purple. That was when his lordship took over. He pushed me out of the way and took the babe's legs in his hands and pulled with all his might. When he was born he was nothing more than a limp rag. He wasn't breathing, wasn't making a sound, so his lordship shook him, commanding him to breath." Maggie looked at her then, tears filling her already rheumy eyes. "He kept shaking that babe until he gasped and cried out his first weak breath. I knew right away something was wrong with him. He kept twitching and jerking and I'd seen enough of babies by that time to know it wasn't right. I didn't think he'd live out the night, but he did, by Jove, and he thrived. He was a miracle from God, but his father didn't think so. The old earl belittled him, threatened him and abused him so badly that there was times I hid him in my room, far away from his father."

"Enough," Madeline cried, covering her ears, refusing to hear anymore of the torture and pain Blaine had endured. No child deserved such treatment and certainly not a babe who was not responsible for the result of his birth.

"If you ask me, his falling sickness is from what his father did to him, shaking him like that, like a wet rag doll to get him to breathe. No one in the family had ever suffered from it. I heard the old earl tell that to the string of quacks he paraded before his lordship. I knew then that what he suffered was from the hands of his father."

Understanding the depths of her actions for the first time, Madeline thought of the horrors her husband had endured. In her selfishness to have a baby she had caused Blaine too much pain, opening the old wounds from his childhood.

"Ssh, Dearest," Phoebe soothed. "It won't do any good to think such things. You did what you thought was right. Come, have a draught of laudanum. You need to rest."

"I don't want to lose this baby. Don't you see? If I lose this baby, I lose whatever I have left of Blaine."

"No, Madeline. You're wrong. Hardcastle loves you. He may be angry but he'll soon see that he can't live without you."

"He told me to get rid of the child," she said at last, exhausted from the crying and the consuming weakness. "And now I'm losing it, just as I've lost him. Had I known the depth of his private hell I would never have seduced him. I would never have willingly submitted him to such pain."

"Maddy," Phoebe whispered, pressing a soft kiss on her cheek. "Go to sleep, Dearest. You may find that things will look better when you awake."

"They won't," Madeline hiccupped, feeling the comforting warmth of sleep making her limbs heavy.

"Remember, Madeline, the road to love is often long and

treacherous, but anything is possible in dreams and love. Never forget that. That thought has seen me through many times of darkness and I'm certain it'll see you through, too."

* * * *

"Madeline," Blaine shouted through the echoing thunder in the distance. "Let me in."

The cold, driving rain continued to come down in heavy sheets around him as he looked up at the dark and barricaded façade of Montgomery House.

God damn it, he swore, rapping the knocker against the wood with such violence his fingers stung. Where the hell was everyone and why the hell wasn't anyone coming to answer his summons? Didn't they know his wife was in there, bleeding--possibly dying?

"Madeline," he roared again, not caring that a candle flared to life in the window of the neighbor's. "Let me in, God damn it, or I swear I'll kick the door in."

The cold rain quickly soaked through his greatcoat, running in icy rivulets down his neck. In anger and frustration he threw his hat against the window, the rain drenching his hair, the water running into his eyes. The fear clenching his insides, refusing to let go of him.

"Madeline," he thundered, pounding his fist against the thick pane of glass. "Let me in this instant."

Another candle flared to life, this time across the street. An elderly couple, dressed in nightclothes and caps appeared in the window, watching him with interest.

He was on display, his emotions bared--naked for all to see. And he didn't care. He only cared that Madeline and his child were slipping through his fingers and that he was losing them due to his own selfish pride and stupidity.

"I'll stand here all night, Madeline. I don't care who hears me," he shouted, cupping his hands around his mouth so that his voice would carry above the wind and the rain. "I won't give a damn about making a scene. *Damn it, Madeline, you're my wife, and I demand my rights as a husband.*"

The lock clicked and the rusty hinges sounded through a crack of thunder. "You fool," a quiet voice said through the darkness. "You'll have all and sundry gossiping about this."

Ignoring the scathing remark uttered by Phoebe Knightly, Blaine stepped over the threshold, heedless of the large puddle he was creating on the floorboards.

"What the devil do you mean by standing out there and creating a stir? For the love of God-"

"I've come for my wife," he said, shrugging out of his coat. "I suggest you stand aside and let me find her."

"My lord," Phoebe halted him with trembling fingers. "You mustn't-"

"I fear I must, Miss Knightly. You see, I cannot bear to stand to be without her for another minute. Stand aside, if you please."

She studied him a long while before nodding and stepping away from him. "She's in my room, the last on the right side, my lord. Let us pray you find her well."

"I'm afraid I've forgotten how to pray, Miss Knightly. Perhaps you will see to the task for me, for I fear that God has never listened to my prayers."

"He's listening," Phoebe smiled up at him. "And he'll answer them, too. Remember, my lord, anything is possible in dreams and in love."

Chapter 21

Blaine stood frozen in the doorway, the ashen appearance of his wife halting him from stepping into the room.

"My lord," Maggie Noland jumped as the sound of the bedroom door connected with the wall.

"Is she…." his throat was dry and he licked his lips, trying again to say the words. "Is she dead?"

"Heavens!" Maggie cried, waddling over to him and pulling him into the room. "Yer soaked to the bone. Get by the fire and out of those wet things."

Ignoring her protests, Blaine walked to the bed, his eyes nervously studying the white figure. He could perceive no movement of her chest beneath the blankets. Her face, ashen, almost gray, blended into the faded white sheets, terrifying him. "Is she dead," he asked again, his voice cracking. "Am I too late?"

"She sleeps deep," Maggie said, tugging his soaked coat down his arms. "I gave her some laudanum."

"Is … is…." Jesus, he couldn't talk, couldn't think. Not with Madeline looking like she was at death's door, ready to leave him in misery forever. "Is the babe all right?"

Maggie made a clucking noise while she placed his coat along the back of a chair, drying it by the fire. "It is a matter of time, my lord. The bleeding seems to have stopped, but one can never tell."

"But do you think?" he asked, staring at his wife, wishing she would open her eyes, wishing he could take back his words.

"I think the matter is in God's hands, now. It is not for me to say."

"Leave us," he ordered, finally taking a step closer to the bed.

"Perhaps I should stay," Maggie said anxiously. "You might need me."

"I'll call for you if I need you."

"Really, my lord, this is not the place for you. This is woman's work."

Finally he looked at Maggie, showing her what he had never shown another soul since he turned twelve--tears. His eyes were brimming with them and Nanny was now just a blurry specter before him. "It is a man's right to take care of his wife. I demand that right."

"Young master," she sighed, using the familiar endearment in the same soft and soothing voice she'd used with him as a child. "There's nothing you can do. She might need…" Maggie grimaced and looked away from him. "She might need to be cleaned from time to time."

"Then I shall clean her. Leave us. I need to be with my wife."

He waited for what seemed like forever for Nanny to take her leave. When she closed the door softly behind her, he pulled up a rocking chair and sat in it, staring at Madeline, unable to touch her for fear he'd find her cold and lifeless.

He sat that way for a long time, allowing the tears to spill from his eyes and down his cheeks as he watched her sleep, remembering what he'd said to her, recalling the anguish on her face. God help him but he didn't know what to do, or where to begin. He loved her so damn much and yet he couldn't even touch her. What the hell was wrong with him? Why could he not reach out to another human being?

Madeline turned, restless, whimpering before clutching her belly and moaning in her sleep. He looked at her through his veil of tears and brushing her hair away from her cheeks, he noticed she felt warm and very much alive.

Emotion, frightening and unfamiliar filled him and he had to force himself not to pull away from her. She was alive, she was still with him and she was still his. While the knowledge made him exultant he tempered it with the memories of their argument. Perhaps Madeline would never forgive him. What if she blamed him and his words for miscarrying the babe?

Refusing to think of it, he pulled the blankets down and saw she wore a thin white nightrail, the hem raised and tangled between her thighs. Her hand, pale and fragile was placed protectively on her belly. His eyes gazed lower and his breath caught as he saw the streaks and smearing of blood on her thighs. His eyes went to her face as if trying to decide if she would be snatched from him, then slowly he let his gaze rest on her hand.

Before he allowed himself to think the matter through, he moved her hand to lay atop her hip and gently, so as to not awaken her, he raised her nightrail, revealing red curls, darkened with blood, and the still flat of her stomach.

His fingers hovered above her for the barest of seconds before he reverently placed a hand over her womb, his fingers stroking and caressing, the motion expressing the feelings he could not bring himself to utter.

Tears, hot and scalding burned his cheeks and he let them come, unashamed to be crying. He wanted this baby. He'd thought of it for the past week, wondering why he'd said such a vile thing. He'd tried to talk himself into hating her. He told himself she'd betrayed him; that she'd deliberately deceived him and gotten with child but he hadn't been able to believe it. He wanted this babe. Somehow, Madeline had managed to give him what he thought he'd never wanted--love and a family. He couldn't lose either now, not now that he'd just realized their worth.

His lips met her belly and he placed a kiss on her warm, smooth skin. His tears trickled along her flesh and he brushed them away with his thumb, but they kept coming, and he realized he couldn't stop weeping. He simply couldn't bear the thought of losing either Madeline or his child.

Giving vent to his feelings, he gathered her closer to him, and buried his face in the folds of her gown and began to pray. Pray to whatever God would hear him that Madeline and the babe would be spared.

* * * *

Sometime in the middle of the night someone had wandered into the room, covering him with a blanket as he lay with his face pressed against Madeline's belly. Squinting at the bright morning light, Blaine stretched, wincing at the stiffness in his shoulders and legs. The bowl and cloth he'd used to wash Madeline was now replaced with fresh ones, a vase, filled with daises and dandelions stood on the table beside her bed. A picture with the words, 'get well' leaned proudly against the vase, the names of the children scribbled in varying degrees of legibility.

He smiled, feeling a strange emotion filling his heart when he saw the simple gift. He wasn't the only one who loved her. Madeline made everyone she had ever met love her and her children were no exception. She had saved them all, including himself.

The door opened and a young woman whom he knew to be the vicar's defiled daughter passed through the room carrying a breakfast tray.

"Mrs. Noland thought you might be hungry, my lord."

"Thank you," he said, watching as she gave him wide berth before placing it on a table before the window. "What is your name?"

"Abby, my lord."

"Thank you, Abby."

She looked at him with a mixture of interest and mistrust before curtseying and fleeing from the room. She obviously feared men, he thought, striding over to the table and lifting the lid off one of the plates. No doubt her notorious suitor was responsible for that. He wondered if she'd ever be able to trust another man again.

He straightened and looked out the window. Would Madeline ever trust him again? Hadn't he mistreated her just as badly as the rogue responsible for taking young Abby's innocence? Would Madeline ever look at him again with anything but contempt and hatred?

The lid dropped, covering the eggs and bacon. He was no longer in the mood to eat. Staring out the window, he watched the activity in the street, busy with carriages and the tradesmen scurrying down the cobbles headed for a day of work. He stood there for a while, feeling the sun on his face, trying to forget about the way his stomach knotted and tightened whenever he thought of what he'd done to Madeline.

Feeling a strange tremor snake down his back he glanced over his shoulder to see Madeline propped in bed gazing at him, her eyes, usually glittering and tranquil were cool and watchful.

"How are you feeling?" he asked, his mouth dry as straw.

"Improved," she said quietly, her gaze resting on her hands. "I hadn't any idea they sent for you."

"They didn't." He turned his attention once more out the window. "I came for you."

"Oh." The silence stretched on until at last she broke it. "How are *you* feeling?"

He stiffened, knowing she was asking him about his fits. He remembered the way she'd looked at him, remembered how he must have looked as he fell to the floor. He felt as though his cravat was strangling him, and then he remembered he'd discarded it during the night. The suffocating tightness in his throat was not from a tight collar, but the culmination of his fears, his pride.

But if he was to gain her forgiveness, if she was ever to believe in his love then he needed to be open and honest. He needed, for once in his life to reach out to another.

Clearing his throat he spoke, quiet and slow, testing the words on his lips, refusing to give in to the fear that engulfed him. "I usually only feel poorly for a day or two after my ... er ... episodes."

"Does it hurt?" she asked. "The episodes, I mean."

"No." He watched as a vegetable vendor wheeled his cart down the street. "I have no recollection of the event. I have what they call an aura--a warning sign. I remember events up till then, but not after."

"Do you...." she hesitated and he heard the rustling of the blankets as she pulled them up around her. "And after it ends, do you feel pain?"

"Just tired and weak. Occasionally I suffer from the headache, but not pain." He glanced over his shoulder and saw her watching him, a mixture of sadness and something else on her face. He prayed to God it wasn't pity he saw in those lovely eyes. "You should know there is no cure."

Silence hung thick in the room and he had the disconcerting urge to bolt. She was looking at him strangely and he feared that it might indeed be as he feared, she pitied him and his pathetic state.

"I should imagine you've seen a physician?"

He snorted, unable to hide his disgust. "A whole host of them, along with quacks and mystics and anyone else my father thought could cure me. Nothing can be done, I am what I am, and will always be this way. You should know that."

"Why would you have me know that you will never be cured of this?"

He whirled around, his feelings and fears finally getting the better of him. "I want you to understand that what I have will never go away. What lurks in me might be passed on to my children. I want you to know that you might...." he choked on the thought, but forced himself to say the words. "You should know that the babe within you might be like its father--a monster like me."

"You are not a monster."

"There is a darkness in me." He prowled about her room like a caged beast. "I can't hide from it--it won't let me. I can't crawl out of the depths and reach for the light. You know this, you've seen it. This...." he stopped and faced her, his face tight and jaw rigid. "This darkness is what I am, Madeline."

Memories of how he'd spent the night with her, carefully washing the blood from her thighs, brushing her hair from her face and weeping quietly when he thought she was sleeping, flooded her mind. He was no monster, of that she was certain. And the darkness he claimed would consume him was fear. Fear that she would leave him, that she would toss him aside as his father had done. He was not evil, merely frightened of being rejected once again.

Whatever he had felt a week ago when she'd told him about the baby he clearly regretted, she saw that now. The demons where still there, plaguing him, but there was something else, too. He was reaching out, trying to tell her, trying to show her that there was more to him then the harsh words he'd spoken to her.

"I should never have married you." He pounded the windowsill so that the glass rattled. "I knew damn well the pain I'd cause you and yet I couldn't help myself. I *had* to have you," he mocked, mirthlessly laughing as he peered out the window. "I just had to take you, to bury myself in your warmth, to feel a bit of you, no matter how small, fill my soul, despite the fact I'd do nothing but make you miserable."

"Blaine," she whispered, feeling the pain and emotion all but pouring from him.

"I told myself even as I made love to you that I it was wrong. That I wasn't good enough for you, that I'd only hurt you. And look," he said whirling around, his hand trembling, pointing to her in the bed. "Look at what I've done to you. I had no right to bring you into my life. I should have let you go to Tynemouth."

"I didn't want Tynemouth. I wanted you."

"I was a cause," he scoffed, raking his hand through his tousled curls. "A lost pup you found amusing and wished to bring out of the cold."

"You were never a cause, Blaine. I wanted you because you were the only man that made me feel passion. Every time I was with you, you made me aware that I was a woman. No man has ever done that before. No man has ever made me think of giving up all I've worked for in my life in order to have him."

He stopped his pacing and whirled to meet her. "What are you saying?"

"That I had already decided to give up Montgomery House in order to have you when I gave you my promise. I'm telling you I would have promised the devil my soul that night if only to have you make love to me."

When he didn't speak but continued to stand in the doorway, his face lined and worried, his stance open and unsure, Madeline did the only thing she could, she opened her arms, tears trickling down her cheeks and motioned for him to come to her.

He did. Swiftly, without thought, he crossed the distance from the door to the bed and swept her up into his arms, holding her tightly, burying his face in her unbound hair and rocking her against him.

No words were said, none were necessary. The gentle sound of her weeping, combined with the wetness from the tears she felt sliding along Blaine's cheeks and onto hers, let her know that that they were in tune with their sorrow and fears.

She wept for the child he'd been, frightened and alone, terrified to confide in someone. She wept for the man who tried so hard to carry the burden of his secret and keep it hidden from her. She wept for the man she loved and feared losing.

"Maddy," he breathed at last, "don't leave me now, not after I've just found you. Stay with me," he whispered harshly. "Who will save me if you leave me? I can't lose you."

"I'm not going anywhere, my love," she whispered, kissing his cheeks.

"I can't lose you." He buried his face once more in the crook of her neck. "I need you beside me, to feel you near. You don't know how much I needed you those times I pushed you away from me. Every time I forced you away I feared that I'd been successful, that you'd never come back to me."

"I'm here," she whispered, raking her hands through his hair, soothing him with her touch. "I won't leave you. Not ever."

"Will you ever be able to forgive me? Will there ever come a time when you will be able to forget what I've said to you?"

"It is already forgotten," she said, cupping his face in her hands. "It is me who should be asking your forgiveness. I purposely betrayed my promise to you."

"You did it because you thought it was best for me, did you not? Madeline," he kissed her roughly before releasing her. "I love you, and what I've done tears me up inside. I have to know, will you ever love me or have I ruined any chance I ever had to make you love me?"

"Silly man," she cried, hugging him fiercely, reveling in his declaration. "I love you, I've always loved you."

"Maddy, I've been so blind, so stupid."

"Ssh," she whispered, allowing him to put his arms around her waist, and his head in her lap. "Everything will turn out all right," she said, smoothing his hair.

"You saved me, even when I didn't think I wanted you to--when I wouldn't let you," he murmured, his fingers tracing her belly. She stilled his hand, not wanting to be reminded of the babe and its uncertain fate. He glanced up at her, knowing what thoughts were in her mind. "You've saved me from my demons, Maddy, from a life of loneliness. You knew what I needed before I did and I will never forget it."

"I would never turn away from my child if it were to suffer as you do. I cannot bear the fact that you think I would turn from you because of your condition." Closing her eyes, Madeline refused to see the look in his face. "I would never do that. My heart breaks to think of what you have had to suffer through. And yet, I know that had you not, you would not be the man I love today."

He looked at her then, a shadow of a smile curling his lips. "Come home with me," he asked, pressing a kiss to her belly. "It's where you belong. It's where our child belongs."

"I do not know if I still carry the child. Maggie says 'tis possible to continue to carry after bleeding, but I'm not sure."

"Then we shall wait. And if it turns out that you are not, we'll make more."

"Are you certain?"

"I won't say it's going to be easy for me, Madeline. I've lived too long in darkness and shadows, but if you're willing to stick by me, to give me a chance, I'll give you whatever you wish."

"My wish has already come true," she said, smiling into his upturned face. "It was you, after all."

* * * *

Sanbourne Hall, Sussex

The warm summer breeze carried with it the scent of roses and honeysuckle as it whispered across Blaine and his sleeping son. Lounging in a hammock, his three-month-old son tucked safely in the crook of his arm, Blaine smiled, well satisfied with the gifts Fate had bestowed upon him.

He was a husband and now a father. His wife adored him--loved him despite his illness and she'd given him the most beautiful and perfect child a man could ever hope for.

His son stirred, bringing his tiny fist to his mouth, sucking vigorously, not to mention loudly.

"I suppose, my little man, we should find your Mama."

His son opened his eyes and looked at him. He had the eyes of his mother, those deep green pools that made him feel peace and tranquility whenever he gazed into them.

"Blaine?" he heard Madeline call from beyond the bushes. "Where are you?"

"Here," he replied, smiling as he heard the hint of tension in her voice. "I'm fine, Maddy."

"Oh, there you are." She stopped to study him swinging back and forth in the hammock. Her gaze dropped to the ground and she smiled, her glittering eyes lit with warmth and understanding. "I think you've managed to pinch every pillow in the house."

"Well, it was necessary, you see. I wanted to bring Michael out for a breath of fresh air and I was worried that perhaps … well, you know. That I might suffer a fit and send him flinging to the ground."

"There's no chance of that," she laughed, scooping his son from his arm and bringing him to her chest. "The grass is covered with pillows. He'd have a soft landing, indeed."

"Indeed." He drew her down to lay beside him. "Can you feed him like this?"

"Of course," she smiled, looking down at their babe. "If you would help me with my gown?"

"A pleasure," he drawled, his fingers slowly unbuttoning her gown before seductively unlacing the strings of her corset. He kissed her back, dragging his lips along he spine. "I particularly enjoy this duty. Had I known that this was an obligation of fatherhood I would have had children years ago."

"Rogue," Madeline said with a grin, fastening his son to her breast. Blaine felt his heart swell at the sight of his wife in his arms and his son between them busily suckling.

"I love you, Maddy," he blurted, while stroking his son's downy black hair, a feeling of completion and acceptance engulfing him. "You've made me whole."

"So you've forgiven me, then?" she asked, brushing back a lock of hair that slipped over his brow. "You're no longer afraid?"

"There's nothing to forgive, my love. But I am still afraid. Mother says that will never go away now that I'm a father. Apparently constant worry is a parent's curse."

"He doesn't have it, Blaine. You needn't worry. The physician declared him perfect, did he not?"

"I only want what is best for him, and for you, Madeline."

"Well, my lord, you're what is best for us."

They lay still for a few minutes, the gentle breeze making the hammock sway, lulling them into a soothing sleep.

"Maddy?" Blaine stroked her hair from her face and smiled as her eyes fluttered open. "Thank you for saving me."

She kissed him then, a deep loving kiss that sent his blood on fire and filled him with longing. "Thank you for letting me."

"Maddy," he breathed against her mouth, his hand finding the roundness of her bottom. "Do you think my son is finished eating? I fear I'm disinclined to grant him much longer with you."

"Well, he has drifted off to sleep. I suppose I could send him back to the nurse."

"Or perhaps your father will want to tour him around the grounds again. Or my mother, I have no doubt she'd like to rock and spoil him beyond what is good for him."

"Perhaps I'm disinclined to agree to your request."

"Perhaps," he growled, pinching her bottom. "I should show you what happens when a wife does not acquiesce to her husband's demands."

"I'd like that."

"So would I."

"Where are you going?" she laughed as he slipped from the hammock and reached for the sleeping babe.

"Off to find one of the doting grandparents."

"I'll be waiting for you."

He looked back at his wife and smiled. He was alive, free of his demons, and it felt wonderful--empowering. Everything was going to be all right. There were still moments of uncertainty and fear and embarrassment when he suffered an attack. But he had Madeline with him now, who loved him no matter what. He truly was a saved man.

And as he strolled back to the house, his son sleeping sated in his arms, his wife awaiting his lovemaking, he said a silent prayer of thanks to whatever God brought Madeline into his life.

The End

Printed in the United Kingdom
by Lightning Source UK Ltd.
109838UKS00001BB/1